C000244335

Cured
by the
Dragon

(Stonefire Dragons #8)

Jessie Donovan

Cured by the Dragon
Copyright © 2016 Laura Hoak-Kagey
Mythical Lake Press, LLC
First Edition

Cover Art by Clarissa Yeo of Yocla Designs.

ISBN 13: 978-1942211433

As Always, To My Readers

You make writing stories for a living possible and I thank you from the bottom of my heart for that.

Other Books by Jessie Donovan

Stonefire Dragons
Sacrificed to the Dragon
Seducing the Dragon
Revealing the Dragons
Healed by the Dragon
Reawakening the Dragon
Loved by the Dragon
Surrendering to the Dragon
Cured by the Dragon

Lochguard Highland Dragons
The Dragon's Dilemma
The Dragon Guardian
The Dragon's Heart
The Dragon Warrior (Feb 2017)

Asylums for Magical Threats
Blaze of Secrets
Frozen Desires
Shadow of Temptation
Flare of Promise

Cascade Shifters
Convincing the Cougar
Reclaiming the Wolf
Cougar's First Christmas
Resisting the Cougar

Chapter One

Dr. Cassidy "Sid" Jackson gripped the sides of her head as she curled into a ball on her bed. The incessant pounding was bad enough, but it felt as if something were trying to punch through her brain.

It was almost as if a dragon were trying to break free.

However, no matter how much she reached out or tried to break down the wall to stop the pounding, nothing happened. After three hours of fighting, Sid was close to giving up.

Gritting her teeth, she pushed aside that feeling. She'd been waging this internal battle for over twenty years and she wasn't about to give up. The people of Stonefire relied on her. While a new junior doctor would be arriving in a few weeks, if Sid embraced the madness now, Stonefire would be left unprotected.

As memories of births, deaths, and even setting bones flashed inside her mind, the pounding eased a fraction. Sid was the reason so many clan members had pulled through and survived. Giving in to the madness would be selfish.

Letting out a growl, she pushed against the invisible wall in her mind. *Stop it! The clan needs us.*

The banging paused a second before it began again, albeit more quietly. The change in volume usually signaled that Sid was close to getting a grip on herself.

I need to check on Nikki and Samira's babies. Also, I need to check Bram's heart after his chest pains yesterday. Any and all of them could die if I can't work.

The ghost force ceased pounding.

Counting to sixty, Sid released her head and rolled over as she took a deep breath. Unless the pattern had changed from all of her previous episodes, she had won the battle for the time being.

Staring at the ceiling of her bedroom, Sid wondered if she would win next time. The increased frequency of her spells was one of the reasons she'd pushed to take on a newly minted doctor from Clan Snowridge. While Bram had doubts about the Welsh dragon clan's loyalty, Stonefire's head Protector, Kai, had thoroughly vetted Trahern Lewis and cleared him.

Sid slid off her bed and went to her dresser. Dawn might be two hours away, but there was no way she'd be able to sleep. Only a run would help her focus and allow her to regain her wits. She might even gain some semblance of peace, too, even if it didn't last long.

Changing her clothes, she glanced at her reflection in the mirror. Her cheekbones were more pronounced than she liked, and the smudges under her eyes were darker than usual. The more frequent internal fights were taking their toll. If she were her own patient, she'd recommend a holiday.

But she wasn't just anyone—she was Sid Jackson. Work kept her grounded. It gave her the energy to fight. A week or two without it could be the end of her.

She turned from the mirror and began a series of stretches. While she had no desire to give in to madness and live out her days tied to a bed, it would happen sooner rather than later. All she could do in the present was continue to fight until she trained the junior doctor to take her place.

She only hoped she wouldn't be a danger to anyone until that happened.

After tying her running shoes, Sid exited her room and went down the stairs. As soon as she snuck out the back door, she looked up at the sky. The clouds kept the stars hidden from her, but she knew they would be shining through regardless. After so many years stargazing with her younger brother and father growing up, Sid knew them like the back of her hand.

Rather than think of her long-dead family, Sid jogged toward the edge of the clan's land. The wind against her cheeks, combined with the steady rhythm of her arms and feet, helped to ease her nerves. This was the closest thing to flying she could accomplish without riding in a blasted helicopter.

No. She wouldn't think of flying. Whenever she thought of anything she missed from being in dragon form, it often brought back the infernal pounding.

Blanking her mind, she kept up a brisk pace and followed the edge of the clan's lands, wishing she could reach out and touch the trees and undergrowth with her fingers. But over the last year and a half, Stonefire's leader, Bram, had built up their defenses and nature was out of reach. Not that she could blame him given the amount of attacks on Stonefire.

Maybe she could sneak out and run up the hill adjacent to her clan's lands.

No. She wouldn't risk it.

Sid headed back in the direction of her cottage when the top of her head stung, and pain raced through her body. As she fell to the ground, Sid made out the small shape of a flying drone before the world went black.

11

~~~

Dr. Gregor Innes of Clan Lochguard listened a few more seconds to the heartbeat of wee Jamie MacDonald-MacKenzie before pulling back with a smile. "The lad is as healthy as a full-grown dragon."

Fergus MacKenzie, the bairn's adopted father, frowned. "Are you positive? His temperature is a bit warm."

"Since I've had years of medical school and nearly two decades of practice, I'm fairly sure I know what I'm doing," Gregor drawled.

Gina MacDonald, Fergus's American mate and Jamie's mother, patted Fergus's chest. "Don't mind him. He's been really protective lately. I think it's a result of him fighting the frenzy."

Fergus growled. "Wee Jamie is only four months old. You need a rest."

"You won't hear any complaints from me. But it's still making you moody."

As Gregor looped the stethoscope around his neck, he kept a smile plastered on his face. Just because he'd lost his own son and mate during childbirth all those years ago didn't give him the right to be jealous of others.

His dragon spoke up. *We could have another mate, and you know who it is.*

The sharp gaze and no-nonsense manner of Cassidy Jackson flashed into his mind. *No, we can't. Even if she would look at anything but her work, she's nearly forty and the risk of childbirth is too great.*

Isn't that for her to decide?

12

Ignoring his beast, Gregor focused back on the arguing couple. He cleared his throat. Once the pair looked at him again, he said, "Take Jamie home, cuddle him, and let him sleep. He's just a growing lad. Small fluctuations in temperature are fairly normal at this age." Gregor stood. "If his temperature goes up any higher, then you have my number."

Gina nodded. "Thanks, Dr. Innes."

Fergus merely grunted before he picked up his son. Cuddling the boy with one arm and looping Gina close with the other, Fergus guided his family out of the room. The instant the door clicked shut, Gregor sighed and closed his eyes. While he worked hard to ensure everyone in the clan was healthy, working with the bairns was the most difficult. But he'd be damned if he let anything take another mate and child from another couple on Lochguard.

His dragon huffed. *Sometimes, it's out of your control.*

Gregor didn't see it that way. There were always scientific advances and new methods to try.

However, rather than argue, he turned to the computer to type out his notes. Just as he saved the information, someone knocked on the door. He raised his voice, "Come in."

The door opened to reveal Finlay Stewart, Lochguard's clan leader. After walking inside, Finn closed the door and asked without preamble, "Do you have any cases Layla can't handle on her own?"

Layla MacFie was Lochguard's junior doctor. "No. After all, she's nearly completed her training. Why?"

Finn lowered his voice. "I'm sending you to Stonefire."

Stonefire was the northern English dragon clan and Lochguard's closest ally. "Care to tell me a few more details?"

Finn shook his head. "Not here. We need to head to the Protectors' central command where it's more secure."

While Finn was young and had only been clan leader for a few years, he had more than earned Gregor's trust. "Aye, well, what are we waiting for?"

Finn slapped his bicep. "I knew I liked you. Maybe you could give my mate a few lessons in how not to ask a million questions."

The corner of Gregor's mouth ticked up. "You enjoy it. You just don't like how she calls you out on your crap."

"Maybe." Finn's face turned serious. "We can discuss Ara later. My matter is time sensitive."

The two men exited the room and walked briskly toward the fortified building near the front of the clan. While Gregor was content with the silence, his bloody dragon spoke up. She *is on Stonefire.*

No, dragon. I'm not pursuing Cassidy.

We shall see about that.

Thankfully, his beast remained quiet for the rest of the walk. No doubt his dragon was scheming in secret, which took some doing considering they shared a brain.

The science behind the two personalities inside one dragon-shifter had always fascinated Gregor. Once Layla was ready to become a full-fledged senior doctor, he might be able to pursue his interest in more depth. There were too many questions lingering about the science of his own kind.

Yet as the fortified front of central command came into view, Gregor forgot all about his interests and focused on the issue at hand. Finn had never sent him to Stonefire before and he only hoped it wasn't because the English dragon-shifters had been attacked. That was usually the only time doctors from one clan helped another. At least, until recently. Layla was working on building relations with a few others, and Gregor supported her efforts.

After walking down one corridor and then another, Finn finally led him into a small conference room. Grant, Lochguard's head Protector, was sitting at the small table. The second the door clicked closed behind Gregor, Finn started talking again. "Stonefire's doctor was attacked."

Gregor frowned. "Cassidy is hurt?"

"Aye," Grant answered. "It was in the wee hours before dawn. Although, no one heard anything and Stonefire doesn't know what happened. Dr. Sid was found by a clan member not long after the sun came up."

Gregor's dragon roared. *We need to take care of her and find whoever hurt her.*

Steady on, dragon. Let's get the facts first.

"If you're sending me, then I guess she's unconscious?" Gregor asked.

Finn replied, "Aye. Bram has asked you to drive to Stonefire. Until he finds out what happened, all dragons are restricted to the ground. How soon can you be ready?"

"Twenty minutes. I want to pack some of my medical kit, too."

"Good. Iris is going to ride with you, just in case. She is also going to help Stonefire investigate what happened."

Iris was one of Lochguard's Protectors and their best tracker. "I'd trust Iris with my life."

Grant spoke up again. "Also, before you leave, I'm going to give you some information to pass on to Stonefire's head Protector, Kai. Just in case this attack is related to the one we had on Lochguard four months ago."

The devastation of the attack lingered with Gregor. Not just because of the massive amount of injuries, but the attack had taken his sister and niece from him. "If it's the bloody Lochguard traitors or the American dragons, so help me, I'm going to go after them myself."

Finn crossed his arms over his chest. "No, Gregor. Your skills are needed as a doctor. Until Dr. Sid recovers, you're the only person who can keep Stonefire together and in fighting shape if there are more attacks."

His beast chimed in. *He's right. Besides, our place is with Cassidy. We need to look after her.*

"Fine. But if one crosses my path, I won't hold back, Finn."

"Fair enough," Finn stated. "But enough talking for now. Gather what you need and meet us back here in twenty minutes. The sooner you leave, the sooner you can look after Dr. Sid."

With a nod, Gregor exited the room. Making his way out of the building and toward his cottage, he tried not to picture Cassidy unconscious in a hospital bed with tubes running out of her body.

He clenched his fingers and picked up his pace. Even though Gregor had no intention of claiming Cassidy, he didn't like the thought of her being injured and helpless. While she wasn't officially his mate, Gregor would be her protector during his time on Stonefire. The female had suffered enough with her silent dragon; she didn't need long-lasting physical injuries as well.

The hard part would be staying near Cassidy for an extended period of time and resisting her.

His dragon laughed in the back of his mind. *Just wait until she wakes up. You won't stand a chance.*

Bloody dragon. Whose side are you on?

Mine.

16

Cured by the Dragon

Some people had cooperative or clever dragons. Gregor's always seemed out to make his life difficult.

His beast huffed. *I am clever. You're just stuffy and afraid to take a chance.*

Rather than admit there was some truth to his dragon's words, Gregor stormed into his cottage and packed. Cassidy needed his help and he wouldn't deny her.

Chapter Two

Sid was trapped in darkness. With no sounds, no wind, and no smells, she wondered if she was buried alive.

She'd been stuck in this small, empty prison for who knew how many hours. If she stayed much longer, she might go crazy.

Then the pounding started and increased with frequency to her left. Out of curiosity, she rapped on the wall. After a brief pause, the same beat she'd tapped out echoed from the other side.

Something intelligent was there, but what?

Feeling around the space for the tenth time, her fingers felt only smoothness. There was nothing to grip on to or even a small hole to try and pry a wall apart. The emptiness extended to the floor, with only her own feet to disturb the surface.

She was trapped.

If only she still had her dragon, then Sid could extend her talons and rip through the wall.

The exact second she finished her thought, a desperate pounding started again from the mysterious source. A small part of her thought it could be her inner dragon imprisoned inside her mind, with no way out. However, wishing for it to be true was dangerous; the next time she had an episode, Sid might embrace the pounding and lose her sanity. She needed more information.

Placing her hand on the wall, her palm warmed. Something large and radiating vast amounts of heat had to be on the other side of the wall.

As she tried to think of a way to communicate further to determine

*what was there, an icy air swirled around her and she was yanked toward a
bright light.*

Sid gasped as she opened her eyes, only to promptly close
them against the brightness.

A male Scottish brogue rolled over her. "Good morning,
sunshine."

That voice brought up memories of a naked, muscled chest
sprinkled with blond chest hair. "Innes?" she croaked.

"Aye, although right now, I'm Dr. Innes, and I'm here to
take care of you. Open your eyes if you're able, lass."

As Sid slowly opened her eyelids, she tried to wiggle her
fingers and toes. However, nothing happened. Wishing she could
articulate herself and get to the point, all she could manage to ask
was, "What?"

Gregor Innes's strong jaw, dark blond hair, and gray eyes
filled her vision. As he leaned down to check her pupils, she
reveled in the heat of his body. For a split second, she wanted
him to lay on top of her.

Get a grip, Sid. Since Gregor still hadn't said anything, she
grunted. The bastard chuckled and leaned back. "You were right
before. Doctors really do make the worst patients." She frowned,
and he continued, "I'm still not sure what happened to you. There
aren't any physical injuries apart from the bruises associated with
falling over. The test results didn't show any poisons or toxins,
just a sedative. Everything is normal, apart from your dragon-
shifter hormones being low, but you usually take a supplement
and I don't think that's what caused your unconsciousness."

"I can't move."

"Your lips are moving just fine, lass."

Growling, Sid said, "I'm not a lass."

19

"Ah, but you are to me. That's all that matters." He took her wrist and looked at his watch as he took her pulse. Most doctors' hands were smooth, but Gregor's held a hint of roughness. She wondered what caused it.

But she pushed that question aside. "Do your job."

While he raised his brows, Gregor never took his gaze from his watch until he finished taking her pulse. "You're awake, aren't you? Even though I'm curious as to why I had to fight the nurses to give you any drugs at all."

"I don't like drugs," she answered quietly.

He searched her eyes for a second and she thought he might ask why. But he shrugged and picked up her chart. "I rarely use them, but sometimes, they're necessary. If I think you need them, I will pin you down and administer them myself if I have to. My job is to ensure your health and look after Stonefire until I deem you fit for duty."

Sid tried again to wiggle her toes, and the big ones moved. "Believe me, I will be out of this bed in two days."

Not looking at her, he jotted something down. "Even if you can get out of bed and walk, you need my permission to return to work."

Sid wished she could clench her fingers. "I need to work, Innes."

His sharp gray eyes met hers and his pupils flashed to slits. "And why is that, Cassidy?"

Since her dragon had fallen silent, no one but Gregor had called her Cassidy. After all, Cassidy was a carefree young dragonwoman with a playful dragon; that part of her had died as a teenager. Calling herself Sid had provided a clean break.

However, for some strange reason, she liked how he said her full first name.

A brief pounding went off in her head and she gritted her teeth. She couldn't afford to have an episode. Gregor would ask too many questions and delay her return to work even longer, if ever.

Drawing on every bit of strength she possessed, Sid roared inside her head. *Stop!*

~~~

Gregor itched to touch Cassidy's soft wrist again but focused on writing his notes. The menial task kept him occupied. More importantly, it was a good distraction.

His dragon spoke up. *Toss aside the bloody papers and touch her skin again.*

No.

Throwing his beast inside a mental maze, he waited to see if Cassidy would answer his question. However, when she clenched her jaw and squeezed her eyes shut, alarm bells went off inside his head. "What's wrong, lass? Tell me."

She remained silent a second more before her body relaxed. "It's nothing."

"Stop being bloody stubborn, woman. I can't treat you if you don't tell me what's happening."

Opening her eyes, she met his gaze and sadness flashed. "There's nothing you can do, Innes."

When it came to dragon-shifter patients, there were times to push and times to be gentle. Cassidy Jackson would deny it with her dying breath, but she needed gentleness.

He lightly brushed a strand of hair off her face. "There might be, lass. If there's one thing to know about me, it's that I never give up on a patient of mine. That now includes you."

21

As they stared at one another, he lost himself in her dark brown eyes. In that second, he wanted to know everything about her. Maybe then he could chase away her sadness.

His dragon banged against the maze, but the walls held.

Cassidy sighed. "If I don't tell you, I have a feeling you'll never clear me for duty, will you?"

"Now there's an idea."

Her gaze darted away and back. The sadness had been replaced with steel. "My work is who I am. Without it, I'm lost, Innes. Just like you defied my orders on Lochguard when I came to help and you went back to work early, I'm the same way. I can't abandon my clan any longer than necessary."

He studied her for a few seconds. There was more to her story; he was positive. However, he had some time to drag it out of her.

Placing his hands on his thighs, he leaned forward. "You tell me everything that's going on, and I mean everything, even if it's an ingrown toenail, and I will clear you as soon as you're physically and mentally ready. Can you do that?"

"Only if you agree to keep what I'm about to say to yourself."

"Unless it endangers your life or either of our clans, then aye, I'll keep it to myself."

Cassidy took a deep breath and the words spilled from her lips. "There's often pounding inside my head that I can't control. It's not a migraine or a headache, but something else." She paused, and he thought she wouldn't say anything else. Then her low voice added, "It's almost as if something is trying to break free, but can't."

"Is it your dragon?"

Cassidy blinked. "My dragon is long gone. Everyone knows that, even on Lochguard. Besides, the pounding comes from behind an impenetrable wall. I've never heard of a dragon being trapped for decades that way before."

Gregor had a few theories but decided he'd air them later. "Then tell me the whole story, lass. I need to know it all."

As the dragonwoman searched his eyes, Gregor held his breath. He had a feeling Cassidy didn't talk about her past often. Would she really share it with him?

His dragon roared some more but still couldn't get free. No doubt his beast wanted to help find a way to bring her dragon back, if it were possible.

The question was whether it was or not.

Just as ideas raced through Gregor's head, someone knocked on the door. Relief flooded Cassidy's face at the interruption. Little did she know he would pursue it again later. "Come in."

Stonefire's clan leader, Bram Moore-Llewellyn, stood in the doorway. His eyes latched onto Cassidy's and he stated, "You're finally awake, Sid." Bram crossed the distance to Cassidy's bed and Gregor gripped his knees to keep from growling at Bram's nearness to Gregor's dragonwoman.

He resisted blinking. Cassidy would never be his. The risk was too great. He needed to remember that.

Bram spoke up again. "Can you remember anything that happened, Sid?"

Gregor stood. "She just woke up. Can't your interrogation wait until later?"

Bram's light blue eyes met his. "I understand you're doing your job, but Sid can speak for herself."

As he sized up Stonefire's leader, Cassidy's voice broke the silence. "I only remember one hazy detail, Bram."

23

Stonefire's leader turned back toward the dragonwoman. "Anything will help, Sid, no matter how small."

"After a flash of pain, I fell to the ground and noticed the faint outline of a small flying drone."

Bram frowned. "Drone? You mean one of those flying contraptions human males seem fascinated with?"

Gregor smiled. "It's the closest they can get to flying themselves, so of course they'll be fascinated."

Shaking his head, Bram shot Gregor an exasperated look. "This isn't a lighthearted matter, Dr. Innes. Start taking it seriously."

Cassidy's voice beat Gregor to a reply. "Focus on what's important, you two. Are Stonefire's defenses guarded against small flying machines?"

"I'll need to talk with Kai about it and I'll have Evie reach out to the DDA. The splinter we found embedded in the top of your head might also be a clue, so we'll look into that, too."

Evie was Bram's mate and a former employee of the UK Department of Dragon Affairs, or DDA.

Gregor jumped in. "Right, then go do that. I need to talk with Dr. Jackson more about her condition."

Bram glared at him, but Gregor didn't flinch. One of the main requirements for being a dragon-shifter doctor was being able to put up with and stand up to alpha personalities. For whatever reason, dragonmen in particular had alphaness in spades.

Although Cassidy seemed to have her fair share, too.

Bram finally spoke up. "Fine. But just know that once Sid's cleared for duty, I'm sending you to Lochguard the next second."

The corner of his mouth ticked up. "We shall see."

"I'm leader here, Doctor. I don't know how Finn runs things, but I don't allow strangers to run amok," Bram warned.

"I'm hardly a stranger. Cassidy can vouch for me."

Cassidy sighed again. "Can you two stop it, already? Just because I'm the patient doesn't mean I won't kick the pair of you out until you can behave."

Gregor's dragon finally escaped the maze. *Yes, yes. I like her strength. How can you resist it?*

While he did admire a lass who could stand up for herself, Gregor couldn't have Cassidy. *Because I don't want to kill her, that's why.*

His beast huffed. *Never taking risks makes life boring.*

Aye, you call it boring, but I call it ensuring the health of everyone I can, which especially means protecting Cassidy Jackson.

Bram's voice interrupted Gregor's inner conversation. "Are you quite finished with your dragon, Dr. Innes? After all, you claim it's urgent to examine Sid."

He opened his mouth, but Cassidy beat him to it. "Out, Bram. I'll never heal with you two constantly arguing."

"I'll go for now and update you when needed." Bram's gaze moved to Gregor's. "You tell me the instant there's a change in Sid's condition, understand?"

"Great to see you appreciate my help," he drawled.

His dragon spoke up. *Why antagonize him? Bram is mated. He is no threat.*

His beast's words helped to cut through the haze. There was no reason to keep arguing. His change in temperament must be because of his proximity to Cassidy.

His dragon added, *Of course it is. Our instinct is to protect her.*

I somehow think she can protect herself from Bram.

The dragonman in question shook his head and mumbled, "The bloody Scottish dragons are always a pain in my arse," before exiting the room.

When the door clicked shut, Cassidy's voice filled the space. "Your pupils keep flashing."

Turning back toward her, Gregor noticed for the hundredth time the circles under Cassidy's eyes and the sharpness of her collarbones peeking out of her skin.

In that instant, he decided part of his mission would be to bring her to full health in addition to working out a way to awaken her dragon.

His dragon swished his tail in anticipation.

Before Gregor could think too much on the reaction, Cassidy wiggled in her bed. "Stop staring at me with the flashing eyes."

He took a few steps closer. "Care to tell me why, lass?"

She looked away. "Because it reminds me of what I can't have."

~~~

With anyone else, Sid would be able to keep her thoughts to herself. Never once in her adult life had she let something slip she shouldn't have. Yet with Gregor, she kept blurting things out.

His flashing dragon eyes and growly nature around Bram only strengthened her growing suspicions about the Scottish dragonman.

She had a feeling she was his true mate.

But Sid would never be able to take a mate. Not that she wasn't curious about having someone to laugh and cry with, because of course she was. Ever since matings had been increasing over the last two years in her clan, she'd started wanting one herself.

The only problem was Sid didn't have many years of sanity remaining. The only way to protect herself and others was to remain unattached for her entire life.

The thought of having an episode and falling into insanity while pregnant was a nightmare. Since all true matings resulted in at least one pregnancy, Sid had to be careful. Even if it was becoming more difficult to avoid noticing Gregor's full lips or how she wanted to laugh at his sarcastic humor, she would resist.

Gregor's voice was low as his Scottish vowels rolled over her. "If it's your dragon you're after, you may have given up hope, but I haven't."

Whipping her head around, she frowned. "You have no idea what you're talking about and I'm about this close from kicking you out of my room. I've lived with this for over twenty years, and you just waltz in here and make it seem as if I gave up too soon." She gave the double-finger salute. "Well, fuck you, Gregor Innes."

Gregor closed the distance between them and took her chin between his fingers. She tried to jerk away, but his bloody strong grip didn't budge. His voice was steely as he murmured, "Someone's touchy. I never meant to imply you gave up too soon, Cassidy. But I'm a very determined dragonman and I'm not through with you yet."

She swore his words held a double meaning, but Sid could barely put two thoughts together as Gregor's hot breath caressed her cheek. Despite every reason why she should resist, her body heated at his touch and she leaned a fraction closer. Only when his pupils flashed again did it break the spell. Leaning back, Gregor released his grip and Sid scooted to the far edge of the bed.

JESSIE DONOVAN

She'd nearly kissed him. She'd have to be more vigilant from here on out.

In response to her thought, the pounding started inside her head again. Not wanting to alert Gregor to it, she kept her face neutral, much like she'd done for short periods of time with her patients in the past.

"You tensed just now. Why, lass?"

Was Gregor Innes a bloody mind reader?

Clearing her throat, the noise intensified in her mind. She kept her gaze averted as she replied, "I just need to rest."

"Liar."

She looked back at him. "You keep saying that. If anything that concerns you crops up, I'll tell you."

"Everything about you concerns me, Cassidy. Now what the fuck is going on?"

Exasperated, she bit out, "The stupid noise is back, okay? If you don't leave me alone to fight my battle, I may never recover."

"Then let me help you, lass. I have a theory and would like to administer something to you. If my theory is incorrect, it won't affect you at all. It can't hurt to try."

She searched his eyes. "You're being vague. Just tell me what you want to shoot into my body."

"You want honesty? Then I'll give it to you. I think the pounding is related to your inner dragon. The drug that silences a dragon for a few days might make it stop."

At the mention of the dragon-slumber drug, as it was known colloquially, Sid was suddenly fourteen again. Lying in a hospital bed, her limbs kept flashing between dragon ones and human ones. Her dragon had taken control and wouldn't give it back. Not even the dragon-slumber shot had worked.

One of the doctors finally gave another dose, and then another. He repeated the process until her dragon finally retreated and her mind went blank.

Her dragon never returned after that.

"Cassidy. Why are you crying?"

Wiping her cheeks, she was surprised to find them wet. "No reason."

Gregor sat down on her bed and took her hands. She pulled back, but he didn't let go. "Bullshit. You might be able to dismiss anyone else in the clan, but it won't work with me."

His demands stoked her temper. "Look, I don't care if you think I'm your mate or what have you. I wholeheartedly refuse you, so stop with the overprotective crap."

"You can't refuse me, lass, as I already refused you."

She blinked as his rejection coursed through her body. "What?"

He squeezed her hands. "You heard me. Not because of your silent dragon, so get that bloody ridiculous thought out of your head. I lost a mate once in childbirth, and I vowed to never do it again. So while you're safe from my cock, I am your doctor and I plan to find a cure for your condition, Cassidy. I've been gentle up until now, but if you don't start cooperating, I'm going to pull out all the stops to make you talk."

CHAPTER THREE

Gregor's dragon wouldn't stop roaring. *I don't refuse her. She is ours.*

Used to his beast's tantrums, Gregor ignored him. He focused on Cassidy. Her anger had melted into pity, which was the one look Gregor couldn't stand. "I've lost two people important to me, and you've lost your dragon. I'd say we're on par for loss and tragedy, so unless you want me to pity you, stop it now, Dr. Jackson."

"You're wrong, you know. We're not even." He opened his mouth to reply, but she beat him to it. "I know about your sister and niece, Gregor. I've dealt with many patients over the years experiencing the death of a loved one, and I know you're still grieving, no matter your outer exterior."

At the mention of his sister, Nora, and his young niece, Gregor's dragon fell silent out of respect. "Aye, I am grieving. But this isn't a contest of who has the most tragic life. This is me trying to help you and how you keep pushing me away."

Searching his eyes, Cassidy finally said, "I'm used to being in charge. Asking for help is difficult for me."

He resisted blinking at her straightforward admission. "Am I dreaming or is Cassidy Jackson telling me something without a fight?"

She rolled her eyes. "It seems I'm damned no matter what I do when it comes to you."

His lips quirked. "Aye, but that's the fun part." He sobered. "But if you want my help, I need all of the facts. Tell me exactly what happened leading up to your dragon's silence and what was done after."

Cassidy remained silent. He wondered if she'd actually open up to him or not. Just as he was about to speak, her low, detached voice filled the room. "I was fourteen years old. My dad and younger brother, Wyatt, and I had taken a trip to the White Cliffs of Dover. Back then, Clan Skyhunter had been neutral to us and the DDA had granted permission for the trip." She glanced at him. "And if you think Cassidy and Wyatt are strange names for British dragon-shifter children, then you're right. But Dad had a thing for the old American Wild West and Mum gave in to his choices."

Gregor wanted to tease her for probably being named after Butch Cassidy, but he merely nodded. She continued, "Any of the cliffs on the coast were one of the few places humans liked to see dragons flying. Probably because dragons diving over the sea ensured they weren't threatening villages, or at least that's the way they thought.

"Even though I was promised the first go by Dad, Wyatt was so excited to dive off the cliffs that we agreed to go together. I wasn't exactly thrilled to be flying with my ten-year-old brother in front of all of the young dragonmen around, but it was together or nothing.

"I jumped at the end of Dad's countdown, but Wyatt hesitated. I flapped my wings and rode the currents back up. I was quite the tormenting sister in those days, and twirled and flipped in front of Wyatt to show off. Finally, he jumped, but as he dove downward, a large piece of the cliff slid off and landed on his wing. In the blink of an eye, he was sinking into the water."

Cassidy closed her eyes, and Gregor knew she was twenty-four years in the past, watching her brother possibly sink to his death. Touching her arm, he kept his voice low as he asked, "What happened next?"

She shook her head and opened her eyes, but kept her gaze averted. "I dove after him. As soon as Wyatt hit the icy waters, the shock forced a shift back into his human form. He was too young to shift back under the circumstances and he sunk quickly.

"However, as I hit the water, I kept hold of my dragon inside my mind and forced her to keep us in dragon form. If I'd been a little older, I could've controlled my shifting without such force. But at fourteen, finesse was the farthest thing from my mind. I fought my dragon inside my head as well as the chill of the Channel, and pushed my muscles to swim toward my brother."

Taking Cassidy's hand, he squeezed. She finally met his gaze again and answered the question in his eyes. "I wasn't able to save Wyatt. By the time I reached him, he was unconscious. As I fought my way back to the water's surface, his heart stopped beating. Even when I surfaced, Dad was there to take him back to land. But it was too late."

"I'm sorry, Cassidy. I truly am."

She nodded in acknowledgment. "It might be more than twenty years since it happened, but in my mind, the memories are as fresh as if it happened yesterday." She paused, and then added, "That whole incident is the reason I became a doctor. If a dragon-shifter doctor had been on-site, Wyatt might've survived."

CURED BY THE DRAGON

~~~

As Gregor rubbed the back of her hand with his thumb, the pounding in her head eased. They might have sworn off each other as mates, but she was grateful for his touch.

Not only his touch but his near silence.

Wyatt's death was the one thing in Sid's life she wished she could change. She would even take the lack of an inner dragon all over again if it meant her younger brother would still be alive.

But what had happened to Wyatt was only part of the story. If she wanted Gregor to know the full truth and attempt to help her, she needed to get out the rest.

Taking a deep breath, she moved her gaze to her hand engulfed in Gregor's large one and forced herself to finish. "As you may have guessed, my story didn't end there. Once Dad carried Wyatt up to the top of the cliff, I finally lost control of my dragon and she thrashed at the water's surface. Every time she tried to jump up, I roared and tried to restrain her again. I knew that if my dragon went rogue, flew up, and started attacking the humans, I would be shot down."

Gregor never ceased his caresses on her hand. The pounding had disappeared in her mind. Daring to look up, she saw curiosity in his eyes.

It was as if he truly wanted to hear it all so he could help her.

If things were different, and Sid had her dragon and Gregor hadn't already refused her, Sid might've considered giving the male a chance. Of course, wishing for someone didn't make it so.

Sid couldn't change the circumstances, but if Gregor could help her stop her episodes, she might actually have a chance at living her life.

33

"My dragon and I kept fighting. Soon, I started flashing between human and dragon. Even when Dad scooped me up, he had to be careful because some of my limbs would grow, or my tail would extend. He finally placed me on the ground. The other dragon-shifters in the area had formed a circle and extended their wings to shield my dad and me from view. If the humans had seen a flashing dragon, panic would've broken out and they might've tried to kill me.

"Dad could do nothing but keep me in place until the nearest dragon-shifter doctor arrived and sedated me. I fell unconscious and woke up in a hospital bed. My limbs were flashing more erratically and one doctor gave me the dragon-slumber drug. When it didn't work, he gave another dose and then another until I remained in my human form." She met his gray eyes. "After that, my dragon never returned."

For one long minute, Gregor said nothing. Sharing her past had sapped her energy and her patience, so Sid said, "Well? That's everything. Usually, you talk as much as any of the Scottish dragons I've worked with. Why the silence now?"

The corner of his mouth ticked up. "I'm thinking."

"Care to share those thoughts? Because if you're waiting for me to plead or offer money for them, you'll be waiting a long time."

"Did your attack also affect your patience?" She flipped him off, and Gregor chuckled. "I'm enjoying this side of Dr. Cassidy Jackson. However, just a warning, lass. If you're going to salute me every time I tease you, your fingers will be so tired you soon won't be able to move them."

Sid, the dragonwoman who could keep her wits about her during a twelve-hour surgery, stuck out her tongue.

Gregor's laugh echoed inside the small room and she couldn't help but smile. It'd been more years than she liked to admit since she'd made anyone laugh.

The Scottish dragonman finally spoke again. "Thanks for that, Cassidy. Once you're well, I'm going to have to repay the favor."

"Do you ever make any sense?"

"Oh, come on, now. You're clever. You can figure it out."

"Just because I can doesn't mean I want to waste the time," she pointed out.

Gregor reached out and took a small section of her long hair and rubbed it between his fingers. "Maybe it's having your hair down that lets out this more playful and lively side of you." His intense gaze met hers and Sid's heart skipped a beat. "You'll keep it down until you recover, doctor's orders."

His words broke the moment. "I'm starting to think all of this power is going to your head."

"Aye, well, at least you didn't argue back. That's progress." She tried to reply, but he cut her off. "You need to rest, so I'm going to do a quick examination, watch you drink some water, and let you sleep. And before you ask me, I've already seen some of your patients. Samira and Nikki's pregnancies are on target and I plan to hunt down Bram shortly after this."

"Good luck with that. I've known Bram my whole life and can barely get him to allow a check-up."

Gregor flexed his arm. "I keep in shape for a reason. I've had to tackle a clan leader or two in the past."

Sid snorted. "I'd pay to see that."

"Oh? Maybe I'll get someone to record it and I can use it as a reward for compliance."

"Do you bargain with all of your patients?"

Gregor leaned close until his breath tickled her cheek. "No, only you." He tucked hair behind her ear. "You require a special touch, Cassidy."

As they stared into one another's eyes, Cassidy itched to stroke Gregor's lightly whiskered cheek.

She might touch patients every day, but it would be different with Gregor; he wasn't her patient. She would also enjoy it and think of where else she could stroke him.

Gregor's eyes darted to her lips and he immediately pulled back. His distance shouldn't sting, especially since Sid couldn't afford to let a mate-claim frenzy happen, but she desperately wanted more time with the teasing Scot.

More than anyone, he helped her to forget her past and her shortcomings.

Clearing his throat, Gregor picked up her chart and moved to the door. "I'll check on you later today and do your exam then. I'm going to trust you to drink some water on your own."

Rather than focus on what she couldn't have, Sid would enjoy what she could with the Scot before he left. "You can tell me how it goes with Bram, too. If you come back with two black eyes, I just might laugh."

"Laughing at a male's wounds isn't kind."

She tilted her head. "Well, you're the one who has confidence in spades, so you shouldn't be worried."

He stood a little taller. "I'm not worried."

"Good, then I look forward to the video."

Shaking his head, Gregor clicked the door shut behind him.

Silence stretched and Sid quickly drank a cup of water before laying back down. Despite her exhaustion, she stared wide-eyed at the ceiling. For the first time in her life, she hated the quiet.

The next few days were going to be the longest of her thirty-eight years on the planet. Each day might entice her more to kiss Gregor and deal with the consequences later.

No. If it were only herself, she might be tempted. However, the frenzy would mean a child and Sid wasn't about to be the cause of someone's pain and tragedy again. Her parents gave their lives to try t17o heal Sid. No one else would suffer because of her.

The sooner Sid recovered, the sooner she could show Gregor his attempts to help her were useless. She'd briefly fallen for his confidence and determination, but Sid's pessimism was back in full force.

Once she could send him back to Lochguard, she could quietly accept her fate of going insane and slowly die alone.

~~~

Gregor finally tracked down Bram's whereabouts at his cottage. Yet as he knocked, it was the human female, Evie, who answered the door. After giving him a quick once-over, she smiled. "You'll do nicely."

"Er, what for?"

She waved a hand. "Never mind. But I'm glad you're here. I need you to check over my stubborn mate before he tries to sneak out the back door."

"Ah, but you see, I have Ginny stationed out back."

Ginny was Stonefire's oldest, toughest nurse.

Evie laughed. "Good. She and Sid are usually the only ones who can handle him. Let's see how you do."

Evie walked and Gregor followed. Judging by what little he knew of Evie and her connections to the DDA, she might be an ally when it came to Cassidy. Gregor couldn't be the only dragon-shifter who suspected the DDA conducted research and kept the results confidential.

His dragon spoke up. *We don't need an ally. She would've let us kiss her earlier.*

She might have, but I caught myself. It's not going to happen, dragon.

His inner beast huffed. *Just because Bridget died in childbirth doesn't mean it'll happen again. Cassidy is a much stronger female. After all, she survived more than twenty years without a dragon.*

Being mentally strong isn't the same as physically strong. Besides, she's too thin. Any child of ours would kill her.

Evie stopping in front of a door caught his attention. "Bram will resist, but"—she opened the door and stared at her mate across the room—"if he ever wants to share my bed again, he's going to sit through your exam."

Bram sat at his desk. Across from him was Stonefire's head Protector, Kai Sutherland, who had visited Lochguard a few times in the past.

Bram sighed. "I've told you, love. I'm fine. It was just a muscle spasm."

Evie crossed her arms over her chest. "Any pain in your left arm could be something vastly more serious, Bram, especially when combined with chest pain." Her voice softened. "Think of Murray and Eleanor."

Gregor half-expected Evie to produce a giant photograph of her children to complete the guilt trip, but she didn't.

Kai spoke up. "You'd better listen, Bram. Evie is as stubborn as Jane, and I could easily imagine her tying you up and locking you away until she deemed you healthy."

Gregor couldn't help but add, "If it's tying up you want to do, it all sounds a bit kinky. Should I leave and come back later?"

Bram met his gaze and growled. "If I'm going to sit through an exam, it's going to be without your commentary."

Gregor took a few steps toward Bram's desk. "I'm afraid that's part of my treatment. You'll get used to it."

Evie cut off Bram's reply. "Kai, you should leave. And on the way out, ask Ginny to watch the door."

Bram raised his brows. "You brought Ginny?" Gregor nodded and the corner of Bram's mouth ticked up. "Clever dragonman."

Laying down his medical bag, Gregor opened it and replied, "Aye, well, if I had a second doctor, I would've brought them. It's strange that you don't already have a junior doctor in training."

"Now you're going to tell me how to run my clan?"

"When it comes to medical practices, aye, I just might."

"I can take a lot of crap, but Sid is a fine doctor. Don't criticize her. She made the call about needing one or not."

Gregor held up his stethoscope. "Cassidy is a fantastic doctor. I have my suspicions about why she didn't take on a junior doctor until recently, but that's none of your concern."

Evie grinned. "So Sid's opened up to you already? That's brilliant."

"Evie," Bram warned.

She waved a hand in dismissal. "We'll discuss this later, although you won't be able to dissuade me. I've waited a long time to help Sid and I'm going to give 120 percent. I owe her my life."

Gregor looked at the pair. "Cryptic couple conversations. You could just wait five minutes and hash it out then to not make your guest uncomfortable."

Bram was about to reply when Gregor lifted up the other dragonman's shirt. Without another word, he quickly placed the stethoscope over Bram's heart. "Shush. You can scold me later."

Ignoring the loud grunt, Gregor focused on Bram's heartbeat. The rhythm was steady.

Standing, Gregor pointed to Bram's shirt. "Take it off and let me take your blood pressure. Since you don't have an arrhythmia, I bet it's stress." He raised his brows. "Given all the shouting you've done at me in such a short time, I'm surprised you haven't had a heart attack years before now."

Evie moved to Bram's side and yanked off his shirt. "Bram needs a holiday, but refuses to take even a day off."

Bram's voice softened when he answered his mate, "I will as soon as I can secure the clan, love."

"You'll be taking time off sooner rather than later. I'll make sure of it." As Gregor wrapped the cuff around Bram's arm, he added, "And then I'm going to visit your head Protector as well. You Stonefire lot are workaholics."

"Just finish the exam," Bram muttered. "And let's hope Sid heals soon."

"Well, until then, you'll have to deal with me." After placing the stethoscope, Gregor pumped up the cuff. "Now, shut it. I need to listen."

"Use your dragon-shifter hearing," Bram stated.

Gregor ignored him and thankfully the clan leader kept quiet.

The Stonefire Dragons were going to take a special touch. All of them liked to argue more than Gregor was accustomed to. It explained Arabella MacLeod, the former Stonefire dragon-shifter female mated to Lochguard's leader, and her tendency to be contrary.

His dragon spoke up. *All the more reason to woo Cassidy. Stonefire listens to her. If we were her mate, the English dragons would listen to us, too.*

That's a rather complex way of getting patients to listen to us.

You're the one being difficult. I'm just trying to find logical ways to convince you to kiss Cassidy.

Gregor ignored his dragon to focus on the systolic and diastolic readings.

Finishing up, Gregor removed his equipment. "Your blood pressure is extremely high. If you don't get it down, you will have a heart attack. I'm going to draw some blood as well, to make sure it's not something more serious."

Evie wrapped her arm around Bram's shoulders. "I told you." She met Gregor's eyes. "What will help the most, Dr. Innes?"

Gregor tightened a tourniquet around Bram's bicep and took out a blood draw kit from his bag. "Reducing your workload and therefore your stress is what will help most. And if you're like any clan leader I've met before, you probably don't exercise as much as you should."

Bram grunted. "I don't have the bloody time to do that. My clan's safety is the most important thing. Going for a swim in a lake comes somewhere toward the bottom of the list."

Gregor raised his brows as he removed the protective plastic from the needle and blood collection tube. "I would hope your clan's safety is first, given you're clan leader and all." Bram glared and Gregor stopped teasing. "Learn to delegate, then. You can maybe take on an understudy."

Evie asked, "Is that done? A clan leader taking a deputy leader? I truly don't know."

"Aye, it's been done in the past," Bram answered. "But as our numbers decreased over the centuries, the practice stopped."

Gregor found the vein and stuck in the needle before attaching the tube. To his credit, Bram didn't so much as grunt.

"Those born from the early years of the sacrifice system are more than old enough to help. You should start looking there."

Evie answered before Bram could. "Oh, he will. I'll make sure of it."

"Evie…"

"No, Bram. You don't need to prove how hard you work. Everyone knows it. A little help would do you good. You could also spend more time with the children."

"Aye, to change their nappies, I suspect," Bram answered dryly.

As the pair continued to banter, jealousy tugged at Gregor's heart. He and Bridget had once had similar arguments. The only difference was that they had never had the chance to actually see their plans through. Gregor would've changed all of the nappies if it had meant Bridget and their son were still alive.

His beast chimed in. *We will always love Bridget and the bairn. But even she would've wanted you to be happy. After more than a decade, don't you think it's time? Cassidy might be our last chance.*

You're being a bit dramatic.

Stop with the drawling and focus. Finding two true mates in a lifetime is a gift. Don't be a stubborn arse and hide behind something you can't control.

For a few seconds, Gregor's reasons for staying away from Cassidy slipped and an image of her leaning against him, their entwined hands over her protruding belly flashed inside his mind.

His dragon hummed. *If you want it, then you need to go after it.*

Then an image of Cassidy in childbirth, screaming in agony as complications sapped away her life replaced the image and restored his resolve. *No, dragon. Until there is a guarantee or way to ensure a female doesn't have complications, I won't risk another life.*

42

His beast sighed. *Then our second chance will soon slip through our fingers.*

So be it.

As his dragon fell quiet, Gregor knew it wasn't the end of it.

He removed the tube and needle before applying a bandage. Clearing his throat, he garnered Evie and Bram's attention. "I'll come back tomorrow to check up on you and to hear about your plans to reduce your stress load."

"I'll wear him down by then, Dr. Innes," Evie answered.

Rather than stay to hear the couple argue, Gregor picked up his bag and exited without another word. He headed back to the surgery to check on Cassidy.

The happy image from before, with her leaning against him, returned and Gregor savored it the whole way back because it was the closest thing he would ever have to a mate again.

Chapter Four

Sid was half asleep when she felt something brush her temple. Opening her eyes, she saw Gregor looming over her with something clutched in his palm. "What the bloody hell are you doing?"

"Making sure your brain activity is normal," he said innocently.

Narrowing her eyes, she stared at his clutched fingers. "Show me what you have."

"No."

She blinked. "What?"

"You heard me. I'll go over your EEG readings with you after I have a chance to look over them. And before you toss out more orders, just ask yourself if you'd cave in to a patient's unreasonable demands. Because I don't and I suspect you're the same."

Damn the man; he was right. "My biggest concern is you drugging me without my permission."

"I didn't drug you."

She frowned and resisted touching the things attached to her temple. "But you obviously had to put the electrodes on my skin. I'm a light sleeper and would've woken up at the first touch."

"Aye, well, you must like my gentle touch," he said as he winked.

"More likely I blocked it out because it was traumatic."

Gregor chuckled. "Tell yourself that, Cassidy. You're just upset you missed the whispers of my manly fingers."

Not wanting Gregor to know how right he was, she changed the subject. "Speaking of which, why are your fingers so rough? Every dragon-shifter doctor I've met has soft hands."

He shrugged. "I like to carve wood. Since I do it by hand, my palms had to roughen up over the years or they would always be raw."

"You carve."

"Yes," he said with a grin. "Are you about to ask me to carve you in the nude?"

"I—of course not. That's bloody ridiculous."

He leaned in a fraction. "Someone doth protest too much."

Sid's cheeks heated and she mentally cursed the dragonman. The longer Sid was around Gregor, the more she yearned to feel his fingers caress every inch of her body. It would be even more erotic to have him caress her slowly with his eyes.

Get a grip, Jackson. Clearing her throat, Sid sat up in her bed. "Does everyone know about your naked statue collection?"

"Sadly, I don't have any naked ones yet. I mostly carve animals and dragons. Lochguard is planning to have a fair later this year and I can finally sell off some of them. They take up an entire room in my cottage."

Sid was grateful for the distraction and pounced on it. "The DDA might change their tune about your fair if the drone attacks continue or intensify. I'm fairly confident the drone is related to what happened to me."

A few months ago, the new DDA Director, Rosalind Abbott, had encouraged dragon clans to hold gatherings with the local humans. Because of security concerns, Stonefire still hadn't made any plans to do so.

"One random attack does not make a war. For all we know, it could be one local teenager trying to prove themselves," Gregor said.

"Or, it could be a trial run for a bigger attack. You should prepare the staff for one."

"I already have."

"But you just said—"

"Just because I like to be optimistic doesn't mean I'm not grounded. Lochguard was bombed last year. Believe me, I'm aware of the possible threats."

When Gregor turned his back to her, Sid guessed it was to hide his emotions about the death of his sister and niece. As Sid knew too well, doctors rarely looked after themselves. No matter how much Gregor might goad her or irritate her, she couldn't let him suffer unnecessarily. She needed to try and help him.

"Gregor."

He turned, his eyes expressionless. "That's the first time you've used my first name."

She wasn't about to be distracted. "Tell me about your sister."

To her surprise, Gregor gave a sad smile and said, "Nora was quiet, especially for an Innes. She liked to keep to herself and either watch the birds or read a book. It drove our parents crazy because they could never get her out of the house."

Sid smiled at the image of a bird-watching bookworm curled up in the corner of a cottage. "And given my experience with Lochguard, I bet she probably hated most clan gatherings. You lot are nosey."

46

"Aye, she detested them. She usually hid in the corners of the great hall with a book. That's where she met Harry, her mate. He'd been searching for insects and spiders. The odd male is known worldwide for his work with the creatures."

"The bookworm and the insect bloke. That is quite the pair."

"They were and spent most of their time away from everyone else. Nora helped him with his work, you see. And Harry understood what it was like to have a family try to discourage an interest. He always supported Nora." Gregor gave a sad smile. "Their daughters grew up with spiders, dragonflies, and beetles painted on their bedroom walls and loved it. The only time I tried to visit my surviving niece, Fiona, after the death of her sister and mother, Fiona had scratched over each one with a marker. When I asked her why, she said the wee critters had died out one by one from sadness."

"Oh, Gregor."

"So, aye, I'm grieving, but my niece and brother-in-law are grieving harder. I'm strong for them and the clan. Me breaking down would benefit only myself."

As she watched him turn to pick up her chart and his tablet, Sid suspected he was about to flee. If she was to ensure his health, she couldn't let that happen. He needed to talk more until he felt safe enough to break down. Only then would he be able to move on.

So, she blurted out, "I did something similar when my brother died."

Gregor turned back around and raised his brows. When he remained silent, Sid continued, "I was a teenager and should've put on a brave face, especially since my grandfather always told me dragon-shifters needed to be strong, but when no one was looking, I would sneak into Wyatt's room and nick one of his stuffed animals or toy planes. I then started putting them in boxes and burying them. It was stupid, but I felt that if Wyatt couldn't have them, no one should. Eventually my dad stopped me, and that's the day I finally let out all of my pent-up anger and sadness." She tilted her head. "When you need to do the same about your sister and niece, come find me. Breaking down with me won't affect your image. I'll deem you my patient and thus we'll have doctor-patient confidentiality."

She fully expected for Gregor to wave his hand in dismissal and say dragon-shifters males didn't need to break down. However, he merely nodded. "I'll keep that in mind."

As they stared at one another, a sort of understanding passed between them. Both she and Gregor had so much sadness and loss in their pasts. They were a rare breed in that they understood one another better than most anyone else.

If only she had her dragon, she might hold him close and never let go.

The noise started in her head again, but on the third beat, it exploded. She grabbed her ears as she cried out. In the next second, Gregor was at her side. "Tell me what's happening, Cassidy."

"Noise, so much noise." The sledgehammer turned into a wrecking ball. "Make it stop. Please make it stop."

~~~

The sight of Cassidy in pain brought his dragon roaring to life. *Help her.*

I don't know how.

There's one thing that might help.

I can't do that. There must be another way.

48

Not right now. Do it.

Sid fell into him and Gregor wrapped his arms around her. As he rubbed her back, each whimper shot straight to his heart.

He hadn't had time to study her scans or brainwave readings. While he had his suspicions, Gregor had no proof of what caused the pain.

"Gregor, please." Cassidy screamed and arched back.

With a curse, he laid her down and cupped her cheek. "Forgive me, but I have to try this. It might help."

Leaning down, he placed a gentle kiss on her lips.

Lust and need shot through Gregor's body, but he managed to keep his dragon at the back of his mind. He'd deal with the bloody beast later.

Cassidy relaxed and he swiped his tongue between her lips. Damn, the heat and her taste made him want to demand more, much more.

However, her wellbeing was more important. Drawing back, he searched her eyes. "Is the pain gone?"

"Yes and no," she whispered.

"Care to tell me what the bloody hell that means?"

"Kiss me again."

"What?"

"Gregor, please. Just do it."

His dragon paced inside his prison, urging him to kiss her. She was theirs. They should claim her.

Ignoring his beast, he focused on the pleading in Cassidy's eyes. He leaned down and took her lips in a rough kiss. To his surprise, Cassidy kissed him back as she placed her hand on the back of his head and pulled him closer.

With a growl, he explored every inch of her mouth since it could be the last time he ever kissed her. No matter what, he couldn't allow things to go further than kissing.

His dragon banged against the invisible wall, but it held.

All too soon, Cassidy pulled away with a sigh. Keeping the disappointment from his eyes, he searched hers. "Well, care to tell me what that was all about?"

She smiled. "When you kissed me, the pounding turned into a hum."

"Then I was right. The pounding is related to your dragon."

"I want to accept that, but there're still too many unknown variables."

"Said like a true doctor."

She ignored his remark. "I may need to keep you around to kiss me and stop the pounding when it crops up again."

"Gee, glad to be of service," he drawled.

"Stop it, Gregor." Her expression faltered. "Unless you don't want to kiss me again."

"Och, woman, of course I do. But I need to lay something out right here and now." His beast increased his tantrum, but Gregor wasn't going to let him out. "I will gladly give such a beautiful female a few kisses. But."

"But what?"

"If it's your dragon and we succeed in freeing her, I will need to return to Lochguard straight away."

"I don't understand."

"Mate-claim frenzies always result in at least one pregnancy. I killed a female once before with my child and I won't do it again."

His beast ripped a gash in the wall. *I'm stronger. I will make it happen. She will be ours.*

Gregor constructed a complex maze full of pits, fire, and dead-ends before tossing his beast inside. That would keep him occupied for a while.

Since Cassidy's expression was free of any emotions, Gregor waited to see what she would say.

~~~

Sid's excitement at what had happened inside her head was quickly replaced with confusion. She had no idea how such a rational male like Gregor could have such an irrational fear. Just because one female died in childbirth didn't mean it would happen the next time.

Not that she would be having any children. Gregor's kiss may have been the first time the pounding had morphed into something pleasant, but she still wasn't looking for a mate. Until she had a sentient, talking presence in her head to guarantee her sanity long-term, Sid wasn't making any plans for her own future.

Still, until Gregor left for Lochguard, she would have to add getting Gregor to share about his past to her list of things to do. Judging by his stance, he still hadn't fully accepted his mate's death or his own grief. Just because Sid might not have a future didn't mean Gregor should be deprived of a happy one full of family. If she could heal him, then he might at least have a chance at it.

A low pounding started in her head, but it was manageable. She wouldn't ask Gregor to kiss her until it became unbearable.

She focused back on him. Keeping her tone light, she shrugged. "Fine."

He blinked. "Just like that?"

"I rather thought giving a male the license to kiss me—in private, of course—with no strings attached would be a welcome suggestion."

After a brief pause, Gregor replied, "Aye, then I'll help." He grinned. "Although I'll have to dole them out slowly, so you can enjoy them."

She didn't miss how he used humor to change topics. "Slow is good. That means I can document the changes more easily."

"You mean 'we' can document the changes. If you're using my lips to run an experiment, then I'm your research partner, end of story."

Sid was used to working alone. "I suppose it will be good practice for when the Welsh dragonman arrives."

"What Welsh dragonman?" Gregor bit out.

"Don't start acting like a caveman. Dr. Trahern Lewis is going to be Stonefire's junior doctor. Given how our species tends to have more males than females, it shouldn't be a surprise that a dragonman is coming and not a female."

"Of course," he answered flatly. "But enough about the doctor. I want to hear from your lips that we'll be working on this together."

"But our lips will be working together."

The corner of Gregor's mouth twitched. "I think you're trying to be funny."

"Just because I'm a doctor doesn't mean I can't poke fun."

"Aye, but when was the last time you did it with someone besides me?"

She raised her brows. "Since that has nothing to do with my health, I'm not going to answer that."

He ran a finger down her cheek and the noise increased inside her head. "Retreat behind that defense for now, but just know that I'm going to enjoy both kissing and teasing you, Cassidy Jackson. In fact, I'm going to give you a freebie right now."

Before she could reply, Gregor pressed his lips to hers. At the contact, the humming returned to her mind. Unlike the stabs of pain with the roaring and pounding, a sense of tranquility coursed through her body. Almost as if kissing Gregor was just…natural.

Ignoring the feeling, she nipped his bottom lip before pulling away a few inches. "Now, since I allowed the kiss, I expect to hear the results of my brain scan the instant you have them."

He grunted. "Bloody woman, do you ever think of something apart from work?"

"Of course I do. But since I'd like to remain sane, the results of my scans are important."

Gregor's voice turned steely. "I won't let you go insane, Cassidy Jackson. So stop teasing about it."

Concern and determination flashed in his eyes. Despite their short time together, he cared greatly about her wellbeing.

But of course he would. Gregor was as dedicated a doctor as she was.

Something clawed the inside of her brain, and she winced. Gregor's eyes turned concerned. "What's wrong?"

"It feels as if something is trying to claw its way out of my head."

"Aye? Then let's monitor it. It may support my theory."

"It won't be my bloody dragon. Stop bringing that up."

Gregor picked up an electrode and lifted it to her temple. "Until you prove me wrong, I'm going to bring it up as often as I like. If anyone deserves to have their dragon, it's you, Cassidy."

Tired of fighting him, she allowed him to affix the electrodes to her temples. "Then you owe me some cheesecake."

"Cheesecake?"

"Your hearing is perfectly fine. That's my price."

He leaned back. "Well, if cheesecake is what the lady wishes, it's what she'll have. Unfortunately, I don't have time to fly to New York for the best kind, so Stonefire's bakery will have to do."

"Do you ever—"

Gregor cut her off. "Shush. What triggered the new response?"

"Certain thoughts."

"I'd gathered that," he answered dryly.

"Give me a second and let me try something."

Gregor sighed but motioned with his hand for her to carry on. She wondered if she were the first person to get so far under his skin. To be honest, it was rather fun.

At the thought of having fun with Gregor, the clawing inside her brain started again. Closing her eyes, she bit her lip to keep from screaming and focused. Thoughts of Gregor seemed to trigger the responses, so she imagined swimming with him in the lake and dunking his head under the water. Then laughing as he came up with bits of plants in his hair.

As she imagined plucking away a twig, the pain increased tenfold.

The response made her think Gregor's theory might be correct. If she were his true mate and her dragon was trapped, the beast would do anything to get out and fulfill the mate-claim frenzy.

She fixed the image of kissing Gregor in her mind and the pain remained the same as before. Images didn't have the same effect as the action.

As if reading her thoughts, Gregor's warm lips touched hers and the pain morphed into pleasure. She sighed into his mouth and simply enjoyed the warm strokes of his tongue.

CURED BY THE DRAGON

~ ~ ~

Gregor had clenched his fingers so hard he'd nearly broken them as he'd watched Cassidy's body tense and her heart rate increase. Thankfully he hadn't removed her EEG sensors and he could see that her brainwave activity was also unlike anything he'd ever seen.

Yet as her face grew paler, Gregor forgot about the science and results and kissed his doctor. As she relaxed, both man and beast mentally breathed a sigh of relief.

His dragon was still inside the maze, but as Gregor took the kiss with Cassidy deeper, lustful thoughts seeped through the walls and coursed through him, straight to his cock.

Easing Cassidy back on the bed, he half covered her body with his. The second her hard nipples pressed against his chest, he growled and took a possessive grip on her waist.

He half expected his doctor to push him away, but she drew him closer until he was almost laying on top of her. The feel of her breasts and smaller frame beneath him turned his cock to stone.

His dragon's lust increased and with a growl, Gregor moved a hand up to one of Cassidy's breasts and cupped her. She fit perfectly into his palm. He bet her nipple would fit perfectly in his mouth.

At the thought of sucking her nipple deep, a flash of reason returned to Gregor's brain. With Herculean effort, he drew back and let go. The distance should've cooled his thoughts and lust, but the sight of her kiss-bruised lips and flushed cheeks only made him want to strip her and explore every inch of her soft skin.

Taking a few more steps back, he cleared his throat. He would never have Cassidy for his mate, let alone explore her naked body. The end result was too dangerous.

His dragon finally broke free. *I want her. She seems to want us. Let her decide.*

No. I'm her doctor and it's my job to protect her.

His beast hissed. *We are more than her doctor. She is our true mate. Why do you brush aside a future you want as much as I?*

It took everything he had not to think about Cassidy round with his child. *Because it's more important to help Cassidy heal. Or, do you want her to live in pain forever?*

Of course not.

Then control yourself and let me help her.

"Gregor?"

Cassidy's husky voice interrupted his conversation. He studied her face for signs of pain, but he didn't see any. "Are you all right?"

"Am I all right? From what? Too much kissing?" She leaned forward. "What happened to you? Is your dragon close to breaking free?"

He tilted his head. "Between me fondling you and laying on top of you with a hard cock, I think you know the answer to that."

"Gregor, stop with the vague comments and just answer my question straightforwardly."

His beast growled, but Gregor ignored it. "My dragon and I have different priorities." She merely raised her brows, and he added, "Yes, he wants you, okay? Considering how bonny and clever you are, it shouldn't be surprising."

She smiled. "I am clever." Her expression turned more serious. "But if he's getting difficult to control, then you'd better leave. Once you've studied the results and have something to share, you can come back."

"Do I need a secret password to enter?"

She rolled her eyes. "Be serious for a second. You don't want the mate-claim frenzy, and neither do I. I'm just trying to think of the best compromise. Of course, if it's too much for you, then go back to Lochguard and I can sort out my own problems."

The thought of leaving his doctor behind caused a bad taste to fill his mouth. "I'm not bloody leaving. Just try not to tempt my dragon so much and we'll do fine."

Something flashed in her eyes but was gone before he could blink. "If you want to better control your beast, then talk to Bram. He held his in line for quite a while until he finally gave in to Evie's charms."

"I'm not asking Bram for any fucking advice," he muttered.

Cassidy shrugged. "Your loss."

"Are you always this infuriating, woman?"

She smiled slowly. "Only with you."

He couldn't help but smile back. "Good."

She widened her eyes in surprise, and he wondered what it would be like to surprise Cassidy Jackson every day of her life.

No. He wouldn't give his dragon any fodder to use.

His beast chuckled. *Too late. We share a mind and you're horrible at keeping secrets.*

Gregor picked up his clipboard and moved to the door. "I'll go over your readings and see if I find anything. In the meantime, you need to rest. If the pain returns, hit the panic button and I'll come running."

"So, it's more like a 'kiss emergency' button," she answered.

Gregor's dragon flashed a video-like image of them kissing Cassidy's neck, her breasts, and even between her thighs.

Gritting his teeth, he banished the image. "Something like that. I'll be back later."

Without another word, Gregor walked as quickly as possible away from the female who tempted him like no other.

Hell, if he weren't careful, he might even give in to his dragon and claim her, which would only sign her death sentence.

Chapter Five

Sid lay in her bed several hours later and studied the patterns on the ceiling.

No matter what she did, her thoughts kept returning to Gregor Innes. More specifically, to the feel of his body and how he made her forget she wasn't a complete dragonwoman.

To be honest, she was merely a woman; she didn't deserve the title of dragonwoman.

Of course, if Gregor had his way, he might be able to make her whole again.

Sighing, she looked back to the patterns above her. As a child, she'd always made up stories from the shapes she saw, to distract from thinking about Wyatt's death. Maybe she could do the same to forget about Gregor and the prospect of having a dragon again. Hope could break her if it turned out her mental anomaly was a rare disease or form of mental illness and not her dragon after all.

Just as she made out an old man with a beard she thought could be a wizard, the voice of the male she was trying to forget about drifted through the door. "Cassidy? Are you awake?"

The unknown presence in her mind perked up and Sid braced herself for pain. "If you have something to report, come in. Otherwise, you'd best stay away and not tempt your dragon."

The door opened. "I can control my bloody dragon."

She smiled at his petulant tone. "Do you want to bet on it?"

Gregor's pupils flashed, but soon became round again and stayed that way. "Do you want to waste time betting or do you want to discuss what I found?"

Sid sat up. "Tell me what you discovered."

The corner of his mouth ticked up. "I like it when you're eager." For a brief second, she expected him to make a joke about being eager when naked, but he merely cleared his throat and continued, "My first question is how much do you know about the science concerning the dual personalities of dragon-shifters?"

"The basics. The human and dragon halves tend to use slightly different areas of the brain for certain tasks, but I'm not an expert. Not only is surgery my specialty, but not much in-depth study has been done on our dual personalities due to lack of funds and resources."

Gregor pulled up a chair next to her bed. "Well, I've been dabbling for years, whenever I have the chance. While my focus has been on children and emerging dragon personalities, since our dragon halves are silent for the first six or seven years, most of the brain activity patterns seem to follow the same areas into adults. At least, for those few I've monitored."

"And?"

Gregor opened his tablet and brought up a chart. He pointed to an intense spike in the middle. "This is when you experienced the greatest amount of pain." He brought up another chart. "The pattern almost exactly matches a female fighting the mate-claim frenzy here." And another one. "And this is a child arguing with their dragon for the first time and the dragon tried to take control."

Sid flipped between the three images. The spikes were almost identical.

60

Yet she wasn't about to get her hopes up just yet. "It could just be similar brain activity. It doesn't mean I have a dragon."

"Ah, but I knew you'd say that. I've gone through every record I can find, and the pattern matches strong emotions between the human and dragon halves."

"Even if that's true, it doesn't give us a solution."

"But it means we can try to bring out your dragon."

"Gee, why didn't I think of that," Sid answered.

"Stop it, Cassidy. This means your dragon is probably still a part of you, albeit separate. I think all of the dragon-slumber shots given to you as a teenager had an adverse side effect."

She had thought that as well until she'd dug further into the research. "That's great and all, but no other cases have been documented."

Gregor raised his brows. "Do you think it would be? After all, what doctor wants to admit their mistake? Unlike the humans, dragon-shifter doctors don't have to report to an overarching authority or abide by any set of common practices."

"Which is bloody dangerous, in my opinion."

"Aye, I agree with you. But that's not important right now. What's important is that you still have your dragon, Cassidy, and I plan to find a way to bring her out."

~~~

Gregor nearly missed the brief flicker of hope in Cassidy's eyes before it vanished. His doctor was more than a wee bit skeptical.

His beast spoke up. *I still say we should participate in the mate-claim frenzy. That will bring out her dragon.*

No, I'm not about to return her lost half only to take her life in nine months' time.

61

His dragon huffed. *She will be fine.*

That's what you said about Bridget and the bairn.

Cassidy's voice brought Gregor out of his head. "Let's say you succeed in bringing out my dragon, then what? Being trapped for over two decades would make the beast insane. I'm not sure I can fix that."

"You can and you will."

As they stared into each other's eyes, Gregor silently vowed to bring hope and happiness back to Cassidy's eyes.

Looking away, Cassidy asked, "And how do you propose you do that?"

"So, you're going to let me try?"

She met his gaze again. "Maybe. If you can find someone else who has experienced the same problem as me and returned to health, then we'll talk about this again. Until then, I just want to be cleared for work and get back to my life."

Clearing Cassidy would mean Gregor had to return to Lochguard.

His dragon chimed in. *Convince Bram we should stay and help her. Finn will probably say yes, too. Layla can handle things.*

His beast was correct about Layla and that gave Gregor an idea. "It's still too early to clear you for work. However, I may be persuaded to clear you tomorrow, provided nothing goes wrong."

She raised her brows. "And what must I do? I'm sure there's a catch."

He smiled. "Oh, aye, there is. Agree that I can stay with you in your cottage to continue to monitor your progress, provided Bram allows me to stay, and you'll be cleared as soon as possible."

"You staying in my house isn't such a good idea."

"Why not? If you have an episode, you have easy access to my lips. I can also keep track of any changes in brain activity. It's a win-win for both of us."

She studied him a second before asking, "And what about your dragon? I imagine it's getting harder and harder to control the frenzy. Can you really sleep under the same roof and keep your hands to yourself?"

No, his dragon roared.

Gregor ignored him. "Of course. The second I can't control my beast, I'll leave. The last thing I want to do is have you die in childbirth."

Cassidy opened her mouth but promptly closed it. Gregor leaned forward and waited to see what she would say.

His silence paid off and she spoke up again. "Convince Bram and clear me as soon as possible, and I'll allow you to sleep in the surgery." He was about to protest, but she shook her head. "I usually sleep here. There's nothing to argue about on that point."

"Stonefire is lucky to have you," he murmured.

Cassidy shrugged. "Of course they are."

"I love when your confidence shines. You should allow it out all of the time."

"More importantly, you need to talk to Bram." She smiled. "Maybe you should invite him here so I can watch."

"You really do revel in my discomfort, don't you?"

She shrugged. "How often do I get to see the big, bad alpha doctor squirm? Besides, it might make me heal faster. After all, laughter is a powerful medicine."

"Aye, is that so?" In the next second, Gregor reached out and tickled Cassidy's side. As she laughed and tried to lean away, he only stood to keep at it.

When she was finally out of breath, he stopped and put his hands on the mattress to either side of her body. "There's your dose of laughter for now. I expect to see a much speedier recovery because of it."

He winked and Cassidy grinned. The happiness in her eyes, which were free of pain, made both man and beast content.

It would be easy to wake up to her face every day and find new ways to make her laugh.

His beast spoke up. *Not just laugh. I would like to take her wrists and pin them above her head as we thrust into her.*

He focused on Cassidy's lips. It would be simple to take her wrists, cover her with his body, and kiss her until she was breathless.

"Gregor." At her husky voice, he met her eyes again. She continued, "The pounding is starting up again. I need you to kiss me."

The lack of tightness of her jaw or pain in her eyes made him suspicious. Did Cassidy want to kiss him for herself?

Of course she does. We are her true mate.

His dragon's words were a warning, but he didn't heed them. "As my lady wishes."

And he kissed her.

~~~

Sid wasn't sure what had compelled her to lie, but at the feel of Gregor's warm lips, she forgot about everything else but his heat, scent, and touch.

As he nibbled and sucked her bottom lip, he maneuvered to her side and laid down. Turning toward him, Sid grabbed his shoulders and pulled him close.

64

CURED BY THE DRAGON

The humming started in her head and faint bursts of lust soon followed. While there was no dragon egging her on to fuck Gregor, the wetness between her thighs and the tightness of her nipples made her ache to be filled in a way she'd never wanted before.

Moving a hand to his arse, she hitched her leg over his hip and shimmied closer. The feel of his hard cock against her lower belly increased the humming and her lust tenfold.

Just as she started rubbing against the Scot, he pulled away and murmured, "Stop it, love. My restraint is starting to slip."

In a voice almost not her own, she answered, "No. I need you. Now."

Gregor froze. "That's not you, Dr. Jackson."

The use of her title cleared the lust haze a fraction. Pulling away, she put a few inches between them. Intense pain exploded into her head and she screamed.

Stop, stop, STOP. Please, just stop.

If anything, the pain increased to the point a sledgehammer against her skull would be relief.

Something pinched in her upper arm. Opening her eyes, she saw Gregor pulling out a needle. She should be furious, but peace returned to her mind bit by bit until she slumped back on the bed.

Gregor's Scottish burr rumbled in her ear. "Every time I see you in pain, it breaks my heart. Working together, we can find a solution quicker, I know we can. I'll talk to Bram straightaway."

He moved to leave and she reached out to grab his hand. "Not yet. Stay, Gregor, and tell me something I don't know to distract me. The sedative is working, but my mind is raw. I need something to forget the pain."

"I'm not sure talking about myself will do that."

"Then tell me why you're so afraid of childbirth."

His pupils flashed and Sid wondered if his dragon would convince Gregor to talk. It might be a bit selfish using her own pain to draw out the truth from Gregor, but she had a feeling he might not talk about it otherwise.

Besides, she couldn't help him heal if she didn't have all the facts.

With a curse, he removed his hand and pulled up a chair. "I'm not sure I like my bloody dragon always taking your side."

She smiled weakly. "Most of the dragon halves tend to take my side as I usually talk sense." She put out a hand and he engulfed it with his own. At the contact, her pain numbed a fraction. "Tell me, Gregor. I won't tell anyone else."

He sighed. "I know." Lightly brushing her cheek, he murmured, "I killed my mate." Rather than protest, Sid merely waited. Eventually he continued, "It's true. If not for my seed, she'd probably still be alive. You see, I knew it would be difficult for Bridget to have children. Every doctor told her to be careful. While the mate-claim frenzy might happen, she needed to not risk another pregnancy after that, even if she miscarried.

"Bridget and I knew straightaway there was a connection and it wasn't long before both of our dragons banged on about being true mates. Knowing what I did about her health and the risk of pregnancy, I suggested that I could transfer somewhere else and she could go on birth control with another bloke and possibly live risk-free. There was also the possibility of tying her tubes and me having a vasectomy to prevent pregnancy, but Bridget was stubborn and yearned for a child. And not just any child, but my child."

Sid squeezed his hand in hers. "So you gave in to the frenzy."

"Aye, despite my better judgment, I did. I was young and in love; I wanted to give my mate everything she desired. If she wanted a child, we'd try.

"She conceived in just over a week. I was a young doctor then and was maybe a bit overzealous in my protection and restrictions. But in my mind, I wanted to give Bridget the greatest chance of survival. While there were a few scares, she was fairly healthy up until the day I found her dead."

~~~

Gregor remembered finding Bridget in their bed with blood on the sheets. The image would haunt him for the rest of his life.

Cassidy's voice was soft as she asked, "What happened, Gregor?"

As he met her brown eyes, he knew he could refuse to say anything. After all, he'd done a good job of not talking about that day since it happened.

His dragon spoke up. *Tell her.*

The next bit spilled from his lips. "When I came back from a twenty-four-hour shift at the surgery, I found Bridget in our bed with blood everywhere. Her mother was supposed to have stayed with her, but had gone out to get some supper and ended up staying out longer than expected."

Gregor shut his eyes and clenched the fingers of his free hand. If only his mother-in-law had stayed, Bridget and their son might still be alive.

His beast spoke up again. *They will always be with us, but we can't change the past. Every decision could result in death. Worrying or placing blame on a random act of fate is a waste of time.*

It's still my fault.

67

Rather than argue, his dragon fell silent. When Cassidy remained silent as well, he opened his eyes to make sure something wasn't wrong.

But her eyes were merely studying him. For once, it was nice not to be bombarded with questions, false platitudes, or to be pitied. No doubt, Cassidy had gone through that most of her life.

And without the comforting presence of her dragon.

Gregor could at least be honest with her. "It was a placental abruption brought on by a genetic disorder. It came on suddenly and even if her mother had stayed, Bridget might not have lived." He took a deep breath and whispered, "But even so, I should've been there for her. Bridget had trusted me to take care of her. I might've been able to save her."

Cassidy finally replied, "Maybe, maybe not. I've thought the same thing over and over with my brother's life, and always wondered if I had been stronger, I could've saved him in time. But the longer I worked as a doctor, the more I began to realize that sometimes, no matter what you do, it isn't enough. I know it's not the most comforting thought, but even if you had been glued to Bridget's bedside, the bleeding could've been too much too quickly. You did everything you could. You both knew the risks, and she accepted them. To blame yourself for everything is ridiculous."

He shook his head. "I should've resisted. Bloody hell, I was a doctor when I met her. I knew better."

"Listen, Gregor Innes, doctors aren't gods or wizards. We don't have magic that can instantly wipe away any small chance of complications or death. Your mate knew what she was getting into, just as you did. There is no blame to place."

"I appreciate you trying to comfort me, but—"

"No buts. I'm stating the facts. You both loved each other and made a decision together. I'm sorry she died, I truly am. But from my experience, whenever a dragon-shifter has left their mate behind, their dying words were always for the other one to eventually find happiness again. I imagine Bridget would've wanted the same. You've denied yourself for long enough, Gregor. Keep your mate and son in your memory, but don't let the past barricade your heart from others."

His dragon growled. *Listen to her. She says what I have been saying for years. You wanted your second opinion, and there it is.*

It's not that simple.

Isn't it? Wanting happiness doesn't mean we will forget Bridget or the bairn. They will live with us. And if you give Cassidy a chance, we might be able to start again.

That almost feels like betraying Bridget.

Why? She wasn't selfish. She would've wanted us to embrace a second chance. Finding a second true mate is rare. Are you really going to throw away what could be your last chance for happiness?

Searching Cassidy's eyes, which had lingering signs of pain, he made a decision. *If I can make her whole, then I will consider it.*

Good. Then let's hurry up and get to work.

Gregor cupped Cassidy's cheek and murmured, "Once we free your dragon and make sure she's stable, we'll revisit this conversation."

She frowned. "Hoping isn't the same as having."

"No, but I'm not going to leave Stonefire until I've tried everything I can think of to make you happy again, Cassidy."

"I'm not sure Bram is going to like that," she replied.

He squeezed her hand. "That doesn't matter. As long as you want my help, I'll fight your bloody clan leader if I have to. So the question is, do you want my help?"

She leaned against his hand and whispered, "I think I do."

"Good. Then I'm going to call Bram to come here so I don't have to leave your side."

"I'll be fine for a short while—"

He shook his head. "No. I'm staying."

At Cassidy's smile, Gregor couldn't help but notice how beautiful his doctor looked when she was happy.

Releasing her cheek, he pulled out his mobile phone and dialed Bram. The sooner he told Stonefire's leader he was staying, the sooner he could take care of his female.

His dragon hummed. *Ours?*

Yes, ours.

Good.

Ignoring his dragon's smug tone, Gregor waited for Bram to answer the phone so he could start planning the next phase of his life. Because if he was ever going to try and be happy again, he needed a certain strong dragonwoman at his side.

Chapter Six

For the first time in a long time, Sid wished she had her dragon and a guarantee for a mostly certain future.

She'd been a doctor for so many years, taking care of others, that she had forgotten what it was like to be taken care of. Gregor's sheer determination to challenge her clan leader if need be made her think she needed someone to kick her arse and point out when she needed a break. Bram had Evie, but as much as Bram tried to make Sid stop and take care of herself, she'd never really listened.

Yet with Gregor, taking a break was something she could get used to. And not just because it would mean forcing Gregor to take a break as well, which he needed as much as she. But rather, he could work with her both professionally and personally. That idea appealed to her in a way she almost couldn't resist.

If only she had her bloody dragon in her mind and sane, then Sid would kiss him and not care about the mate-claim frenzy.

Gregor hung up his phone and grinned. "Bram's coming, so you can have your front row seat."

She rolled her eyes. "You could've asked him over the phone."

"And give up a chance to see his facial expressions? I think not. Besides, you'll be a witness and my standing up to Bram will win points with Finn."

Finn Stewart was Lochguard's clan leader, who irritated Bram like a younger brother.

"Shouldn't you ask Finn first about staying?" she asked.

"Finn told me to stay as long as I like. Layla can handle things. Besides, Clan Seahaven has a doctor who helps Lochguard every once in a while, too. They won't miss me."

"I somehow doubt it. I bet your patients miss you already."

He smiled. "I do miss them, but you need my help more. I'm sure they would understand."

She tilted her head. "Why are you so determined to help me? I sense it's more than you just being a doctor."

He leaned down until he was a few inches from her face. "Because I'm starting to picture a future I want and I can't have it if you're not there."

Her breath hitched at the huskiness in his voice. When his pupils flashed, Gregor pulled back and added, "But for now, I must resist your sweet lips or my dragon may take control."

At the mention of his lips, her gaze shifted to them. She wanted to taste them again, which was ridiculous since Sid was thirty-eight years old and should be able to control herself. She needed to stop acting like a randy teenager.

A low warning hum sounded in her brain, but the sedative kept it from being full-blown. If the presence were indeed her dragon, Sid needed to avoid tempting her until she had a solution to ending her episodes.

Hope was a dangerous thing for someone like her, but Gregor's confidence and determination made her want to believe she could be cured.

Bram's voice muffled voice boomed down the hallway. "Where the hell is that bloody Scot?"

Ginny's steely voice answered, "Keep your voice down, or I'll toss you out." A pause and Ginny added, "They're in Room 4."

A few seconds later, Bram walked into the room and looked straight at Gregor. "What's so bloody important that I needed to come here in person?"

Gregor tsked. "Remember about your blood pressure. You need to stop yelling."

Bram narrowed his eyes, but his voice was more of a normal volume when he replied, "Why am I here, Innes?"

"You're here because Cassidy wants you to be."

"Don't drag me into this, Gregor," Sid hissed.

Bram looked between them before asking again, "Why am I here? You may have forgotten, but I'm clan leader. I have shit to do."

Gregor took Sid's hand and Bram watched the motion. Sid could've pulled away as Gregor had no claim on her. But she rather liked having someone know the Scottish doctor wanted her.

Hell, she rather wanted to hold his hand in front of the entire staff to signal he was off limits.

Before she could think too hard on that thought, Gregor's voice filled the room. "I'm staying on Stonefire until I find a way to bring Cassidy's dragon back."

"Is that possible?" Bram asked.

"I don't know," Gregor answered. "But we have a few ideas. Two doctors working on the case in close proximity means a greater chance of succeeding."

"By 'close proximity' do you mean living together?"

Sid wasn't surprised Bram had pieced that together so quickly. "Yes, although not quite in the way you think," Sid said. Gregor squeezed her hand, signaling he didn't agree with that, but

73

she ignored him, for now. "While you know I suffer from terrible headaches from time to time, there's something I've been keeping from you." She took a deep breath and added, "I have episodes of intense pounding and pain, as if something is trapped in my mind and can't get out."

"So every time you disappeared because of a headache, it was because of this?" Bram asked.

"Yes. I didn't mean to deceive you, Bram, but I didn't want to be locked away. Besides, when they started to increase in frequency, I requested another doctor," Sid stated.

Bram searched her eyes and sighed. "You should've come to me, Sid. I would've done anything I could to help."

The corner of her mouth ticked up. "Well, doctors don't often like to admit something's wrong with them."

Gregor jumped in. "Which is exactly why I'm going to stay. I'll make sure she takes care of herself."

Bram searched Gregor's eyes for one long minute. As easy as it was to wind up Bram, her clan leader based all of his decisions on the possible outcome rather than his emotions. Well, except for a few cases regarding his mate.

Sid hoped his emotions didn't get in the way this time.

She blinked and tried not to think of how much she was rooting for Gregor to stay, especially since her condition might only deteriorate. Not even the most determined dragon-shifter in the world could prevent the inevitable from happening through sheer will.

Bram finally grunted. "Aye, I'll let you stay. But, don't think it gives you free rein. I want to be updated on Sid's progress and anything you find. If we need to bring in more doctors, I'll find a way. But I can't do that if I don't know what's going on."

Sid's voice choked with emotion. "Thanks, Bram."

He waved a hand in dismissal. "You're clan, which makes you family. Of course I'm going to help you." He looked to Gregor. "I'm going to be watching you, though."

Gregor shrugged. "You'll soon realize my skills and grow to love my charm."

Bram mumbled, "Bloody Scot," before speaking to Sid again. "I'll put in a request for the Welsh dragonman to arrive as soon as he can. That way it will free up Innes's time to help you." She nodded. "And take care of yourself, Sid. Stonefire won't function properly without you."

Unused to praise and the talk of feelings, she bobbed her head. Before she could say anything, Gregor jumped in. "And right now, Cassidy needs to sleep. I'll call you again if anything changes."

Bram looked like he wanted to say something, but merely turned and raised a hand in parting.

After she heard Bram leave the surgery, Gregor pulled the blanket up around her body. "I was serious, love. You need to sleep."

"But the data—"

"I'll study it some more and investigate the dragon-shifter medical databases. Some of the research is locked up tight, so I might need Arabella's help to retrieve it."

Arabella MacLeod was a former Stonefire clan member, who was now the mate of Lochguard's leader. She was also a fairly skilled hacker.

"Just make sure none of you are caught."

"Well, if anyone comes to investigate, I'll just have to bring out my charm." He winked. "Few can resist when I really try."

Smiling, Sid said, "I may have to prove you wrong later."

"Oh, love, I'd like to see you try." He tucked her in. "However, sleep first. And in case you're worried, I'll be right here, watching over you. I won't let anything happen to you on my watch."

Snuggling into the bed, Sid wholeheartedly believed him.

As he stroked her forehead and hummed a tune, her eyelids turned heavy. Before she knew it, she was fast asleep.

~~~

Aaron Caruso, one of Stonefire's Protectors and Kai's second-in-command, drummed his fingers against the desk as he waited for the video conference call to go live. "Where is the bloody female?"

Another Protector at his side, Quinn, answered, "It's one minute past the time. Maybe something came up. After all, Teagan O'Shea has an entire clan to look after."

"I'm sure one of her people could inform us that she's running late."

A familiar female Irish accent filled the room. "She would have if she were late. However, I'm exactly on time."

Looking at the screen, Aaron's dragon hummed at the sight of the green-eyed, black-haired female. It was Clan Glenlough's leader, Teagan O'Shea.

His dragon spoke up. *She is just as pretty as I remembered.*

Ignoring his dragon, Aaron raised his brows. "It's not very leader-like to argue."

Before Teagan could reply, Quinn jumped in. "Thank you for agreeing to talk with us, O'Shea."

Teagan's gaze moved to Quinn. "Maybe I should ask Bram to make you our main liaison instead of Caruso." She flicked a gaze at Aaron and back to Quinn. "We could get things done a lot faster."

Cured by the Dragon

Clenching his fingers under the desk, Aaron growled out, "How about we put aside our differences for a minute and focus on what's important? Your brother mentioned something about a similar attack to what happened to our doctor, but said only you could tell us the details."

Teagan leaned back and crossed her arms over her chest. Thankfully, the camera wasn't pointed low enough to show her breasts or his dragon would've started throwing a tantrum again.

His beast growled. *Why do you ignore the obvious?*

Because I can. Life was complicated enough in Italy, and I need a break.

Teagan's voice prevented his dragon from replying. "It happened a few weeks ago. Something in the sky attacked a child."

Aaron frowned. "A child? Putting aside only a low-life would do such a thing, why? Targeting a clan's only doctor seems more strategic."

"Unless they were testing it out on an easy target," Teagan answered.

Anger flashed in Teagan's eyes and Aaron approved. Dragon-shifters treasured children. He couldn't imagine anyone hurting one.

Pushing aside his own anger, Aaron said, "I hope you have specifics."

Teagan lifted one arched eyebrow. "I'm not sure how the English dragon-shifters run their clans, but we document everything."

"Of course we bloody document everything. You just take too long to get to the point."

Quinn stepped in. "Ignore him, Ms. O'Shea. The cloudy weather affects his mood."

Aaron was going to punch Quinn the next time they were alone.

The corner of Teagan's mouth ticked up. "Is that so? You're living in the wrong country then, boy-o."

Rather than growl he wasn't a boy, Aaron drew all of his irritation deep inside and forced his voice to be neutral as he asked, "What did you find out about the attack on the child?"

Teagan's eyes widened a fraction but quickly turned fierce. "While there weren't any toxins or visible puncture wounds, our doctor finally found a tiny splinter-sized piece of wood embedded in the boy's scalp. Once we were able to remove it, they ran tests and found it was coated in an unidentifiable substance that mostly still remains a mystery."

Aaron leaned forward. "How's the boy now?"

Concern flicked in Teagan's gaze. "He's alive, but his inner dragon has become unpredictable and he's under constant watch."

Quinn chimed in, "That sounds more like the result of a targeted attack than a random teenager having fun with a new toy."

Teagan nodded. "Aye, although we still haven't discovered who did it."

"Send us the information you have and we'll see about spotting something you missed," Aaron said.

Teagan leaned back in her chair. "Putting aside the fact you just insulted my clan doctor's abilities, isn't your doctor the one who was attacked?"

"She was, but Sid can still take a look. There's another doctor here, as well," Aaron answered.

"I'm not sure I want to share this information around. If Clan Northcastle gets wind of this, they might try to seek out the attackers and target Glenlough."

Clan Northcastle was the dragon-shifter clan in Northern Ireland. Northcastle and Glenlough had a history of being allies for a few decades, becoming enemies, and then allies again. Currently, they were suspicious of each other.

Aaron answered, "As much as I don't want to admit it, I trust Lochguard. If you need to talk with Finn Stewart to ease your worries, we can arrange it. However, each second that ticks by with the political bullshit is a second lost to finding out what the bloody hell is going on. Our doctor lost her dragon, and if this unknown substance affects inner dragons, waiting could end up making things much worse for her."

Teagan studied him a second before adding, "You care for your clan's doctor."

Aaron growled. "Of course I do. Why is that a surprise? Sid has kept our clan together for nearly half my life."

His dragon spoke up. *There's no need to attack her. She is doing her job. A clan leader should always be cautious.*

And what about Sid? She's taken care of all of us, and it's more than time we take care of her.

Teagan's voice prevented his beast from answering. "I will send the information. However, my stance on keeping your Protector, Brenna, here until I meet with Bram in person won't change."

Brenna had accompanied Aaron on a mission to Ireland and remained with Clan Glenlough.

Aaron wanted to say Teagan's statement was childish, but Quinn beat him to the reply. "Of course. Once we sort out this mess, I'll personally talk with Bram and try to set up the meeting."

Teagan nodded. "Good." She looked to Aaron again. "If you were clan leader, you'd understand the necessity of keeping Brenna here. Try to think things through rather than lash out."

Before Aaron could do more than open his mouth, the screen went blank.

He growled. "That bloody female lives to put me down."

"She's not putting you down so much as trying to point out your lack of patience." His friend studied Aaron a second before adding, "Although given how much your dragon chimes in whenever she's near, I think there's another reason she gets under your skin so easily."

Aaron stood. "As I've said before, I'm not talking about that. Now, let's make sure that woman sends the information as promised."

"Suit yourself," Quinn murmured before exiting the room.

As Aaron followed, his beast poked his head out again. *Her pupils flashed too. We need to find a way to see her again in person.*

You just want to kiss her.

Of course. But she probably wants to kiss us too.

Ignoring his dragon, Aaron headed in the direction of the Protector's IT specialist, Nathan. He needed to focus on helping Sid. After all, Aaron had just returned home to Stonefire less than a year ago. Was it too much to want to merely enjoy his friends and family and forget about females? They only brought trouble and he wasn't sure he ever wanted to face it again.

Chapter Seven

Gregor frowned at the computer screen. There had to be at least a hundred files to sort through.

While he appreciated Arabella's hard work, finding something to help Sid might take longer than he liked.

His beast spoke up. *Acquiring what we want most in the world is almost never easy.*

It's not about me, dragon. The longer it takes to sift through everything, the longer Cassidy risks an episode that might steal her sanity.

Then we'll just have to stay close to her side. Even if she sleeps in the surgery most nights, we can stay in the same room.

She probably won't go for that.

So? We won't give her a choice.

Gregor smiled at his dragon's confidence. *You have a lot to learn about the human sides of females.*

Since his beast huffed and fell silent, Gregor opened the first file and scanned its contents, about the adverse effects of a specific sedative.

As he finished the first and worked his way through five more files, he rubbed his temples. Each case was idiosyncratic and spoke of rare reactions to drugs, not unlike with humans. All dragon-shifter doctors were partially trained at human universities, so Gregor was quite familiar with human biology. Maybe one day his kind could start up their own universities and instill the desire to share knowledge amongst all dragon-shifter doctors.

Or, even better, establish some sort of professional network to help answer questions and lend assistance.

But all of that had to wait. Helping Cassidy was all that mattered.

Just as he opened the next file, he glanced at the clock in the corner of his computer screen. It was time to check on his most important patient.

Exiting the room he used for research, Gregor rushed down the hall. While he'd hoped to have something to share with his doctor, he wasn't about to lose hope.

Entering her room, he found her asleep on her side. With a hand under her cheek and her mouth slightly open, Cassidy looked as if she didn't have a care in the world.

His dragon spoke up. *We need to work harder. Our female deserves the same peace when awake.*

Oh, so now you want to win her approval?

Cassidy's eyes fluttered open. When she met his gaze, she smiled and the sight stole his breath away.

He quickly recovered to catch her words as she said, "I'm surprised Ginny let you in here when I was sleeping."

Moving to the side of her bed, he brushed a section of hair off her face. "Oh, aye? She can try to keep me away, but I have a special touch with older females. After all, Lochguard has plenty of strong, older dragonwomen who run the clan in the background. If I can handle Lorna MacKenzie, I can handle your Ginny."

Cassidy snorted. "Lorna MacKenzie has known you your whole life and probably has some weakness when it comes to you. Ginny doesn't and she'll do what's necessary."

82

"Right, I'm sure she's a secret black belt who can pin me down."

She rolled her eyes. "Enough about Ginny. Did you find out anything yet?"

The eagerness in her voice stoked his inner fire to find an answer. "No, but Arabella found me plenty to look through. As I thought, the reactions that seem isolated sometimes have a pattern. Two cases concerned an allergic reaction to a certain sedative."

Sid raised her brows. "The dragon-slumber drug?"

He shook his head. "I haven't found anything about that yet. Still, I bet the more I comb through the records, the more patterns I'll find. Once we get you well again, maybe we should ask Arabella to look beyond the UK. Combined, we can put together some kind of reference for dragon-shifters."

"Between that and your desire to study brain activity surrounding our dragon halves, you might just have enough to do until you're old and gray."

The corner of his mouth ticked up. "Oh, I have another idea to squeeze in—a dragon-shifter university. I may need your help on that one."

Gregor winked, and Cassidy laughed before replying, "Anything else I should know about?"

He didn't miss how she ignored his comment about needing her help in the future. Given his cautious doctor, she wouldn't accept the possibility of a sane future until it happened.

His dragon growled. *I still think the frenzy will bring out her dragon.*

I won't risk it.

I thought you'd moved past your ridiculous fear of childbirth.

It's not that, although I won't completely discount that possibility, but Cassidy will stress over remaining sane if she ends up pregnant. That increases the risk of a dangerous delivery or complication.

Cassidy reached out and grabbed his hand. "Tell me why your smile faded, Gregor. If it's bad news you've been hiding about my case, then just tell me straight. I can handle it."

~~~

Sid had momentarily forgotten about all the things that could go wrong and had simply enjoyed talking with Gregor. Hell, she even mustered up the courage to tease him.

Then a frown creased his brows as his pupils flashed and worry crept into her mood. Had he been merely preparing her for the worst?

Gregor finally answered her question. "I haven't hidden anything, love. My dragon and I are still working out a few things."

For a split second, Sid longed to have an inner dragon to argue, discuss, and even laugh with. Memories of her beast were distant, but her dragon had been the easygoing one out of them.

However, if Sid had kept her beast, she may have strayed from her path of becoming a doctor. She loved being a doctor above all else. That was one positive thing, at least, about being half a dragon-shifter.

Gregor's deep voice cut through her thoughts. "If talking about my beast is too painful, I can put it off. But I think you're strong enough to handle it."

"I can. I've done it for years as a doctor, after all."

84

"Aye, you have. Although, given my dragon's tantrums, I sometimes wonder if you're not the lucky one to have a silent mind."

Whenever someone had brought up her dragon in the past, Sid had always changed the subject. Yet as she met Gregor's curious gaze again, the words spilled from her lips. "As a teenager, I would've agreed with you. My dragon never stopped going on about adventure. To be honest, I'm surprised I survived the seven years I had with my dragon. I snuck off Stonefire's land more than once. One time, I wanted to find the mythical dragon egg."

Gregor sat on the edge of her bed and stroked the back of her hand with his thumb. "As in the legendary necklace from the first dragon-shifter to set foot on the isle of Britain? You do realize that's a myth, right?"

Sid changed positions until she sat against her pillows. "Of course I do. Dragon-shifters don't lay eggs, yet the myth says the female wearing the necklace spawned three dozen eggs that we all descended from. It still doesn't mean that it's not tempting to go looking for it, especially for a teenager. After all, the necklace could be real even if the myth is rubbish."

"So, did you find it then?"

She blinked. "No one ever asked me that, not even my parents growing up."

"You're a very capable female, Cassidy Jackson. If it does exist, you have as good a chance as any of finding it."

The Scottish dragon-shifters were a charming lot and if it had been anyone else, Sid would've dismissed the compliment. But Gregor's eyes were sincere.

Although why he'd put so much faith in her after such a short period of time, she didn't know. Did it work that way with all true mates?

A dull thud started in the back of her mind. Sid winced, and Gregor touched her cheek. "What's wrong, lass? Is the sedative wearing off already?"

For the first time, a roar sounded off inside her head. Sid arched her back as the pressure increased.

She was barely aware of Gregor's lips on hers before her mind ripped in two. Screaming so loud her throat hurt, the world went black.

~~~

Five seconds after Gregor tried to kiss Cassidy, she screamed and slumped onto the bed unconscious.

Drawing on twenty years of practice, Gregor pushed aside his panic and forced himself to look at her vital signs. Her heart rate was slightly erratic, but not dangerous. All of her other signs were still within acceptable ranges.

Opening one of her eyelids, he discovered a slitted pupil; just as if a dragon were in control. For one second, he merely stared.

Then his beast snarled. *Help her.*

I will once I bloody well know what's wrong.

Checking her other eye, the other pupil was the same.

Had her dragon finally broken free? And if so, would it be insane?

As Gregor tried to think of what to do since he'd never been in this type of situation before, sharp points dug into his arms. Looking down, he saw the tips of Cassidy's fingers had extended into talons and were embedded in his skin.

He tried to loosen her grip, but rather than remove her hand, the talons dug in deeper.

"Cassidy, if you can hear me, you need to fight your dragon."

In response, her eyes opened and she hissed. As he moved to pin her top half down, she pounced and sent them tumbling to the floor.

Gregor managed to pin Cassidy underneath him, but one of her arms snaked loose and ripped off his shirt as she hissed in a voice not quite her own, "Mine."

Shit. He was probably dealing with her dragon. And not just any dragon, but possibly an insane one, hell-bent on completing the mate-claim frenzy.

The door opened and Ginny's voice drifted in. "What's going on?"

Dragon-possessed Cassidy snarled. "Get out. My male. I'll kill anyone who tries to take him."

Gregor finally succeeded in pinning Cassidy's arm down. He never severed eye contact with his doctor as he told Ginny, "We need to sedate her. The sedative that worked before is still on the counter. Hurry."

"No!" Cassidy yelled before her arm grew into a dragon's forelimb. She pushed against his chest and her increased strength sent Gregor flying across the room.

He thudded against the wall, but not hard enough to do permanent damage. Still, it took him a second to regain his wits enough to stand. By the time he did, Cassidy was gone.

He raced to Ginny on the floor, but she was conscious and murmured, "Find her. I'll alert the others."

With a nod, Gregor raced down the hallway. He followed the trail of scratched walls and furniture tossed to the side. He hoped she didn't do the same damage to any of her clan members or Cassidy would never forgive herself.

Pushing his muscles to run faster, he tried not to panic. Even if she didn't severely hurt anyone on her way out of the surgery, if Cassidy made it outside and succeeded in shifting, he might lose her forever. Not because she could fly away, but rather if she reached a human settlement and terrorized it, the DDA could shoot her down.

His beast roared. *We must stop her.*

Aye, so be ready to shift as quickly as possible.

While he felt his dragon pacing and waiting, Gregor followed Cassidy's trail. As he reached the reception area, he caught a glimpse of her long hair disappearing out the front door.

Gregor didn't have time to check the clan members huddling on the sides of the room. He only hoped Cassidy hadn't killed anyone. She may never come back to him if she had.

The late day sun hit his face, and he spotted Cassidy's tall form dashing toward the rear entrance to Stonefire.

"Cassidy," he yelled out. She looked over her shoulder, but rather than stop, the bloody female ran faster.

In the distance, he spotted Nikki Gray entering from the back gate. Before it could close, Cassidy pushed Nikki aside and darted out the entrance. While his dragon urged Gregor to follow their doctor, Nikki had landed front first on her stomach. Since she was several months pregnant, Gregor stopped. He couldn't risk the lives of two people for one, even if he wished it differently.

Just as he crouched and murmured, "Nikki, are you okay?" her mate, a human named Rafe Hartley, dashed toward them.

"Nikki," the human male yelled before crouching down and turning her over.

Nikki's eyes fluttered open and Gregor motioned toward the rear entrance. "Rafe, you need to go find Cassidy, and quickly. I'll look after Nikki."

"There's no fucking way I'm leaving her," Rafe bit out.

Nikki's voice was soft as she said, "Go, Rafe. I'm okay. I think Sid's dragon-possessed. If we don't stop her, the DDA might kill her."

Gregor met Rafe's gaze. "Please find her. If I had your skills, I'd go in your place. But I don't. I'll look after your mate. My skills will help more than comforting words from you."

After sharing a glance with Nikki, Rafe kissed her gently and stood up. "Fine. But if anything is wrong with Nikki when I get back, I will have your hide, dragonman."

Nikki pointed toward the rear entrance. "Just go, Rafe. And hurry."

With a nod, Rafe punched in his code and disappeared. A few seconds later, two dragons soared overhead and circled around the nearby forest and mountains.

His dragon hissed. *We should be searching for her.*

We're not trained soldiers. They will find her faster than we could.

Nikki's voice prevented his dragon from replying. "Rafe will find her, Dr. Innes."

He met the younger female's eyes. Her conviction reminded him of his duty. "Aye, let's hope so. Now, tell me where it hurts."

As he examined Nikki, Gregor wished with everything he had that Stonefire found Cassidy before the DDA or dragon hunters did.

Chapter Eight

Sid ran her hands against the mental prison wall for the hundredth time, but nothing she did budged it even an inch.

As her beast tackled Gregor, all Sid could do was watch. She wondered if her dragon had been this way for twenty-four years—allowed to see everything that happened but powerless to do anything about it.

She was grateful Gregor had her pinned to the floor. Yet with his body over hers, her dragon wanted to do one thing at any cost—mate.

But at the mention of the sedative, her dragon roared and snarled. *NO. Not again.*

As her beast escaped the exam room and made her way out of the building, each person her dragon tossed aside made Sid cringe. She was supposed to heal others, not hurt them. She only hoped her clan would forgive her.

Well, if she survived this escapade.

No. She wouldn't allow negative thoughts. She needed solutions, not a constant stream of what-ifs.

Eager to try something, Sid put on her sternest doctor voice and said inside her head, *Stop it and let me out of here, right now.*

Her dragon laughed maniacally and made them run faster.

Damn. She didn't have a dragon; she had a crazed beast.

CURED BY THE DRAGON

Sid had no idea what to do. All those years wishing she had an inner dragon were coming back to haunt her.

She actually gave a strangled laugh at all those wasted wishes. The beast in the front of her mind wasn't a friend or ally. She completely ignored her and kept repeating four words over inside their head: *Run. Hide. Find. Fuck.*

Yet, if Sid didn't do something, her beast would find Gregor, ravish him, and who knew what else would happen in the interim. For once, she wished she'd dug more into the research behind the psychology of the two halves of a dragon-shifter.

Taking a deep breath, she pushed aside the negativity. Dr. Sid Jackson didn't wallow. No, she needed to think of ideas to test out and find a solution. Because there was no way she was going to allow her beast to kill and terrorize. Even if it meant her life, Sid would find a way to stop her dragon.

As Nikki was pushed out of the way, Sid clenched her fingers and said, *Stop it. Even a dragon should want to protect a child. Nikki is pregnant.*

After a beat, her beast answered, *I won't be contained again.*
You won't be. I'll make sure of it.
Liar!

The dragon went back to ignoring her and weaving through the trees of the forest. Just as Sid searched her brain for an idea, her beast caught the scent of a familiar human male: Rafe Hartley.

Sid wondered if her beast would have access to Sid's memories, but as her dragon roared, *He won't catch me*, she had her answer.

Sitting down in her mental cell, Sid closed her eyes and tried to remember what her teachers had taught her as a child about working with and containing her dragon-half. There had to be something she could do to stop her.

Because once her dragon shifted and relearned the basics of flying, that would sign Sid's death warrant.

~~~

Back in the surgery, Gregor finished checking the last person injured by Sid's dragon's dash and slipped into the hallway. However, not two seconds later, Bram's voice filled the corridor. "Come with me."

"Is Cassidy okay? Did you find her?" he asked.

"Not here. Come."

Gregor shook his head. "I can't leave my patients. Nikki, in particular, needs to be watched closely."

Bram motioned with his head. "We're staying in the building, but just a few doors down. Ginny can keep watch and let us know instantly if anything is wrong."

Gregor looked at the door to Nikki's room. "Nikki is one of your Protectors. No matter what it is, she should be privy to it."

"Look, Innes, I don't want to argue. But the last thing we need to do is cause Nikki any stress. For once, just trust me."

Searching Bram's eyes, Gregor's dragon chimed in. *Nikki is fine. Everything checked out normal. You're just worrying more than necessary because she's pregnant. I want to trust Stonefire's leader.*

Gregor's dragon rarely trusted so quickly, which spoke volumes about his beast's opinions of Bram.

With a sigh, Gregor took a step toward Bram. "Then let's hurry up."

He followed Bram's lead to a room a few doors down. As soon as Gregor shut the door behind him, Bram spoke again.

"We're still trying to locate Sid. Thank fuck she hasn't shifted yet, or we might be having a grimmer conversation."

"Just tell me why you called me in here. Neither one of us has time to beat around the bush."

Approval flashed in Bram's eyes. "Aye, you're right. What I need for you to do is think of how to coax Sid back from the edge."

"I would love nothing more, but usually the dragon-shifter teachers have a better grasp on how to do it."

Bram nodded. "Tristan MacLeod is going to help, but so are you. From what I heard from Ginny, Sid wants you for the mate-claim frenzy. That could work to our advantage."

Gregor clenched his fingers. "I won't impregnate Sid without knowing she'll be fine afterward. A pregnant, out-of-control dragon would do too much damage. I also won't take the choice of whether or not to have a child away from her."

Bram studied him a second before replying, "You're a much better male than I originally thought."

"Bloody hell, Bram, don't you understand how serious this situation is? Stop wasting time thinking about me and think about Cassidy."

"I am," Bram growled. "Snapping at me won't help Sid. Instead, work with me. You don't have to complete the mate-claim frenzy, but if you can entice Sid into your arms, we can sedate her and have Tristan and the other teachers work with her."

The thought of kissing Cassidy so she could be shot full of the drugs she hated so much made his stomach churn.

Gregor cleared his throat. "If we do this, we do it my way. The teachers may have the greatest chance of bringing Cassidy back from the brink, but I can help, too. Promise me I can stay as long as I want and keep me in the loop about anything to do with Cassidy Jackson, and I'll help."

He half expected Bram to argue or throw back his words about the seriousness of the situation. To Gregor's surprise, Bram put out a hand. "I promise."

Gregor took the other male's hand and shook. A second later, Bram dropped his hand. "Kai has a plan, but it means leaving Nikki's side for a short while. Were you serious about needing to watch her or were you just being a good doctor?"

His dragon flicked his tail, as if reminding Gregor of their earlier conversation. Gregor answered, "If my junior doctor on Lochguard had examined Nikki, she would've cleared her. I just like to be extra careful."

"I know what happened to your mate, Innes, and I'm sorry. But Nikki is strong and young, with no history of complications or even ill health. If your other doctor would clear her, then don't feel guilty about doing the same."

He's right, his dragon said. *Let's help Cassidy.*

After taking a deep breath, Gregor replied, "What did you want me to do?"

~~~

Sid watched as her dragon weaved them between the trees. Her beast had been wandering the forest for nearly an hour. While dragons circled overhead, Rafe's scent had vanished.

She knew that Bram wouldn't give up on her so easily, but she kept that thought tightly guarded so her beast wouldn't pick up on it. She had no bloody idea if she could even keep a secret without proper training, but she was going to try.

Their stomach rumbled and her beast murmured, "Food. I need food."

Extending an arm, her fingers extended into talons. Not wanting the shift, Cassidy banged against her prison. *I know where we can get food.*

The beast paused before saying aloud, "Where?"

The clan has food. She paused and decided to add, *Gregor will feed us.*

Yes, our mate. He will feed us and then I'll fuck him.

Sid decided to keep appealing to her dragon's baser instincts. *Yes, food and lots of fucking. Find him. That means in human form as the frenzy can only be completed when human.*

My male, not yours. I want him.

Then go.

Her dragon hesitated. Not that Sid could blame her—they were strangers, after all. She also had no idea how much her beast had learned about Sid during her twenty-plus-year confinement.

Seizing on what might be her only chance, Sid recalled Gregor's naked chest, brushing his blond chest hair, and drinking in the view of his chiseled muscles. Her dragon started humming, so Sid went further and visualized the peek she'd had of Gregor's cock back on Lochguard all those months ago.

Heat raced through her body as her beast took the combined images of Gregor's naked body and visualized them straddled over him and riding him hard.

She should stop her dragon, but deep down, Sid wished she had the chance to do exactly as her beast wanted.

Wait, what was wrong with her? It must be the effects of her dragon's lust seeping into her own thoughts. She couldn't allow the mate-claim frenzy to happen.

Right before her beast had them coming in their vision, the faint trace of a familiar male scent drifted into the air.

Gregor.

The movie stopped in her head and her beast sniffed the air. *He's here. Forget food. I want to claim him.*

Sid had hoped to use the need to claim Gregor as a method to get back to Stonefire. If he were really in the woods, she feared for his safety. An out-of-control dragon could be rough, or so she'd read in a few reports in the past. Fracturing a penis wasn't completely ridiculous.

Well, if it came to it, Sid would do whatever it took to make sure her beast didn't hurt Gregor.

Just as she stood inside her prison and readied herself, a shirtless Gregor stood in front of them. "Hello, lass. Looking for me?"

~~~

Gregor barely noticed the cool spring air as he spotted a wild-eyed Cassidy standing about ten feet away. He'd found her.

His dragon hissed. *Of course we did. Stop doubting me.*

You can throw your tantrum later. Right now, we need to stick to the plan.

His beast remained silent, which told Gregor how much his dragon wanted their female.

He made his way through the underbrush to Cassidy's location. It wouldn't be his first choice to traipse through the woods without a shirt, but he'd needed his scent as strong as possible. Otherwise, Cassidy's dragon might not have picked up their scent until it was too late and the plan could have failed.

Dragon-eyed Cassidy met his gaze. "Mine," she stated in the growly voice before rushing toward him.

Opening his arms, Gregor braced himself for whatever the dragon might do. "Come here, love, and you can have me."

"All of you," she growled as she closed the distance. She reached out a talon, the only part of her that was in dragon form, and Gregor took hold of her wrist. Pulling her up against his body, he nibbled her ear and murmured, "Let's save the rough stuff for later."

Dragon-possessed Cassidy rubbed against his body and Gregor's cock went hard. He should keep his mind calm and focused, but the combination of the friction and Cassidy's delicate feminine scent made him groan. "Cassidy."

His dragon growled. *We can claim her later. Remember the plan.*

With Herculean effort, Gregor released her wrist and took hold of Cassidy's hips to still her movements. He whispered, "Before I strip you naked and claim you every which way, kiss me. I'm dying for another taste of your sweet lips."

"Mine," she said before standing on her tiptoes and taking his lips.

The dragon was definitely in charge. Cassidy would've called him out on his charm.

Yet as the beast stroked and pulled him close, Gregor had trouble remembering it was the dragon and not his doctor doing the kissing.

Maybe someday, he could have both of them.

He pulled away and met her brown eyes. "How do you feel?"

Cassidy's dragon frowned. "What do you mean?"

Stroking her hip, he watched her eyes closely. A few seconds later, they began to droop. She murmured, "What?"

"Shh," he whispered as he held her close and gently laid her down. When she was finally unconscious, Gregor took out his mobile phone and dialed Kai. When the leader picked up, Gregor said, "The drug on my lips worked. She's unconscious, but I don't know for how long."

"We'll be there in a few minutes," Kai answered before hanging up the phone.

As Gregor caressed Cassidy's cheek, he hoped his calculations were correct. If she awoke before the Protectors could contain her, then they might lose Cassidy forever. After all, he'd just drugged his true mate unconscious via a topical sedative. He hoped she understood the need for it. There was also the chance she would have a reaction like with the dragon-slumber drug.

Chapter Nine

Sid awoke on the floor of her mental prison. Sitting up, she tried to see what was happening, but her dragon half was just beginning to stir, so it was pitch-black.

Maybe with her dragon not fully conscious, Sid could find a way to slip out.

Reaching forward, she surveyed the wall again with her hands. The surface was still smooth. Nothing had changed.

Sid sighed and leaned forward against the wall. Yet instead of a solid surface, it gave a few inches.

She had a chance.

Sid pushed with everything she had, and the wall gave a little more. However, it wasn't long before she was breathing heavily. Once all of this was over, she was going to stop neglecting her health and build up her endurance. Dragon-shifters were meant to be strong.

With one last heave, the wall completely enveloped her body. The cool, smooth surface lasted another second before she crashed through.

Jumping to her feet, she looked around for her beast. When she spotted her, the dragon was curled up fast asleep.

While she had little experience containing her dragon, she remembered her teacher's words from over twenty years ago: Build a prison piece by piece in your head, around the dragon.

The stronger the materials and more complex the construction, the longer it will hold.

Imagining steel bars, she constructed a box with bars closely spaced together. When she placed the last piece, Sid panted from the mental exertion.

And to her surprise, the dragon still slept.

For a second, she wondered if Gregor had used the dragon-slumber drug, but then quickly pushed the thought aside. She was more concerned with waking up and finding out if she had a future or if Bram would have to turn Sid over to the DDA for everyone's safety.

Not afraid to find out what her future held, Sid forced her eyes open. She half expected for it not to work. But five seconds later, her physical eyelids parted and light hit her eyes. Blinking a few times, she barely noticed the straps around her wrists and ankles and looked around until she saw Gregor asleep in the chair next to her bed.

His hair lay across his forehead and the stubble on his cheeks was a bit longer. Had he sat next to her the whole time?

There was only one way to find out. "Gregor."

He instantly shot up and rubbed his eyes before meeting her gaze. Cupping her cheek, he searched her eyes. "Cassidy? Is it truly you?"

"Yes, it's me. Tell me what's going on."

"What about your dragon?"

She checked her prison. "She's asleep inside a cage I constructed. I only hope it holds." She paused and then added, "What happens now?"

The corner of Gregor's mouth ticked up. "Between us or in general?"

She frowned. "In general. Now is not the time to tease."

100

"Ah, but you're wrong, lass. I think more than ever you need some lightness and maybe even a wee hug."

She yearned to lean against Gregor's chest and simply listen to his heartbeat. But she couldn't afford that kind of normalcy. "You're aware I have a half-crazed dragon loose in my head and that the second she wakes up, we could all be in trouble. You, most of all, should be careful. For your safety, you should go back to Lochguard."

Irritation flashed in his eyes. "I'm not bloody leaving you. Although I don't think telling you how my heart thudded until you were safe and sound back here would do any good, stubborn woman."

"Gregor—"

"But I have information you need. While Tristan MacLeod is going to help you learn to control your dragon, I'm going to keep looking and digging for information about inner dragons that show up later in life."

"As far as I know, I'm the only one."

"Aye, well, I think there have been others and I'm determined to find them." His voice softened. "You just discovered your beast and I don't want to banish her again."

Sid remembered Gregor's words about wanting a future that might include her. "You don't have to be noble, Gregor. We can both pretend you never said anything about maybe wanting me as your mate." He opened his mouth, but she cut him off. "You've suffered more than enough heartbreak, and I don't want to only cause more grief in your life. I'll accept your help as far as my dragon, but then you need to go back to Scotland."

Gregor remained silent as his pupils flashed to dragon slits. Even when he was unhappy and clenching his jaw, she wanted him more than any male in her life.

But Sid wouldn't be selfish. Even if she could control her dragon a little, her beast could revert to her old ways at any time. She wasn't about to allow anyone else to care for her.

~~~

Gregor resisted the urge to take Cassidy's shoulders, tell her he wasn't going to bloody leave her, and then kiss her to show her how much he meant it.

However, the lass was clearly spooked. While his dragon may argue and fight him, Gregor had no idea what it would be like to have a crazy, uncontrollable presence in his head. Only after he ensured Cassidy's sanity and the woman could be persuaded to think of more than the present, then would he pursue her with full force.

His beast spoke up. *Then hurry up and help her. I don't like waiting to claim what's ours.*

She hasn't said that she is ours yet, dragon.

She will be.

Have some patience. If you had been a prisoner for twenty years, unable to talk with me, you'd be crazy, too.

His beast huffed. *I wish I could talk to her dragon. I would have it all sorted in a matter of minutes.*

Rather than argue the ridiculous point, Gregor finally answered Cassidy, "I'll go back to Scotland when it's necessary."

Relief flashed in her eyes, and he wanted to growl. What his doctor didn't know was that he may return to Scotland, but he'd bloody well come back.

Cassidy nodded. "Good. Now that's sorted, tell me what you used to put my dragon to sleep."

"I'm not sure if I should reveal my secrets."

"Gregor, just tell me."

"All right, all right. I used a variation of the dragon-slumber drug, but reduced the dose." She frowned, but he continued before she could speak. "And no, I didn't use a needle. I applied it to my lips. I supposed you can say it's a reversal of the *Sleeping Beauty* story—my kiss put you to sleep rather than awaken you."

"Clever. Our last kiss was at least a memorable one. I'm sure tales will develop around it if the teenagers get wind of it."

His dragon snarled at the thought of never kissing Cassidy again, but thankfully the door opened and prevented Gregor from dealing with his beast. Ginny's head popped in. "I thought I heard voices. How's our patient doing?"

Cassidy answered, "Let's not do this, Ginny. Just tell Bram I'm awake. I want to know what comes next."

Ginny tsked. "You're going to get well, of course. Keep up with the negative thoughts and I'll withhold your dessert from your meals."

Gregor said in a loud whisper, "Don't worry, I can sneak something in."

Ginny walked up to him and lightly smacked the side of his head. "You're a guest in my surgery. Remember that."

Cassidy snorted, and Gregor couldn't help but grin at his doctor. With her dragon out of the picture for the moment, it was almost as if they could all forget what was looming on the horizon.

But then he remembered that Cassidy had maybe a day before her dragon would wake up. He couldn't afford to waste time. He looked to Ginny. "Ask Tristan to come. I want him to start working with Cassidy straight away."

Ginny's gaze darted to Cassidy. "Sid has barely been awake two minutes. I think she should rest, first."

Cassidy shook her head. "I actually agree with Gregor. While I was lucky enough for you all to bring me back this time, I may not be so lucky next time. I need all of the help I can get."

"Fine," Ginny replied. "Although I'm going to chat with Tristan first, to make sure he doesn't bring his twins with him. Those two cause more trouble than five teenage dragon-shifters and I'm not about to chase them around the surgery."

Sid bit her lip a second before nodding. "Good luck. Jack and Annabel have been glued to his side recently. It may be more trouble than it's worth to force them apart."

Ginny muttered something as she left. When the door clicked shut, Sid smiled. "I almost hope he does bring them. I could do with a distraction."

Gregor leaned forward a few inches and searched her eyes. "Are you in pain? You need to keep me in the bloody loop or I can't help you."

"While my mind is a bit raw from the recent escapade with my dragon, it's manageable. It's just that…"

Her voice trailed off and Gregor took her hand. When she didn't pull away, hope bloomed in his chest. "Tell me, lass. I can keep a secret."

Fear flashed in her eyes. "If my dragon takes control again, I want you to restrain me and keep me sedated as long as it takes to either help me or allow the DDA to take me away."

"No one is taking you away."

"Gregor, please. I've spent so many years keeping the clan healthy and alive that it would tear me apart if I ended up harming any more of them. As it is, what I did today with pushing people out of the way, especially Nikki, will stay with me for the rest of my life."

While he had hope he would never need to do anything, he nodded. "I promise you. But only if you've reached the point of no return. You're going to fight with everything you have, Cassidy Jackson. Because if you don't, then you'll have to deal with me."

"Oh? Am I supposed to be afraid?"

He growled. "I've been Mr. Nice Doctor up until now. But if you need pushing and prodding, I'm going to push you hard. I never give up on a patient until death claims them. You're one of my patients now, so be forewarned."

"I'm almost tempted to see what Mr. Tough Doctor looks like. You Scottish dragons always act as if you're jolly and enjoying life, but I think you have your moments like we do."

"Oh, I'm not denying that claim." He almost mentioned mates but caught himself in time. "But laughing along the way makes life more enjoyable. Maybe with enough interaction with my clan, your clan will learn that lesson."

She frowned. "Don't criticize my clan. Remember, Stonefire is the one who put their necks out and pushed for change. If not for us, you wouldn't be here, your leader wouldn't have a mate, and you wouldn't be able to sell your naked wood carvings to humans."

"I don't have any naked carvings," he growled.

"Maybe I'll ask Arabella to find out for sure."

The amusement dancing in her eyes made him smile. "If you can tease me, you must not be doing that poorly."

"I don't know how much time I have left, so I'm trying to make the most of it."

Leaning forward, he caressed her cheek. Cassidy's breath hitched. He waited, giving her time to pull away.

When she didn't, he dared to speak up again. "Then let me give you one last proper kiss. I don't want you to remember me drugging you unconscious." She hesitated, so he added, "There's nothing on my lips if you're worried. I cleaned them right after I got back. They are pure Gregor Innes."

His dragon growled. *Hurry up and kiss her.*

No. This is her decision.

But she wants us. I can hear her heart racing.

Cassidy murmured, "Just one kiss," before leaning forward to meet his lips.

~ ~ ~

Rationally, Sid knew she should push Gregor away and avoid any sort of contact. As it were, just holding his hand kept her grounded and calmer than she would've imagined she'd be. Hell, she'd been teasing the man about naked carvings. Given the enormity of what loomed, she should be focused on winning against her dragon.

Yet as he leaned close and asked for a kiss, she remembered the warmth of his skin and the sweet taste of his mouth. If she had just one more kiss, she could take her time to memorize every detail slowly so when he returned to Lochguard, Sid could bring up the memory and cling to it. Sid didn't think she'd want any male after Gregor, so she needed to make a memory to last a lifetime.

Trying not to think of how much Gregor invaded her thoughts, she gave her answer and kissed the Scottish dragonman.

She'd barely reveled in the warmth of his lips before his hot tongue swept into her mouth. Wrapping an arm around his back, Sid leaned in and gasped at the contact of her breasts against his hard chest.

Gregor moved until he was on the bed and hauled her into his lap. His hard cock between her legs should've set off warning bells, but Sid didn't care. This was the last kiss she'd have with her Scot, and she was determined to make it good enough to sustain her forever, through all of the hard times ahead.

His large hands moved to her bum and rocked her against him. She gasped, and Gregor took the kiss deeper. The ache between her legs intensified and her nipples tingled. Every nerve ending was sensitive to even the slightest movement. No male had ever set her body on fire like this before.

All she wanted to do was to strip Gregor and ride him like in her dragon's vision from earlier. She had no doubt his skill at kissing was just a glimpse of what he could do with his hands and mouth on her body.

Gregor released her lips and kissed down the side of her neck. Sid moaned as he nipped her skin. She was barely aware of him untying her hospital gown and slipping it off one shoulder to expose her breast. Arching her back in invitation, Gregor took her nipple and sucked hard.

Threading her fingers through his hair, she rubbed against his cock.

However, before she could suggest for him to strip, someone knocked at the door. The sound brought reality crashing back, and Gregor released her nipple.

Looking away from Gregor, Sid scrambled off his lap to the far side of the bed and pulled her gown back into place. She'd come far too close to making a horrible mistake. Gregor was strong, but he might not be able to resist the mate-claim frenzy once it started, especially once her dragon woke up and took control.

"Cassidy—" Gregor began, but Tristan MacLeod's voice boomed from outside the door.

"Hurry up and answer the bloody door. My children are waiting for me at home."

107

CHAPTER TEN

Gregor's dragon snarled. *Challenge the male and chase him away. Cassidy is ours. She wants us. We need to finish what we started.*

Gregor clenched his fingers. *No. She's not ready and would resent us forever if we pushed her.*

She doesn't need much pushing. She was happy enough rubbing against our cock.

Tristan's voice boomed from the other side of the door again. "Last chance to let me in or I'm leaving."

Remembering how much Cassidy needed Tristan's help, he moved to the door. He glanced to make sure his doctor was decent before opening the door. Gregor eyed the dragon-shifter teacher he'd seen on Lochguard before. "Tristan MacLeod."

Tristan grunted before pushing past Gregor to stand at Cassidy's side. "All I was told was that you needed my help, but I'm not sure what I can do."

Gregor opened his mouth to castigate the male's surly tone, but Cassidy beat him to it. "Tristan MacLeod, if not for me, you wouldn't have your mate today. All I ask is for you to cut the alpha bullshit and teach me how to control my dragon."

Tristan crossed his arms over his chest and sighed. "Sorry, Sid. My twins have tested my patience lately. Don't tell Melanie how I snapped."

Cassidy raised her brows. "That depends if you actually try to help me and act at least somewhat friendly to Dr. Innes. We need him."

Tristan glanced over at Gregor. "Since he's not shacking up with my sister like the bloody Scottish clan leader, I'll try, but I can't make any promises."

It was on the tip of Gregor's tongue to tease Tristan about Arabella, but he decided Cassidy's well-being took precedence. "Then let's cut to the chase. We have a little less than a day before Cassidy's dragon stirs. The beast is unstable and she needs to learn how to rein it in."

The corner of Tristan's mouth ticked up. "Well, I agree that *Cassidy* is strong, but I'm not sure even you can manage it in a day, Doc."

"I'm going to try," Cassidy stated.

Tristan shrugged. "Fine. But it's hard to do anything without the beast actually awake."

Gregor growled. "Do what you can."

Tristan studied him a second before his pupils flashed. The Stonefire dragonman finally replied, "I will for Sid's sake, not because you want to fuck her."

Cassidy narrowed her eyes. "Tristan."

"Does he deny it?" Gregor couldn't bring himself to lie, so he said nothing. Tristan smiled. "I thought so." He looked to Cassidy again. "If you want any chance of succeeding, you need to be 100 percent honest with me, Sid. Otherwise, anything I say will be a waste of time." Sid finally bobbed her head and Tristan's brown eyes met his again. "And you need to cut the protective bullshit. I'm happily mated, and while I'm not sure a Scot is worthy of our doc, you have no competition from me."

Gregor's dragon spoke up. *I believe him.*

Nice of you to ignore all the insults.

Challenging him on everything takes time away from helping Cassidy. Are you really going to let your pride get in the way?

Gregor grunted. "Fine. So, let's get started."

Tristan motioned with one hand. "Wait outside. Sid doesn't need any distractions."

Gregor nearly blurted how Cassidy was his patient, but as he met his doctor's eyes, he could see her saying she'd be all right. Regardless of Tristan MacLeod's rough manner, Cassidy trusted Tristan and Gregor trusted her.

His dragon huffed. *About time.*

Gregor spoke aloud, "I'll check on my patients and come back in an hour or two." He sent Tristan a piercing stare. "But if anything goes wrong or her condition changes, you hit the panic button and find me. Understood?"

"Fine," Tristan muttered.

As Gregor exited the room, he wondered how the hell the surly dragonman was a teacher, let alone how he could help Cassidy. But since his dragonwoman trusted the Stonefire male, Gregor would have to do the same. As much as he wanted to hiss and chase any male away from his doctor, he knew Cassidy wouldn't put up with it.

His dragon chimed in. *Keep thinking of her and acting noble and she'll want to mate us sooner.*

We'll see, dragon. We'll see.

~~~

Once Sid and Tristan were alone, she sighed. "Was it really necessary to provoke him?"

"Yes. Any male who wants you had better be able to stand up for himself while also knowing when to let someone fight their own battles."

"Someone's become quite the philosopher."

He grunted. "Melanie has me reading books on childrearing."

She smiled. "Maybe I should have you come in and give talks to the other males." When Tristan glowered, Sid decided to get down to business and changed the subject. "So, I'm ready to learn, Tristan. What's first?"

He studied her before pulling up a chair and sitting next to her bed. "You didn't lose your dragon until you were a teenager, so what do you remember?"

Careful not to let the memories flow, Sid answered automatically, "The basics of how to construct a simple prison. There's no talking with her in her present state, though. When she's not unconscious, all she thinks about is the mate-claim frenzy."

"Did you ever consider embracing it? She might become more cooperative afterward."

She frowned. "I'm not about to give Gregor hope and get pregnant just to appease my dragon."

"Do you want a future?"

She blinked. "What?"

"You heard me. Do you want a future or are you giving up and preparing yourself to die?"

"I almost forgot how blunt you are."

He shrugged. "Tiptoeing around my sister for a decade taught me a thing or two."

"You've grown quite a bit, Tristan MacLeod. Thank goodness for Melanie."

111

His face softened. "Yes." Hardness returned to his eyes. "But you're trying to distract me. From what I know about dragons, once they have an idea, they focus on it and won't change or try to restrain themselves until that idea is addressed. It happens all the time with my students. Your situation is probably similar since you haven't had decades to train your dragon." His pupils flashed and he added, "Or, as my beast puts it, you haven't had time to compile a list of compromises."

"No, I haven't. But surely there's something else we can try?"

"We can try things, but the mate-claim frenzy will most likely overpower any and all techniques you learn. You're a novice, Sid. If you don't accept that now, you don't stand a chance."

Tristan had a knack for making clan members uncomfortable, but in this instance, Sid was grateful for his honesty. "And yet, there's no guarantee my beast will calm down once the frenzy is complete, right?"

"When it comes to dragons, there's no guarantee about anything, except maybe for their determination regarding mates and protecting children."

Which meant there was a chance her beast would behave at least until her child was born. That might give Sid enough time to learn how to control her dragon. It was possible for her to be a mother after all these years of accepting she'd never have the opportunity.

Wait a second. Why was she even thinking of children? She had no doubt Gregor would care for theirs if her dragon eventually took control and Sid had to be imprisoned. However, she didn't want to hurt him and have him lose someone else. It was all too easy for Sid to imagine falling for the Scottish doctor.

Pushing aside thoughts of Gregor, she met Tristan's eyes again. "I'll think about it. In the meantime, I need you to teach me anything that could help."

"Right, then we're going to cover dragon prison basics. If you have even a crack in it, they will find a way out. So, close your eyes and tell me what you built and how."

As Sid did what Tristan asked and described her current prison, Sid's mind kept returning to Tristan's suggestion about embracing the frenzy. If, and it was a big if, she convinced herself it was a viable option, she wouldn't do it without Gregor's consent. The trick would be in participating in the frenzy and mustering the strength to construct a wall around her heart if it didn't calm her beast.

~~~

Gregor read the same paragraph three times before he sighed and rubbed his temples. Between scanning the medical files he'd received from Arabella and the new ones about the unknown substance from the attack on a child at Glenlough in Ireland, Gregor had enough work to keep him busy for months.

And yet, his mind kept drifting to Cassidy Jackson. Tristan had been with her for nearly two hours and only through sheer restraint had Gregor kept from barging into Cassidy's room.

His dragon sighed. *As I keep saying, he's helping her. If there's trouble, the English dragonman will let us know. Smothering Cassidy will only push her away.*

Aye, I know that. Still, I'm afraid something will happen, her dragon will wake up, and we'll lose the human half of her forever.

Stop being so pessimistic. It's not our way.

Gregor looked back to the computer screen. *If I could only figure out the mysterious compound that coated the small sliver found in both*

113

the child and Cassidy, I might find a way to help her. And not just for selfish reasons, but if too many dragon-shifters get this drug in their system, things won't turn out well.

Then reach out to Layla. She has a stronger background in chemistry than us.

A knock on the door interrupted his conversation. "Come in."

Bram appeared in the doorway with a stranger behind him. "Your help has arrived."

"What help?"

Bram stepped to the side, and a young dragonman in his midtwenties with black hair and brown eyes moved to stand next to him. When he spoke, it was with a North Welsh accent. "Hello. I'm Dr. Trahern Lewis from Clan Snowridge."

Gregor moved a little more in front of his computer screen. He didn't need a stranger knowing what he was doing. "While normally I'd welcome you and get you up to speed on my patient list, Nurse Ginny can do that. I have something important to work on."

Bram raised his brows. "Is it to do with Sid? Trahern knows about that."

Gregor eyed the Welsh dragonman and then met Bram's gaze again. "Can I speak to you alone?"

Bram said to Trahern, "While I talk with Innes, find the nurse we met a few minutes ago. She'll help you get settled. I'll find you once I'm done here."

Curiosity burned in the male's eyes, but he merely nodded and exited the room. Once the door clicked shut, Bram demanded, "Tell me why you're dismissing him. Trahern came a few weeks early to help ease your burden so you can help with Sid."

"I appreciate the help, but I don't know him. Unless you want him seeing the recent information we received from the Irish clan?"

"I imagine that's not all you're doing, but I'll play innocent for now. Still, you're going to get Trahern up to speed with your patients, and Ginny will keep an eye on him. While my head Protector was thorough, we all need to watch him to make sure he's not hiding anything."

"I'm surprised you're including me in on this."

Bram shrugged. "Sid has a high opinion of you and I admire your dedication. You're well on your way to earning my trust, so remember that and don't fuck up."

Gregor's dragon preened in the back of his mind. Before his beast could gloat, Gregor nodded. "Thanks, Bram. I have no plan of fucking things up." He hesitated a second but decided honesty with Bram would be best. "Cassidy is my true mate. While neither one of us intends to see the frenzy through, my dragon alone will do anything to help her."

Bram stared at him a second before answering, "Will you tell me why you're so hell-bent on not embracing the gift of a mate?"

Gregor stood to his full height and was happy to notice his gaze was level with Bram's. "I mean no disrespect, but it's none of your fucking business."

For one long second, Gregor wondered if he'd just earned himself a one-way ticket back to Scotland. But when Bram smiled, he relaxed a fraction as the Stonefire leader said, "Aye, I understand that. All I ask is to keep an open mind. While you bloody Scots are always causing me trouble, if keeping you around means Sid can be happy, I'm open to the idea. Don't let my judgment stand in the way."

Before Gregor could say anything, Bram opened the door. "Talk to Trahern. There were several applicants to come to Stonefire, but Sid chose him. Find out why."

The door clicked shut and Gregor turned back to his computer. He would test out the waters with Dr. Lewis, but he wasn't about to trust the bloody man. No matter how much it pained him to delay finding anything that could help Cassidy, Gregor would have to work on the files later.

Chapter Eleven

Several hours later, when Tristan closed the door behind him, Sid sighed and collapsed back on her bed. Looking for cracks in mental prisons and repairing them had sapped her mental energy. Despite her previous determination, Sid wasn't sure she could control her beast when she woke up. Even if she managed to patch any visible cracks, her dragon could be stronger and still break free. She was starting to see why the children needed several years of practice to perfect it. At one time, Sid had been quite adept, but too much time had lapsed. Like with any skill, if a person didn't use it, it tended to fade.

There was always Tristan's other suggestion—to embrace the frenzy and see if it calmed her dragon. After all, the facts pointed toward her beast being mostly contained, at least until Gregor showed up. Of course, if he did say yes and they went through with it, Sid ran the risk of causing Gregor even more heartache in the process.

Growling, Sid punched one of her pillows. She'd known what to expect a few weeks ago. She almost missed the certainty.

But then the thought of never kissing Gregor and knowing what it was like to be desired would also never have happened.

"Why is life so complicated?" she asked aloud.

The handle turned and a familiar Scottish brogue filled the room. "Because it would be boring otherwise."

She glared at the handsome, blond-haired Scot. "I never understand why people say that. I like making plans and hitting goals. Not being able to do that not only irritates me but also stresses me out."

"I think you need a hobby, then."

"I have one—running."

He made a face. "And that is something I don't understand. Running is not a hobby. It's something you do out of necessity."

"Is there a reason you're here? Otherwise, you should just go carve another naked statue."

"Of you? Then I need you to model." He looked her up and down. "Strip if you're offering."

"Gregor," Sid growled out.

He grinned and took her hand. "I love when you growl my name like that. It sounds so primal."

Despite herself, Sid snorted. "So much for the civilized doctor."

"Even civilized doctors need a little wildness."

At the huskiness of his voice, Sid resisted a shiver. All of her reasons for denying the frenzy seemed to fade away when Gregor was near.

Then she remembered the look in his eyes as he told her about his dead mate and Sid sobered. "Did you find anything while I was training?"

Gregor's lips pressed together. "No, although part of it was because of your new doctor."

"So Trahern came early?"

"*Dr. Lewis* is here, aye."

"Then why didn't you bring him?"

"I wasn't sure how much he knew or how much you wanted to tell him."

Gregor caressed the back of her hand with his thumb. Her Scottish dragonman was protecting her.

Sid could get used to someone watching her back. "I should meet him and then decide. I've only ever talked to him via video conferences and it's easier to read people in person."

"Are you sure you're strong enough to do that? You look exhausted, Cassidy."

"Gee, thanks."

He winked. "I'll always be honest, even if you don't like what I have to say."

She softened. "I want to be honest with you, too. However, what I'm about to tell you might scare you off. Brace yourself."

Gregor raised an eyebrow. "Now I'm intrigued."

For a split second, Sid doubted her decision. But she quickly pushed it aside. Gregor had gone above and beyond to help her. If what she revealed scared him away, then so be it. "Tristan suggested something during our session that might be a last resort to taming my dragon."

He raised his brows. "Oh, aye? What is it?"

The easy way would be to avert her gaze, but she resisted. "He said that giving in to the mate-claim frenzy might calm my beast long enough for me to learn to contain her."

Gregor's thumb stilled on her hand. Sid held her breath to see how her dragonman would react.

~~~

The image of Cassidy round with Gregor's child flashed inside his head before his dragon spoke up. *We can have it all and start over.*

Ignoring his beast, he finally answered his doctor, "But what about the bairn? Frenzies result in pregnancy and I know

119

you'd never forgive yourself if the dragon ended up harming you and by extension our child."

More than he liked to admit, Gregor wanted to say "our child" again.

Cassidy's reply garnered his attention. "While there's no guarantee, Tristan thinks even my dragon would want to protect a child." She paused and then added, "I'm not trying to pressure you, Gregor. I know how much you fear childbirth. I just wanted to reciprocate your honesty."

His thumb stroked the back of her hand again. "I'll never help with a pregnancy and be at ease, but my fear has lessened around you, lass. And if it's your only chance at sanity, I'll do whatever it takes. The more time we have, the greater the chance we can find a way to calm your dragon." He lowered his voice. "While the frenzy may be part of it, I think part of your dragon's increased hysteria is a result of the attack. I still haven't identified the substance that must've seeped into your body."

"Have you talked with Trahern about that?"

He blinked. "I just freely admitted I'm open to the frenzy and you're concerned about Trahern Lewis?"

Cassidy rolled her eyes. "He has a strong background in biochemistry. It's one of the reasons I picked him."

"We can talk about bloody Trahern Lewis later. Just tell me if you want me to let the frenzy run its course if your dragon becomes out of control again. After all, it could happen in a few hours, once she finally wakes up."

His dragon hissed. *You could be nicer about it.*

Right, because you've been patient this entire time.

Cassidy's voice filled the room. "I don't want you to do it out of honor or obligation, Gregor. You deserve better."

With a growl, Gregor released her hand and cupped her cheeks. "It's not out of a sense of honor, woman. I care about you and meant what I said earlier about actually envisioning a future with you. That hasn't happened since Bridget. I want the chance to know you better, Doctor. Because I think we'd be bloody brilliant together."

"Gregor," Sid's voice cracked.

"I hear a whisper of doubt in your voice, lass. Tell me why."

"I—" Sid swallowed and continued, "Have you considered the fact it could all go wrong? You've suffered so much sadness in your life. You shouldn't have any more."

"And that right there is why I want to try. You always think of others, Cassidy. Isn't it time to let someone think of you, too?" He leaned closer. "What do you truly want? Tell me."

She leaned into one of his hands. "I always thought I would spend my life alone. I dedicated my life to the clan and taking care of them. They all became my children in a way. But now…"

"Now what?"

She searched his eyes. "I've allowed the possibility of becoming a true mother into my head and I can't seem to chase it out again. I keep thinking I'm weak for not being able to push aside my own desires."

"Stop being bloody ridiculous. It's okay to want something for yourself, Cassidy. The only question is whether you're ready to fight for your future? Because if you think I'm going to throw up my hands and walk away a few months from now, you'd be dead wrong. Once I make a decision, I stick with it. And if we go through the frenzy, I'm going to be growly, protective, and bloody unreasonable at times. But I will protect you with my life and do whatever it takes to ensure my future and yours are one and the same."

"How can you be so certain? You barely know me."

"I know you well enough. You're strong, dedicated, stubborn, and clever. You will be my equal in all ways."

She smiled. "Well, except in the penis department."

He laughed. "Okay, there will be a few differences. I'd much rather enjoy your breasts than grow my own."

Cassidy sighed. "You think you're so clever."

"Aye, lass, I am. And witty, as well as sarcastic. Get used to it." He moved until his lips were a whisper away from hers. "Tell me what you want, Cassidy. I'll make sure to be standing at the ready."

She lightly swatted his chest. "Stop it."

He grinned. "It'll be mighty hard to complete the frenzy if I did."

She snorted, and both man and beast loved the sound. But Cassidy still hadn't given him an answer. He was about to ask again when Cassidy spoke. "If I can't control my beast, then yes, I want to experience the frenzy with you."

"Don't sound too enthused about it."

She rolled her eyes. "Really? You want me to wax on about your glorious penis and its ability to grow?"

"Aye, that's a start." She opened her mouth, but he nipped her bottom lip to keep her quiet. "I would kiss you, but don't want to risk my dragon. However, I'm going to spend as much time next to your bed as possible so I can be here if you need me."

She frowned. "The walls aren't soundproofed."

"Then tell your dragon to keep quiet."

As they stared into each other's eyes, Gregor smiled at his doctor. Each second in her company made it easier to envision spending his life with her.

And even if the frenzy didn't calm her beast, Gregor would find a way to help Cassidy. There was no bloody way he was going to lose her without a fight.

~~~

Happiness coursed throughout Sid's body. It was hard to believe that after so many years of struggle and grief, she might just have a chance at having a mate and family of her own.

Still, she kept most of the happiness bottled deep inside. There was always the possibility everything could go wrong, so she needed to focus on the present.

Reaching out, she lightly touched Gregor's cheek. "Speaking of my dragon, we need to talk about Trahern again."

"You sorely need to learn how to enjoy a moment, Cassidy," Gregor growled out.

"I don't know how much longer my dragon will remain silent. I need to make sure everything is in place in case we complete the frenzy."

"Such as?"

"I want Trahern to analyze the mysterious substance. You don't have to tell him how we procured it, but if he can break down the chemical makeup, then he can try to find a way to neutralize it."

"Do you trust him that much?" Sid opened her mouth to protest, but Gregor beat her to it. "I'm not asking out of jealousy or irrational protectiveness. I've never heard of the male until today, for one. Who is he?"

Sid took one of Gregor's hands and threaded her fingers through his. "He's Kai Sutherland's stepcousin. In other words, he's the nephew of his stepdad. Trahern supported the mating between Kai's mom and stepdad when not everyone was keen to do so. From all accounts, he's clever and hardworking if a little shy."

"I would hazard a guess that Trahern and Kai were never best friends."

"No, but Kai trusts his mother implicitly. Even Bram trusts Lily Owens, as Bram knew her as a boy. If Trahern is trying to deceive us, then he would have to have almost spy-like training to do so," Sid stated.

Gregor fell silent and Sid waited to see if he'd trust her judgment. Because if he couldn't, she wasn't sure she could take Gregor up on his offer to participate in the mate-claim frenzy. Sexual attraction was well and good, but she needed a partner in all things more than anything else.

Her Scot finally grunted. "Okay, I'll ask him to look into the mysterious compound. But until the frenzy is complete, I'm afraid my dragon isn't going to like him much, or any unattached dragonman for that matter."

She smiled. "Since I'm more than familiar with dragonmen and their mates, I can live with that. Go talk with him now. I need to rest anyway."

Gregor kissed her cheek before whispering into her ear, "I'm also going to have a surprise for you when you wake up. Prepare yourself."

"As long as it's not your penis tied with a bow, I look forward to it."

Gregor chuckled. The vibration next to her ear was soothing. "So you'd welcome a naked carving of yourself? I'll keep that in mind."

"I didn't—"

"I'm teasing, love. You need to get used to it." His pupils flashed. "Oh, and my dragon is impatient to play with you. He says you need to hurry up and get well."

For years, Sid had always pasted a fake smile on her face when confronted with another dragon-shifter talking about their inner dragons. However, with Gregor, she smiled for real. "I look forward to meeting him, too. At least then I won't have to worry about sarcasm or teasing since dragons can't talk."

Gregor moved a hand to her hip and squeezed. "Such cheek."

She looked innocent. "What? I thought we could both tease."

He snorted. "I definitely think all of this is because you're wearing your hair down. Maybe we should make it mandatory whenever you're alone with me."

"Or, I could just cut it off."

"Don't."

Sid shook her head. "I've never understood why females should have long hair but males can wear it short. I think males can look handsome, too. You should grow yours out."

"We can argue that point later. I have a Welsh doctor to talk to."

"Then go already. I swear it takes Scottish dragons ten times as long to leave a room as someone from Stonefire."

"I can't help it if we light up the room."

She shoved his side. "Go before I start rolling my eyes again."

He lifted her hand and kissed the back of it. "As my lady wishes."

Sid should scold him, but she couldn't stop smiling.

Gregor kissed her hand one more time and murmured, "Remember, I have a surprise for you," before exiting the room.

As Sid lay back on the bed, she stared at the ceiling. Despite her mental exhaustion from both her dragon exercises and dealing with Gregor Innes, she was almost afraid to fall asleep. Because when she woke up, Sid may no longer be in control and it became a question of whether she would ever regain it again or not.

No. She couldn't think like that. If Sid wanted a chance with Gregor, she needed to fight for him. There was no bloody way she would give up now when happiness was on the horizon.

Her dragon would have to deal with her.

Chapter Twelve

Dr. Trahern Lewis took a deep breath before entering the room of his first patient on Stonefire.

As much as he loved medicine and the ability to heal others, he didn't care for small talk. Some said it was poor bedside manner, but Trahern saw his lack of conversation as devoting his energies on a patient's health.

Since he'd butted heads with Snowridge's senior doctor, Stonefire's call out for a doctor had been the opportunity he needed. Or, so he hoped. Only time would tell if it worked out.

Luckily his first patient was someone he'd met not long ago, when she'd accompanied the human named Rafe Hartley to Snowridge.

Nikki Gray met his gaze and smiled. "What are you doing here, Trahern? I know I made you laugh at Lily Owens's dinner, but you've come a long way to thank me."

He adjusted his glasses and cleared his throat. "I'm Dr. Jackson's new junior doctor."

Nikki raised her brows. "Really? You think someone would've told me about this. I'm going to have a word with Kai when I see him."

"That's unnecessary."

He opened Nikki's chart and scanned the contents. The dragonwoman filled the silence. "There's nothing wrong with me.

Pregnant women fall all the time. Maybe you'll realize that and let me go. I swear Dr. Innes would confine me to my bed for the remainder of my pregnancy if he could. I already have to deal with Rafe. I don't need to battle another male's overprotectiveness."

When he finished reading the chart, he looked to Nikki. "If it were up to me, I'd release you."

She frowned. "Then why don't you?"

"Because no one has cleared me to do so."

Nikki grunted. "Then I'm going to look into that as soon as I'm out of this bloody bed. Otherwise, what's the point?"

Trahern agreed but wasn't about to speak ill of the others doctors until he knew them. Rashness was the opposite of his personality. Not to mention he wanted the chance to learn about Stonefire's medical practices. He might even luck out and be able to communicate with Lochguard in Scotland, too. His clan leader in Wales was of the mind to keep to himself, but Trahern wasn't the only one who saw change coming, even to somewhere as remote as North Wales.

He removed the stethoscope from around his neck. "Let me examine you and add my notes. Maybe the confirmation will help sway the others' opinion about your release."

Nikki sighed. "Fine. Let's get this over with."

As he listened to her baby's heartbeat, he wondered how much of the little one's dragon personality had developed. Trahern was in the minority that believed dragon halves were present and sentient far sooner than most believed. He had a theory about dragon-shifter hormones, but had never had the chance to test it out despite the fact Trahern's dragon was much quieter than most dragon-shifters he'd met.

Even now, he poked but his beast yawned and went back to sleep.

128

He'd just have to be careful that the Stonefire dragons didn't learn of his secret or they may see him as less of a dragon-shifter, which was dangerous for a doctor dealing with dragons in various states of temperament.

Standing up, Trahern moved his hands here and there around Nikki's belly. "Everything sounds and feels normal. I'll make sure to stress that."

Nikki smiled. "Brilliant. Maybe I can get out of this bed sooner. Stick to the facts and you'll win over the females of the clan in no time."

He nodded and jotted down some notes. Before he could finish, someone knocked. "Nikki?"

It was the voice of the Scottish doctor from earlier.

Nikki shouted, "Come in."

Gregor Innes opened the door and looked to Trahern. "We need to talk."

"Not until I'm finished with my notes."

Gregor growled. "Forget the bloody notes. This is more important."

As the tall, blond dragonman glared down at him, Trahern knew that if he gave in now, the Scottish doctor would forever see him as weaker. And since Trahern was determined to make a new start on Stonefire, he couldn't have that.

Trahern shrugged. "In a minute. I'm not about to neglect my patient."

Gregor took a step closer. "Nikki is fine."

He raised an eyebrow. "Is that so? Then I can release her?"

Gregor waved a hand. "She can go as soon as her mate comes to collect her. I don't want Hartley challenging me to a fight if she breaks a toenail on the way home."

Nikki jumped in. "Hello, I'm right here."

Trahern flipped his papers until he reached the page of the release form. "Sign this and I'll go with."

Swiping the pen and clipboard, Gregor signed. "Done, on provision Rafe collects her."

Nikki clapped her hands. "Oh, Dr. Lewis, you're going to do well here."

He smiled at the enthusiastic dragonwoman. "I hope so."

Gregor grunted. "Now, let's go."

As Trahern followed, he handed off the clipboard on the way to the nurse named Ginny. "Nikki Gray's release."

However, before the older female could reply, Gregor dragged him down the hall into his office. The second the door clicked closed, Gregor rounded on him. "I admire you standing up for your patient and doing your job, but you need to know something. Dr. Jackson is my true mate and we both need your help."

He tilted his head. "With what?"

"You're supposed to be a whiz with biochemistry. I need you to identify the compounds in a particular chemical and determine if there's a way to neutralize it."

"Show me what you have."

Gregor blinked. "I was expecting a fight."

"If there's one thing you need to know about me, besides my dedication to my patients, is that I love nothing more than to spend hours in a laboratory to solve a puzzle."

"Aye, well, let's put that love to use because the sooner you can find a way to neutralize the chemical, the better."

"Care to tell me why?"

Gregor shook his head. "I can't. Talk to Bram and see what he says."

CURED BY THE DRAGON

As the Scot showed Trahern the data and what samples they had, he tried not to smile. His first day on Stonefire was going better than expected. And if he could spend the next few days locked in a room with his microscope and other tools, it would be heaven.

Unlike back on Snowridge, he might be able to convince the dragon-shifters on Stonefire that research was just as important as practicing medicine. He might even be able to make a difference.

~~~

Sid awoke to a sharp pain in her brain. Sitting up, she barely noticed the dark room or large bed under her body.

Her dragon was awake and banging against the bars of her prison. Her beast snarled. *Out, out. Let me OUT.*

Ignoring her, Sid concentrated on mending any cracks or bent bars. But as the minutes waxed on, she knew it was only a matter of time before her dragon escaped. There was no way Sid could keep up the repairs indefinitely.

Her beast roared. *I need out to claim our mate. I can't let anyone else take him. I want him.*

Lust shot through her body and she cried out. The prison may keep her dragon from taking control but didn't lessen the urge to mate.

It seemed Sid would have to fall on her backup plan and participate in the frenzy.

Not that she didn't look forward to it, but she wished it could've been under better circumstances.

She shouted, "Gregor," before replacing another bar on the prison. She hoped her dragonman was nearby.

131

The light flicked on and Sid barely noted she was in the bedroom of her cottage before Gregor was at her side. "What's wrong, love? Tell me."

She grabbed his arm as she tried to keep her dragon contained. "Frenzy, please."

"Are you sure?"

"Yes," she murmured as she worked even harder to keep her dragon in the prison. She didn't want Gregor to be forced and she would give him one last chance to back out.

However, Gregor shucked his clothes and quickly went to work undoing her hospital gown. Each movement of the material against her skin only made her burn hotter. The pulsing between her thighs was almost unbearable; if she didn't have Gregor's cock inside her soon, she might burst.

Gregor took her wrists and pinned them over her head as he laid on top of her. His voice was husky as he whispered, "Let her out, love. I'm ready."

Sid took a second to memorize Gregor's face. She would never forget he put aside his fears to help her.

As her dragon thrashed, Sid finally released her beast. As her dragon took control, the pulsing lust increased tenfold, and Sid was aware of her body rubbing against Gregor even though she had no control.

Her dragon was in charge.

Gregor released her wrists before he kissed her and her beast grabbed his shoulders to pull him close. Despite the rough nips and strokes of her dragon, Gregor met her in urgency. No doubt, his dragon had come out to play, too.

As he moved a hand to her breast and gently squeezed, every nerve in her body tingled. She wanted, no needed, the male above her. Only he was worthy enough to father their child.

Gregor released her breasts and lightly brushed between her thighs. Sid moaned and hooked a leg around his hip. The change in position made it easier to rub against his hard cock.

Her beast roared. "Why aren't you inside me?"

With a growl, Gregor brushed her folds a few times before thrusting into her. Sid arched her back at his fullness and raked her nails down his back. A voice not quite her own ordered, "Move."

Gregor nipped her jaw before he retreated nearly all the way out and then slammed back in. "Yes," her dragon hissed.

"Mine," Gregor murmured before he moved in a steady rhythm.

Grabbing his arse, Sid-slash-dragon dug in their nails and Gregor increased his pace. Her beast didn't understand why he delayed his orgasm. They needed his seed to conceive. Maybe they should flip him and ride him.

As if reading their thoughts, Gregor took hold of her hips and lifted slightly before pounding in and out. The feel of his hard length at a new angle hit just the right spot and she moaned, "Harder."

Not fighting her, Gregor complied for a few more beats before he stilled and roared her name. As he came, pleasure exploded and her core gripped and released his cock.

Soon, we will carry his child. More, her dragon stated.

Once she'd wrung the last drop from Gregor, Sid's dragon flipped him onto his back. "My turn. You're too slow."

Gregor's pupils were slitted. He hissed, but as Sid's dragon moved their body again, taking care to circle their hips, Gregor groaned and took her breasts in his hands. His rough palms against her nipples sent a tingle down her spine.

A small part of Sid yearned for him to suck and play with her nipples, but then her dragon pushed it aside. All that mattered was another orgasm, and another, until they carried both Gregor's scent and his child.

As her dragon increased the movements of her hips, Sid merely enjoyed the sensations. She was too exhausted to fight her dragon any longer. With any luck, once the frenzy was complete, she could finally learn to live with her beast.

But then another orgasm hit and Sid lost any rational thought.

Chapter Thirteen

Twelve days later, Gregor lay with Cassidy snuggled against his side and he battled a mixture of happiness and fear.

His lass's dragon had been a lusty thing, but even so, the frenzy had taken longer than most, probably because Cassidy was older. Still, his doctor currently carried his scent, which meant she carried their child and that pleased his beast.

His dragon was half asleep as he murmured, *Of course it pleases me. The others will stay away. We can also have a family again.*

Gregor pushed aside his doubts. *Completing the frenzy is only part of it. We still need to help Cassidy control her dragon.*

I'll leave that to you, his dragon muttered before yawning and curling up in a ball. The bastard was asleep within seconds.

Well, at least with his dragon being exhausted, Gregor could simply hold his female and revel in the brief moment of happiness. Because no matter what happened later, he wanted to be a father.

For so long, he'd hidden the desire. To even think it equated betrayal in his mind.

But looking down at the relaxed features of Cassidy Jackson, a child signaled a future and new start for them both. He couldn't feel guilty for that. He'd just have to remember her words about risks in childbirth were slim for most dragon-shifters.

If he lost another mate, Gregor would never recover.

Pushing aside his thoughts, he focused on the positive and merely kissed her forehead.

Cassidy rolled over and he held his breath. As much as he wanted to share the news, he needed to brace himself in case her dragon was still in control.

The mother of his baby opened her eyes and slowly looked over to him. He nearly breathed a sigh of relief at her round pupils. Brushing a strand of hair off her face, he smiled. "Good afternoon."

She frowned. "We're both in our right minds again and all you can say is, 'Good afternoon.'"

"You're a clever lass and know full well the frenzy is over." He placed a hand over her abdomen. "You carry my child."

She tentatively put her hand over his. "A child."

"Yes, a child. Although in our case, there's a bigger question looming. How's your dragon doing?"

Cassidy sighed. "She's asleep for now. I won't know for sure if she's tame until she wakes up."

"She was determined, I'll give her that."

Sid rolled onto her side and propped her head on a hand. "As if yours was any less so."

He grinned. "I think he did brilliantly." He sobered a fraction. "But are you all right? I haven't contacted anyone yet to let them know the frenzy is over, but if you need a doctor, I'll call Lewis."

"No, I don't need a doctor. But I'm afraid to say anything until I know how my dragon behaves. To be honest, I'm tempted to ask you to tie me up."

"Normally, I wouldn't pass up that opportunity. But I will just this once since sorting out your future is more important."

Sid leaned against his shoulder. "A future is something I dare not hope for. At least, not yet."

Gregor growled as he pulled Cassidy onto his chest. "You will have one, Cassidy Jackson. And you'd better start believing it or I will tie you to this bed until you do."

"And that's supposed to accomplish what? Besides call into question your heritage? Maybe you have some Viking blood in your veins."

"Don't deflect, woman. Anything you say won't push me away. I'm in it for the long haul, no matter what happens."

She met his gaze. "Why? We haven't known each other long."

"I know enough. I haven't felt this at ease with a female for a long time, and not just because you're my true mate. We can discuss medicine one moment and you can tease me about naked statues the next. I'm not sure I can go back to a life where all I do is work and carve alone in my cottage. I want you in my life, Cassidy. The sooner you accept that, the sooner you can start fighting for our shared future." When she hesitated, he added, "Are you having second thoughts?"

"No, not second thoughts. It's just that after thinking for decades I would be alone my whole life, I still can't believe I might have someone to share it with."

He rolled them over until he could trap Cassidy with his body. "There's no 'might,' lass. I'm here and we'll work through this together."

As his doctor blinked back tears, Gregor wondered what the hell he'd done wrong.

~~~

Sid's exhaustion was doing strange things to her. She usually wasn't emotional and she couldn't remember the last time she'd cried. Yet as Gregor vowed to stay by her side and help her win her fight, she wanted to sob in relief.

She hadn't lied about her dragon sleeping, which meant Sid still had no idea what her future held. But knowing Gregor would be there made her want to fight harder for it.

Not just for herself, but their unborn child as well.

Still, as Sid pushed Gregor until he was on his back and held him tight, she knew she'd have to be strong for him, too, when the time came. He would need reassurances that she wouldn't die at the faintest sign of a sneeze or nausea up until she gave birth.

"I'm fine," she murmured.

Gregor stroked her back slowly. "You looked about ready to cry, love. And believe me, if there's one way to put a male on his guard, it's to cry right after the frenzy."

Old Sid would've brushed everything aside and kept her thoughts to herself. However, new Sid trusted the male under her cheek. If it was to work with them, she needed to be honest. "It's a combination of exhaustion and happiness." She propped her chin on Gregor's chest. "I'm so close to having a happy future I can taste it, yet it could still be ripped away from me at any second."

He cupped her cheek. "How about we clean up and find Dr. Lewis? He's had plenty of time to work on that compound. It might be partially to blame for your dragon's behavior. If he has a way to neutralize it, we might be one step closer to our happy ending."

"Ours?"

"Of course, woman. A future without you wouldn't be happy."

"Gregor—"

"I'm not being ridiculous or charming. I'm merely speaking the truth."

"If you'd let me finish, I was going to say I'm glad."

He grinned as his eyes lit up. "You've just made me a very happy dragonman."

"Well, while you're in good spirits, let's hurry up. Maybe you won't bite off Trahern's head when we talk with him."

Gregor leaned down and placed a gentle kiss on her lips. "You carry my scent and my bairn. You're mine. Every male will know it, which means I can be civil."

He kissed her slowly and Sid melted against him. While a frenzy was special, she preferred quiet moments like this, when she could make a memory and cling to it without the taint of her dragon's mental state.

Gregor finally released her lips and murmured, "As much as I'd like to take you one more time for myself, I think we're both a bit sore and need food." He placed a possessive hand on her arse and squeezed. "Still, I hope you'll allow your doctor to do a thorough examination in the shower, just to make sure everything is fine."

She snorted. "How long are you going to play the doctor card?"

"Forever, love. So get used to it."

Tracing his jaw, she replied, "Then I'll be playing my card, too. I need to take advantage of my dragon being asleep and exam every inch of you."

"Aye, is that so?"

"Oh yes. I need to make sure I memorize your current state so I can make a better diagnosis later on."

The corner of his mouth ticked up. "I love when you talk doctor to me."

"Good. Then listen to your doctor and take a shower. Hygiene is important."

He raised his brows. "Are you saying I smell?"

Sid moved to the edge of the bed. "Wouldn't you like to know." Gregor growled and reached for her, but she jumped up and dashed into the bathroom. She made it as far as the shower before Gregor pulled her up against his chest.

After kissing her neck, he said, "Your examination begins now." He moved a hand between her legs and stroked with a finger. Sid leaned against him and drew in a breath. He chuckled. "Your response to sexual stimulation is normal."

"Gregor, don't be—"

He slid a finger inside her and damn her body, she grew wetter.

"I can continue my examination or you can let me inside you one more time."

It took everything she had to concentrate as Gregor slowly moved his finger. "I thought you suggested we rest."

"Sometimes, a doctor can make a mistake. I've revised my decision." His voice turned concerned. "If you're not hurting."

Sid took his hand between her legs and pushed away. Gregor froze for a second, but she took advantage to turn around and wrap her hands behind his neck. "No, but I still think the hot water of a shower would do us both good. Let's multitask."

He grinned. "I love how your mind works, lass."

Gregor reached over and turned on the shower. After testing the water with his hand, he gripped her arse and lifted. Sid wrapped her legs around his waist.

They never broke eye contact as Gregor carried them under the hot spray. The heat felt good against her skin, but she barely had time to register it before Gregor leaned down and licked the water off one of her nipples.

He raised his head and fire danced across her skin. Any thoughts of exhaustion or soreness faded. She wanted to claim Gregor as her own, without her dragon interfering.

And not just because he was the father of her unborn child. No, Sid wanted to make sure Gregor knew that she planned to be as possessive of him as he would surely be of her.

Gregor Innes was her future.

Running a hand through his chest hair, she asked, "What are you waiting for?"

"Just as lusty as your dragon. I see where she gets it from."

Impatient, Sid ran her hand down to the tip of Gregor's hard cock between them. Lightly rubbing the tip, her Scot hissed.

Sid smiled. "Your response to sexual stimulation also appears normal."

"Bloody woman," he said before he took her lips in a rough kiss. As his tongue stroked and explored her mouth, Sid moved against his hard length and swallowed his groan.

She loved the fact she had the power to make him moan.

Gregor pulled away to meet her eyes again. He said nothing as he positioned her and slowly slid his cock inside inch by inch. The initial soreness faded to pleasure and Sid gripped the back of his neck as she moaned.

When he was in to the hilt, Gregor took her chin between his fingers. "Right here, right now, it's you and me, lass. Just know that even without the frenzy or the need to appease your beast, I would still want you."

The truth in his words was absolute.

Emotion choked her throat, but Sid pushed past it. "Then show me how much you desire me, Gregor. Let's make a happy memory together to start replacing the old ones."

"Nothing would please me more than to make you happy," he murmured before backing her gently against the wall. "I'm also the only male who will ever make you scream in pleasure again."

"Oh? Then convince me why I should only look at you."

Determination flashed in his eyes. "I intend to."

As Gregor moved his body, Sid clung to her dragonman and somehow forced her eyes to remain open. She wanted to memorize every feature of Gregor's face as he came. She might even be able to draw strength from the memory later, to wrestle control back from her beast.

But as her Scot increased his pace and the sound of wet flesh slapping against flesh filled the shower, Sid forgot about everything but the male in front of her. It wasn't long before she screamed his name as she came, as if her human half was officially claiming Gregor as her own.

CHAPTER FOURTEEN

An hour later, Gregor and Cassidy stepped out of their cottage into the late afternoon sun. Without missing a beat, Gregor wrapped his arm around his mate.

He half expected for Cassidy to give him a stern look and talk about how they could walk faster apart, but she merely leaned into his side.

His dragon's voice was sleepy as he said, *She is tired but hiding it. This had better not take long.*

I will carry her back if I have to, but we need to talk with Trahern Lewis. Any and all information we can get before Cassidy's dragon wakes up may shape our future.

At least you admit we have one.

Aren't you supposed to be sleeping?

With a huff, his dragon curled up and went back to sleep.

He was about to ask Cassidy if they should slow down when Evie Marshall carrying her son, Murray, as well as an older human woman carrying who he assumed was Evie's daughter, Eleanor, rushed up to them. Evie beamed as she looked between them. "Since I just left Bram, I know you haven't told him the frenzy is over. Let me be the first to congratulate you two." Evie looked to Gregor and raised her brows. "And I'm going to watch you, Dr. Gregor Innes. If you hurt Sid, then I don't care if you're a dragon-shifter, I will hunt you down and make you pay."

The older woman and Sid both said, "Evie."

Evie looked at the woman Gregor didn't know and shrugged. "What, Mum? You've been here long enough to know that Stonefire looks after its own. Gregor needs to be aware of that."

The older human moved her gaze to Gregor and smiled. With Evie mentioning the family connection, Gregor could see the resemblance.

The woman spoke up. "Sorry about my daughter, and not just her rude manners." Evie opened her mouth, but the female cut her off. "My name is Karen Marshall. Nice to meet you."

"Aye, well, the pleasure is all mine." Gregor bowed his head. "It's not often I'm surrounded by such beauty in all ages."

Sid snorted. "Excuse him. Every Scottish male dragon-shifter seems to come equipped with over-the-top charm."

Karen laughed. "Is that so? Maybe I should visit the Scottish clan. Then Evie wouldn't have the chance to chase away everyone before I can have more than two words with them."

Evie adjusted Murray in her arms, who was sucking his thumb. "Dylan is too young for you."

"I didn't say I wanted to sleep with the man, but it's nice to have some attention," Karen pointed out.

"Mum, I don't want to hear about you sleeping with anyone," Evie replied.

Gregor wanted to chuckle but managed to keep it inside. Thankfully, Cassidy spoke up. "Evie, let your mum have some freedom. No one likes to be in a cage. As long as she's on Stonefire, Bram won't allow anything to happen to her. All of this is your doctor's orders. Just as you had time to find your place in the clan, allow Karen to do the same."

Evie sighed. "I'll try."

"Good," Sid said. "Now, we'll visit you and Bram later. Right now, we have some urgent business. And no, not the sex-in-the-woods kind."

Gregor winked. "Although it's always a possibility."

Karen laughed as Evie rolled her eyes. Taking a closer look at the older human female, he didn't notice enough laugh lines on her face. He'd work with Cassidy to ensure the female had a chance to bloom again.

His beast growled. *We can help everyone else later, after we help Cassidy.*

Reminded of why they were out in the first place, Gregor squeezed Cassidy's hip. "Now, if you'd excuse us, ladies, we really need to leave. But make sure to visit the surgery soon, Karen, and we'll think up a list of orders that Bram and Evie will have to follow."

Evie frowned, but before she could say anything, Murray pointed to the sky. "Blue like Daddy."

A blue dragon whooshed overhead. Sid tensed at his side for a second before relaxing.

Hurry, his beast mumbled.

Squeezing Cassidy gently, Gregor nodded at Evie and Karen. "Until later, ladies."

He took a step and Cassidy followed his lead. Once they were out of earshot of the human, he leaned down to her ear and asked, "Are you all right, love?"

~~~

Given all that had happened with Gregor and the progress she'd made, Sid should be okay with seeing a flying dragon. Yet as the male blue dragon soared overhead, a deep longing flooded her body, much as it did every time she saw a dragon-shifter in their dragon form.

And while she had her dragon in her mind, albeit asleep, Sid still didn't know if she'd ever be able to trust her beast enough to shift.

Gregor asked if she was all right and she looked up at him. The concern in his eyes helped to alleviate her fears and doubts. "I'm practical enough to know I'm not completely fine. However, it's not anything I haven't endured before."

"Is that your fancy way of saying you're still scared of what your dragon will do?"

"You're too clever for your own good."

He grinned. "Of course I am." He sobered. "But just remember I'm always here if you need me, Cassidy. Never hold back from me or I may resort to my charm to entrance you into the truth."

She sighed. "If I asked you to tone it down, would you?"

"Charm and sarcasm are who I am. Sorry, love, but this is what you get."

Looking up at him again, she touched his jaw. "Which is all I want."

As they stared into one another's eyes, Sid knew she was in trouble. She was halfway in love with Gregor Innes already.

To ensure he never suffered the grief of losing a mate and child before their time again, Sid vowed to win over her dragon.

Releasing his jaw, she nodded into the distance. "Now, let's hurry up. The sooner we talk to Trahern, the sooner we can come up with a strategy of how to get me into the sky."

"There's my doctor lass." He picked up his pace and Sid matched it. He continued, "But just know that once you have the

CURED BY THE DRAGON

basics of flying again, I'm not holding back. We're going to race and I'm going to win."

"We'll see about that, Doctor. I was pretty good at flight maneuvers in school."

"Then consider it a challenge, lass. The winner claims a prize."

Sid raised her brows. "Since I have no intention of losing, I had better think of something good."

"Oh, never underestimate a dragonman when it comes to winning. If there's one thing I know for certain, you like true competition without platitudes. I plan to please my doctor."

"Good. Now hurry up and try to keep your charm to a minimum for the next hour, okay? I have a feeling Bram will want to see us after we talk to Trahern, and we may need your charm with Stonefire's leader."

"Don't worry about Bram. He'll grow to love me soon enough."

Sid smiled as they approached the surgery. The medical research laboratory was inside.

They entered the building from the back to avoid notice. However, after making a few turns, Ginny spotted them and rushed up to say, "So you two are alive." She scrutinized Sid and then Gregor. "No visible bruises or claw marks, so it couldn't have been too rough."

Sid had seen her fair share of injuries after the mate-claim frenzy. "We're fine, as you can see. Is Dr. Lewis with a patient?"

Ginny's mouth formed a thin line. "He's probably in that bloody room again. He does his rounds early and orders us not to disturb him unless it's an emergency. I hope he isn't taking advantage of our hospitality and doing something sinister."

Sid hated keeping Ginny in the dark, but she couldn't risk the information spreading. "If he's working on what I think he is,

147

it shouldn't be." Ginny raised her brows in question, but Sid shook her head. "I can't tell you just yet. But as soon as Bram gives the green light, you'll be the first of the staff to know."

Ginny harrumphed. "I miss the old days, without all of the secrets and strangers coming into our fold."

Sid touched the nurse's bicep. "I don't keep secrets longer than I have to, and you know it."

Ginny sighed. "I know." She waved down the hall. "Go find out what the Welsh dragonman is up to. If it's something that can help someone recover, he'll need all the help he can get."

As Sid and Gregor moved toward the research room, Sid's heart rate ticked up. It was possible Trahern had found something to help with her dragon

However, she wasn't about to get her hopes up just yet. Knocking on the door, she heard the muffled, "Enter," and turned the door knob.

Inside Trahern peered at his computer screen. Never taking his eyes from it, he said, "So, you two have returned."

Gregor shut the door and locked it before replying, "Aye, we're back and I hope you have good news for us."

Trahern remained silent for a few seconds. Sid was about to speak when the Welsh dragonman beat her to it. "I've identified all of the compounds but one. Unfortunately, that unidentified one seems to affect dragon-shifter hormones and is probably the culprit." He finally met Sid's eyes. "I'd like to confer with a colleague, but Bram said you two were the only ones who could grant approval."

Sid's hard-fought battle to control Stonefire's medical issues had paid off. "I'm not sure we should bring anyone else into the fold at this point."

Trahern frowned. "I thought formulating a way to counter the effects of this compound was your top priority? Doesn't that mean we should use all resources available to us?"

"Who is it?" Sid demanded.

Trahern adjusted his glasses. "My lab partner from university. She's human."

Gregor jumped in. "Giving a human this knowledge is dangerous, Lewis."

Sid patted Gregor's chest and focused on Trahern. "How well do you know her?"

"We were lab partners on and off for a few years at Cardiff University. However, we still keep in touch via email to discuss new breakthroughs," Trahern answered.

Inviting a human was dangerous, especially if she were allowed to come and go back to her life afterward.

Sid had an idea. "Would she consider staying with us?"

"What?" Gregor and Trahern asked in unison.

"Think about it. All of us have mentioned needing more research and establishing a baseline for dragon-shifter care. If Trahern and this woman work together here, with us, Gregor, then we might actually be able to accomplish enough to build a case with other clan doctors. We might even be able to put out regular articles about our findings. No one may read them at first, but with time, others might do the same thing."

Trahern responded before Gregor. "There's the little matter of the DDA and the legality of a human living on dragon-shifter land without being mated."

"Bram had promised the DDA someone could come to study our clan. It was delayed with some of the attacks and other problems, but things have calmed down a bit. Evie might be able to persuade the DDA to accept our suggestion, even if she's not an anthropologist. Maybe your human could bring a friend and divide their research. That's probably more feasible." Sid answered.

Gregor answered, "I'm not sure about things being calm, lass. We've kept the information about the drone attack from the DDA for now, but they're bound to find out soon enough."

"Then we'd better hurry up and get this female approved to come to our land." She looked to Trahern. "What's her name? Do you think she'd accept?"

"Her name is Dr. Emily Davies. And it's possible she would come. She's always been fascinated with dragon-shifters, but was never allowed to pursue the interest."

Sid nodded. "Right, then I'll talk with Bram. Once I have his permission, you can reach out to this female and see if she'd be interested. Make the offer contingent on finding a social science partner, too. But make sure it's a secure connection and that Emily won't share the information before extending the offer."

Trahern tilted his head. "You barely know me. Why are you so trusting?"

"I did my research before selecting you, Dr. Lewis. You and I share similar goals about the future of dragon-shifter medicine. I also know that you love research above all else and I'm confident that you won't do anything to jeopardize your chance of living your dream. Am I right?" He bobbed his head and Sid continued, "Good. Now, reach out to your colleague with a vague offer and send me and Gregor her details as well as her suggested partner. Stonefire will have to run an extensive background check on them and the sooner Kai can do it, in addition to Gregor and my own check, the sooner we can ask for Evie's help."

"You lot do things differently here than back on Snowridge," Trahern mumbled.

150

"Stonefire has been pushing boundaries for nearly two years now. I see no reason why we can't keep doing it. Integrating with humans is important, but finding ways to better ensure the health of our own kind is just as important in my book."

"I'll contact her within the hour. She should be coming off shift soon," Trahern stated.

Trahern knowing the human's schedule told Sid volumes. "Okay. Gregor and I need to check in with Bram. After that, we'll check back."

Trahern studied her. "Are you well enough for all of this work? You just completed a long frenzy and are newly pregnant. You should rest."

Gregor grunted his approval. Sid merely raised her chin. "I can handle a few hours of work without falling over, just as generations of dragon-shifters have done before me."

For the first time since meeting him, Trahern smiled. "I like your dedication. We should get along famously, Dr. Jackson."

"Call me Sid. And I hope so. Just don't fuck up with your recommendation and everything should be fine."

"Yes, Doctor," Trahern answered.

Gregor touched her lower back and Sid looked up at him as he said, "Let's talk with Bram. Given all that we need to discuss, it's going to be a long meeting. Thank goodness I've stored up my charm for the occasion."

Sid smiled. "Then let's see if it works, because this meeting should be interesting."

CHAPTER FIFTEEN

Twenty minutes later, Gregor tried not to laugh at Bram's expression as Stonefire's leader asked, "You want to do what, Sid?"

Cassidy crossed her arms over her chest. "You heard me, Bram. Or, do you not care about the health and welfare of our clan?"

"Just wait a bloody minute. Why would you even ask me that? There's caring for the clan and then being reckless. This walks that line, Sid," Bram growled out.

Cassidy shook her head. "It's not reckless, Bram. Our medical practices are outdated, especially when it comes to sharing information. If anything, I think the DDA would appreciate us being more open and transparent with a human. You also already agreed to have an observer come to the clan, so what's one more? This will foster trust with the DDA's new director as well as fulfill your obligation."

Bram sighed. "If, and it's a big if, I decide to green light this, it still may not happen."

"We won't know until we try," Cassidy pointed out.

Bram looked to Gregor. "And I assume you agree with her?"

Gregor and Cassidy had decided on the walk to Bram's cottage that they would need to divulge all of their secrets. Gregor spoke up. "Of course. After reviewing some files I obtained from other clans, I already know too many things aren't being shared with the dragon-shifter medical community at large. There are probably hundreds, if not thousands, of dragon-shifters who could've been cured over the years if only their clan doctor had had access to the files from other clans. We need to make the first move if we're ever to change the practice."

"I'm going to pretend I don't know how you received these 'files' without my knowledge, as Arabella probably had something to do with it. Still, stealing information on a large-scale basis won't make anyone happy. What's your plan to get other doctors to contribute voluntarily?" Bram asked.

Cassidy answered, "I'm working on that part. What's more important right now is figuring out that substance from the drone attack. Just because another one hasn't happened again to us or our allies doesn't mean it won't or hasn't. We need to be prepared."

"I will on one condition, Sid," Bram replied.

"What?" She demanded.

"You take it easy for a few days." Cassidy opened her mouth to protest, but Bram beat her to it. "You and your Scot can easily work from home. Not only do you need to regain your strength from the frenzy, but we don't know what'll happen when your dragon wakes up. I don't want to put you, the baby, or anyone else in danger."

Gregor took Cassidy's hand in his. "I'll make sure she rests. And if she has trouble with her dragon, I expect Cassidy to tell me."

"Gee, thanks for letting me answer for myself," his doctor mumbled.

Gregor winked. "It's more fun this way."

Bram cleared his throat and garnered his attention again. "I want to be kept informed of anything that happens. You'll also continue meeting with Tristan for lessons. If you agree to these two points, in addition to not overtiring yourself, I'll ask Kai to run the background check on Emily Davies and the social scientist she finds. Do we have a deal?"

"Fine, Bram. We have a deal. Just make sure the background check doesn't take too long. We need the female's help as soon as possible," Cassidy stated.

"Kai will be as efficient as always. However, I won't risk the clan by rushing things just because you asked. You'll just have to live with that." Cassidy nodded, and Bram looked to Gregor. "As for you, I need to talk with Finn. I assume you're going to want to mate Sid and stay? Because there's no bloody way I'm letting Lochguard take another of my clan members away."

Gregor wanted to shout that Cassidy was already his, but since he hadn't asked his dragonwoman yet, Gregor tapped his chin and said, "My staying depends on how Cassidy asks me to stay. I need something to make up for the grumpiness of your clan."

"We're not grumpy," Bram growled out.

"I see you're still in denial," Gregor answered.

Cassidy jumped in. "Can we talk of matings later, Bram? Our plate is quite full as it is, what with the research, the frenzy, and my dragon."

Bram met her eyes. "If Gregor can't handle you, Sid, then I will always have your back."

Gregor leaned forward. "Watch it, Bram. Clan leader or not, I'm about to challenge you over that remark."

Cassidy stood up. "Let's go, Gregor. The last thing we need right now is you and Bram fighting. There's too much to do and I'm hungry."

Gregor's dragon perked up at that remark. *Our mate should never be hungry.*

I'm not going to bother responding to that.
You just did.

Ignoring his beast, he turned toward the door. "You're saved by a hungry female, Bram. You may not be so lucky next time."

Before Bram could reply, Cassidy tugged him out of Bram's office and quickly out of the cottage. She frowned up at him. "Can you at least try not to rile him up?"

He shrugged. "I don't see the point. It's not like he's going to send me away."

Cassidy sighed. "Males."

Her stomach rumbled and he said, "You can sigh and shake your head all you like, lass. But first, we need to get you some food."

"We'll get a takeaway from the main restaurant. That way we can work from home."

"And keep a watch on your dragon in case she wakes up."

Uncertainty flashed in Cassidy's eyes. Gregor looked forward to the day when his female didn't have to worry about something that should be as natural as breathing, such as her inner dragon.

Taking his hand, she answered, "Yes. I should probably contact Tristan as well. His tips were helpful, but I'm mature enough to admit I need a lot more help."

"I'll help with anything you need, love. Just ask."

"I will, Gregor. Believe me, I will."

As she leaned against him, he wished he could snap his fingers and make everything easy from here on out. But fighting for what someone wanted was never easy. What Gregor wanted was to make the English dragonwoman his mate and watch their child grow inside her. With each passing day, he hoped to see happiness and light replace her pessimism and caution.

155

It was a dream worth fighting for.

He hoped Trahern's contact would pull through. If the unknown substance had delayed side effects, Gregor may never have the chance to make Cassidy happy.

His dragon spoke up again. *Has anyone contacted the Irish clan again? The child was attacked several weeks before Cassidy. We might have a better idea of what is to come, if anything.*

While a small part of him was afraid to think about it, Gregor couldn't afford to allow his fears to rule his life or he might lose his doctor. *I'll add it to the list.*

Good. I'll think of other ideas.

So you're an expert on biochemistry now?

I picked up a few things during university. Just because I'm dozing doesn't mean I'm not listening.

Then maybe you should doze more often.

His beast huffed and turned his back to Gregor. He muttered, "Bloody dragon."

Cassidy squeezed his hand in hers. "I should meet him properly soon. That might give you a break."

"More likely he won't shift back and demand you scratch his ears into the wee hours of the night."

He watched Cassidy's face closely, but all she did was smile. "You never know, his presence might be a good influence on my own dragon."

Leaning down, he kissed her before saying, "We'll definitely add it to the list of things to try, love. But not quite yet."

She kissed him back. "I know. Let's deal with radically changing a major aspect of dragon-shifter practice first and work on charming your beast later."

Gregor's dragon grunted, but didn't say anything.

As they entered the restaurant and placed their order, Gregor took a second to place a hand over Cassidy's lower abdomen. "With everything that's going on, we haven't had much time to address a much bigger milestone."

"I know. To be honest, it still hasn't sunk in."

Gregor opened his mouth when Jane Hartley's voice boomed out, "The doctors are back!"

~~~

Sid had barely had a moment to think about her unborn child when the human female's voice garnered her attention.

She was glad for the distraction as the whole motherhood future was still uncertain and brought both good and bad scenarios to mind. Yes, she'd have to deal with it eventually, but it was nice to see her clan members again. Nearly two weeks apart from them was a long time.

The tall, dark-haired human tugged along her mate, Kai Sutherland, who murmured, "They just finished the frenzy. We should let them be."

At one time, Sid would've pinned Kai's reluctance on his own history. But as he gazed lovingly at his human mate, Sid had a feeling it was more out of courtesy than anything else.

Jane grinned at Sid. "So, it's done then."

Gregor's voice was dry as he said, "So much for the hotshot reporter."

Jane raised her brows. "I already have reports of loud noises and the banging of furniture from some of Sid's neighbors. Believe me, Dr. Innes, everyone in your section of the clan knows the frenzy is over because of the silence."

Gregor scrutinized Jane. "A lass with backbone. I can see why you're here."

Kai grunted. "She's my 'lass' as you put it. If you want help with security issues in the future, you'll keep that in mind."

Sid rolled her eyes and then turned toward Jane. "Do they ever grow out of this phase?"

Jane leaned in and whispered loudly, "No, although their attitudes come in handy for chasing off unwanted attention."

"We could hear you whisper fifty feet away, Ms. Hartley," Gregor drawled.

"I know. But it's fun to make you work for it," Jane answered.

Kai moved to stand behind Jane and wrapped his arms around her waist as he laid his chin on her head. "My mate is a little feisty this morning. She had a breakthrough on one of her stories."

Sid tilted her head. "I didn't think you'd launched your videocast yet."

"No, not yet. Maybe someday there won't be an attack, a mating, or some other major event taking precedence and keeping me from doing a proper launch with Gina MacDonald's help. Still, I write stories about dragon-shifters under a pseudonym and post them occasionally. I like to think it helps," Jane replied. "But enough about me. How's Trahern working out?"

Kai grunted. "Jane, they're clearly busy and Sid needs her rest. We can ask later."

Jane frowned. "You just don't want to hear bad things about your stepcousin, if it's not going well."

Not wanting them to argue, Sid stepped in. "He's been quite helpful, actually. And Bram should be contacting you shortly about something, Kai."

"Oooh, a new secret," Jane stated. "I can hardly wait. Even if I can't share them all, I like knowing them all."

Kai ignored his mate and answered Sid, "Whatever it is, I'll make it my top priority. Anything for you, Sid."

She half expected Gregor to challenge Kai, but her dragonman merely caressed the back of her hand with his thumb as he said, "Good. There's our food. You can talk with Cassidy more later. Right now, she needs to eat."

Jane nodded. "Of course. Congrats, Sid. I'm glad to see you happy."

Rather than darken the moment with uncertainties and all the scenarios that could still go wrong, she merely smiled. "Thanks."

Gregor picked up their takeaway and guided them out of the restaurant. The smell of curry wafted up to her nose and her stomach rumbled. She wanted nothing more than to curl up at her mate's side and enjoy a meal together.

Sid blinked but managed to keep walking. She'd never thought of Gregor as her mate before, but the thought of never seeing him again made her stomach flip. In a short time, he'd become an integral part of her life.

For the first time in her life, Sid wished for her own happily ever after.

But all of that could wait until she ate something. Clearly, carrying a large, Scottish doctor's child meant eating the equivalent of three people's worth of food on a regular basis.

A child. Yes, the dragonwoman without a dragon had found her true mate, her dragon, and carried a baby. The trick would be in balancing all three while she continued as Stonefire's doctor. They were her family and had stood with her even when she hadn't had a dragon. Trahern may do a good enough job, but Sid wouldn't abandon her patients.

Looking up at Gregor, she realized she'd never asked him what he wanted. "Are you sure you want to stay on Stonefire forever? Won't you miss your clan?"

"Aye, I will. But once Lewis is settled, we can visit Lochguard every once in a while."

"What about your brother-in-law and niece?"

He shrugged. "Who knows, having them come down here might be good for them. Lochguard is full of memories of my sister and other niece. A fresh start could be the perfect recommendation. I'll just have to think of a way to convince Finn without making it seem as if Bram is stealing away clan members."

"That will be quite the feat."

He winked. "Aye, but I've known Finn his whole life, which gives me a leg up on how to persuade him." Gregor searched her eyes and added, "I want to stay with you, Cassidy. Don't doubt it for a second. Even if your dragon goes crazy and takes time to tame, I'll still be at your side. Whatever happens, we can face it together."

After he leaned down to kiss her, something stirred in the back of her mind. Careful to keep any fear from her voice, she murmured, "We need to hurry. It's my dragon."

With a nod, Gregor tugged Sid along. Because she trusted him, she barely paid attention to where they were going so she could focus on the cage around her beast. While there was no way Sid could spend her whole life building cages, she needed some time to win over her dragon. Her beast had once trusted Sid and she just needed to think of how to build that trust again.

She was vaguely aware of arriving at her cottage and Gregor sitting her down in the kitchen. Only when she had everything reinforced and ready to go did she search out his gaze. The determination shining in her mate's eyes gave her strength.

Gregor nodded toward the table. "Eat, love. You won't be able to do anything if you don't take care of yourself."

Since she'd given the same advice many times over to her patients in the past, Sid focused on eating one bite of curry and then another. Before her next bite, she said, "If things become too out of control, then do whatever it takes to keep me in human form and on the ground. If my dragon makes it into the air…"

He picked up where she trailed off. "I know, the DDA might go after you." He cupped her cheek. "Just promise me you'll fight with everything you have, love. If there's anything I can do to win over your dragon, just say the word, and I will. Even if it requires me to dance naked with scarves, I'll do it to help you."

She smiled. "I don't think that will help my dragon, but I'm curious to see such a dance."

"Aye, well, work with your dragon and I might indulge your scarf fancy."

"I never said I had a fancy."

His voice turned husky. "You've clearly not been using scarves properly in the past."

Her cheeks heated at the image of Gregor caressing her neck, her breasts, and then her lower belly with the edge of a silk scarf. No doubt her dragonman would torture her and make her beg.

At that second, her dragon roared inside her head. *He's mine. I won't share. Let me have him.*

Sid took a deep breath and reinforced her mental reply with every bit of steel she had. *No, he's ours.*

But I claimed him. He wants me. Let me have him.

Images of her dragon taking Gregor flashed inside her mind. If her dragon wanted to play games, she'd do the same. Sid tossed back memories of tender moments with her Scot—gentle kisses, teasing him about his carvings, and even the look of understanding when they'd discussed their pasts.

161

Her beast huffed. *Those will soon be mine, too. You had many years in charge without me. It's my turn.*

As her dragon thrashed against the prison, Sid vaguely noted Gregor taking both of her hands and squeezing. His reassuring warmth made her sit taller. *I didn't imprison you.*

Her beast snarled. *Your actions did, which is the same thing. If I can ever find a way to mentally contain you for twenty years, where you can hear and see everything but never act, I will do it.*

Some might tiptoe around the issue, but Sid would treat her dragon as she would any stubborn patient. *Threats are one thing, actions another. Why aren't you trying to take control now?*

I won't harm my child.

Our child.

No. Mine. I will raise him or her alone. Once he or she is born, I will pounce. You've been warned.

Her dragon turned her back and remained silent. Sid slumped against Gregor's side and he asked, "What can I do, love?"

She shook her head. "Nothing. I'm safe enough for about the next nine months. After that, all hell is going to break loose."

"Over my dead body. Nine months is plenty of time to woo your beast."

Looking up at Gregor, Sid's voice cracked as she replied, "My dragon blames me for her solitude and confinement."

Stroking her cheek with a finger, Gregor said, "As I said, we just need to woo your beast."

Sid sat up. "And how, exactly, are we going to do that? She won't believe anything I say, and I'm not about to be someone I'm not just to kiss her arse all the time."

Her dragon's tail flicked at that comment, but she still said nothing.

Gregor placed a finger under her chin. "Are you giving up before you even start? That doesn't sound like you."

"Of course I'm not bloody giving up. The thought of my dragon stealing our child and raising him or her alone is more than enough motivation for me to keep fighting."

"Good." He released her chin and pushed her food in front of her. "Now, eat. Not taking care of yourself will only irritate your dragon further, not to mention me as well."

"And we can't have you irritated, can we?" she asked dryly.

He smiled. "Someone's picking up on my sarcasm."

Sid merely hit his side before eating a spoonful of curry and rice.

Gregor chuckled. "Don't worry, lass, I love the fact you've been around me long enough to pick something up from me. After a few more months, you may become as charming as any Lochguard dragon-shifter."

"Don't hold your breath."

As Gregor swiped a piece of naan bread, Sid checked on her beast. However, she still sat in silence with her back turned.

Maybe Gregor was right—they could find a way to win her over.

But not in the present. Each bite of food made her sleepy. As always, there was much to do and not enough time to do it. The only difference from the past was Sid could ask not only Gregor but also Trahern for help to watch over the clan's health.

Why she ever thought doing everything herself was best, Sid would never know. All she could do was embrace the changes and focus on her goal of raising her child with Gregor at her side and her dragon as an ally. How the bloody hell she would accomplish that, however, was still a mystery.

CHAPTER SIXTEEN

Later that evening, Gregor sat on the bed with a laptop as Cassidy lightly snored at his side.

She'd fallen asleep in mid-conversation, but he didn't mind. He could watch over her while she rested and also do some work. As much as Gregor would love to be the devoted mate who spent every waking moment looking after their partner, he couldn't neglect the future health of others. Cassidy would want him to multitask since she was as devoted to her clan as he'd been on Lochguard.

His dragon spoke up. *Why do you feel guilty about leaving Lochguard?*

Who says I do?

You can't lie to me. Layla loves them all as much as us. No one back home would begrudge you finding a second chance.

Gregor decided to be forthright. *I know, but Harris is still suffering whilst I have gained a family. It almost doesn't seem right.*

Harris Chisolm was Gregor's brother-in-law and had been mated to his recently deceased sister, Nora.

His dragon tilted his head. *You already found a solution—invite Harris and Fiona to Stonefire. A new start will help.*

Maybe. I should wait at least a few days before asking Bram for more favors.

He will say yes to helping those in pain. He may complain, but Stonefire's leader has a heart.

Still, I want to help our mate first. She needs to be as strong as possible when the bairn comes.

She is strong. She will live.

Gregor glanced at Cassidy's face, relaxed in sleep. His doctor was strong. He needed to believe she could handle a child of his.

His dragon shook his head. *You worry too much. Hurry up and find something to ease your mind.*

Before Gregor could reply, his beast curled up and dozed off.

Looking back to his laptop, Gregor scanned the file names he'd received from Arabella. Since Cassidy's dragon had returned, he'd switched his focus from researching silent dragons to unruly ones.

The problem was quite a bit more common as a simple search turned up four cases. Opening the first one, Gregor read the summary:

After a critical injury, the patient is unable to control their beast. Only positive reinforcement seems to help but hasn't cured the situation.

Further down he saw the treatment had lasted five years before the patient had been reconciled with their dragon.

Gregor didn't have five bloody years to follow the same treatment.

However, positive reinforcement was something he could try, although he suspected earning her trust would be more beneficial.

He clicked the next file but dismissed it as the patient had gone rogue and been shot down by the DDA. That doctor had used negative reinforcement, which only angered Gregor.

"Stupid doctor," he muttered. Prodding a dragon was the quickest way to end up dead. Any school child would know that. He took note that the doctor was from Clan Skyhunter. Since the clan in Southern England had recently experienced a purge and was undergoing a leadership change, he hoped that poor excuse for a doctor had been one of the ones to be booted out. He'd check on it later.

The third one was from Clan Snowridge. Curious since it was Trahern Lewis's clan, Gregor scanned the summary:

Female attempted to save her sister by forcing her dragon. When the patient's sister died, her beast went insane. All options were exhausted until one clan member mentioned the old practice of using of a rare moss found in the Celtic rainforest, among other locations, to help calm the dragon.

With each word, he leaned forward. Gregor continued reading:

With the help of an elder male versed in the ways of plant medicine, the patient was given a dose. Results began within the hour. After a few months of daily doses, the dragon and human halves started to work again. However, when the patient stopped the doses, she went through withdrawal. If using this moss becomes necessary in the future, I would recommend a much slower weaning period. Side effects also need to be explored further.

He read a few more notes about the female's full recovery and release before the file ended.

Gregor leaned back against the headboard. He didn't want to get his hopes up, but he needed to talk with Trahern Lewis first thing in the morning. Maybe the Welsh doctor knew the name of the moss that had been used. He may also know some of the side effects. As much as Gregor wanted to help his mate, he couldn't risk the bairn.

Of course, it would be easy enough to ask Trahern to research more of the side effects. Nine months may be enough time to ascertain the safety of the moss treatment and have Cassidy reconcile, at least in part, with her dragon.

He could track down Lewis even though it was the middle of the night. Yet as Cassidy snuggled closer to his side, Gregor decided he could wait a few hours and simply enjoy the warm presence of his mate.

~~~

Trahern sipped his coffee as light filtered through the small window on the far side of the room. He probably should've slept more than the hour nap on top of his desk, but he needed to figure out the final compound. Granted, it could be a million different things, maybe even a billion, but he wasn't about to give up.

The work also kept his mind from thinking about Emily Davies. It had been more years than he'd like to admit since he'd last seen her. He enjoyed their email discussions, but staring at a computer screen wasn't the same as seeing her smile or how the sun glinted off her dark hair.

His dragon flicked a tail at the memory but then settled back to sleep. Thinking of Emily always stirred his beast.

At one time, he'd wondered about her being his true mate. However, the laws had been different then, and Trahern had learned to push aside the possibility to be friends with her. The more often he repeated she was just a friend, the quieter his dragon had become. Maybe seeing her again would wake up and motivate his dragon.

Provided she responded to his invite in the first place.

Adjusting his glasses, Trahern focused back on his work. He'd learned as a child not to get his hopes up about anything too soon. Besides, if he wanted to stay on Stonefire, he needed to show he was useful.

As the computer scanned through the database, comparing the chemical makeup of the mystery ingredient, someone knocked lightly on the door. Since the nurses knew not to disturb him unless it was a priority, he stood up and said, "Come in."

Gregor Innes's tall, blond form filled the doorway. "I need to ask you something."

Sitting back down, Trahern answered, "I still haven't figured out the compound. You can check back again later."

Gregor shut the door and moved to Trahern's desk. "I'm not here about the bloody compound. Do you know Dr. Arwel Hughes?"

He frowned. "Dr. Hughes retired a few weeks after I began my stint as a junior doctor. Why?"

Gregor laid a few sheets of printed paper on his desk and tapped them. "Do you know anything about this rare moss he used in one of his cases to treat an unruly dragon?"

Trahern read the old doctor's notes before answering, "No, but I might know who the old male he refers to might be." Gregor opened his mouth, but Trahern beat him to it. "He won't talk to you, though. Clyde doesn't care for English dragon-shifters. Something about a feud from several hundred years ago."

"Then you talk to him."

"He probably won't talk to me, either. I'm a traitor for leaving Wales, you see."

Gregor growled. "Then find a way. This bloody moss might be the key to saving my mate. We need to locate it so you can test it for negative side effects. Even if it's the best cure for Cassidy's dragon, I need to make sure it won't endanger my child."

"Look, I'm not good at politics or gathering favors. Many from Clan Snowridge also see me as a traitor. Only about a quarter of the clan want to reach out and build alliances. The rest want to be left alone. So, if you need help, have Stonefire's leader talk to Rhydian Griffiths. That's the best chance you have of getting the information you want."

"Bloody stubborn Welsh dragons," Gregor muttered.

Trahern raised his brows. "If I recall, the Scots didn't always believe in being open, either."

"Aye, well, that was the old leader who eventually got himself killed. Maybe yours will change his mind with goodwill."

"The male who can identify the type of moss respects Rhydian and will do whatever Snowridge's leader says. Use that with Bram. Let me know when you either hear about Emily Davies or if Rhydian convinces old Clyde to talk with us. There's not much else I can do outside of the surgery until Clyde talks."

Gregor assessed him a second before saying, "You could explore the clan's lands and meet a few people before they come to the surgery."

Trahern shrugged one shoulder. "I don't like small talk. The best way for me not to offend someone is to continue my work here."

He expected Gregor to prod again, but the Scottish dragonman nodded. "Right, then I'll let you carry on with your work. Although I'd suggest a shower to wake you up before visiting any more patients. Cassidy has one off her office you can use."

Trahern nodded. When the silence stretched, Gregor raised a hand in farewell and left the laboratory.

Sighing at the peace and quiet of his sanctuary, Trahern opened another window on his computer screen and started researching the different species of moss in the Celtic rainforest.

He might be able to find something even without Clyde, although he hadn't mentioned it to Gregor since he didn't want the other doctor to get his hopes up. Trahern didn't give false promises to anyone.

However, the possibility of finding something new to use with his patients was too good of an opportunity to pass up. If he found anything, he'd share the information. If not, then no one would be the wiser.

Trahern went to work.

~~~

Sid was awake but kept her eyes closed. Her dragon dozed at the back of her mind, and Sid was gathering strength to confront her beast. Just because her dragon wouldn't take complete control until after the child was born didn't mean she would make things easy.

Breathing in and out, Sid calmed her body. As ready as she'd ever be for her dragon, Sid took the remaining quiet moments to think of her baby.

Or, more importantly, the fact she carried one and would be a mother in about nine months' time.

She only hoped she wouldn't screw up her child's life.

No. Sid had worked hard to survive as long as she had while maintaining her sanity. Not only that, she'd gone through her own tragedy as a child and never wanted her baby to go through the same. Sid would protect him or her at any cost.

Her dragon stirred. *Only I can protect the child.*

She debated pushing her beast for more information and decided she wouldn't be a coward. *Gregor and I will do fine.*

170

Her dragon huffed. *I don't care. I will do as I please and you can't stop me.*

Why do you hate me?

Snarling, her dragon spat out, *You didn't help me when I needed it. I won't ever forget that.*

I didn't know how.

Liar. You're a doctor and should've taken risks. Instead, you kept pushing me aside to help everyone else.

Before Sid could reply, her beast roared and thrashed inside her head.

Sid curled on her side. *Stop it!*

No.

She attempted to construct a prison, but her dragon moved around her head and kept escaping. As the minutes ticked by, Sid's strength waned. Rather than risk her baby, she finally said, *Stop or you risk hurting the child.*

After a few more seconds, her dragon quieted. *This isn't over.*

As her beast moved to the rear of her mind and turned her back, Sid relaxed into the bed. Fighting her beast had sapped her energy. If this kept up, Sid would be spending the next nine months bedridden.

She could call out for the nurse downstairs or even ring Gregor, but reaching out would feel like defeat. Yes, if she truly needed help, she would ask for it. However, all she needed was a nap. Recouping energy would give her another chance to try reasoning with her dragon. There had to be a way to reconcile, even if it was to the minutest degree.

One sentence from her dragon kept repeating inside her head: *Instead, you kept pushing me aside to help everyone else.*

To a degree, her dragon was right. But only after Sid had exhausted all of her options. Did she not realize that?

171

Her beast may have been watching for twenty-four years, but she hadn't matured at a normal rate. Maybe Sid needed to approach the situation by assuming her dragon was still an unruly teenager.

Yes, maybe that would work. She could mention it to Gregor later. But first, she needed to rest.

Closing her eyes, Sid recalled sleeping in Gregor's arms the night before. Even the memory of his heat and scent surrounding her made her sigh. Within minutes, she was asleep.

CHAPTER SEVENTEEN

Gregor paced the length of the living room as he waited for Bram to finish his call with Rhydian Griffiths. Even though Stonefire's leader had assured Gregor he'd call him as soon as he was done, Gregor didn't want any sort of delay. Cassidy would be awake and he wanted to greet her with good news.

As he turned to pace the other way, a door opened and Kai Sutherland raced past. Gregor poked his head out of the hall, but he only saw the door to Bram's study closing with a click.

He debated knocking to find out what was going on when Aaron Caruso, Kai's second-in-command of the Protectors, burst through the front door. His gaze immediately zeroed in on Gregor. "There you are. We need you for a medical emergency."

His doctor's instincts on high alert, Gregor nodded and followed Aaron out of the cottage. "What's wrong?'

"We've found another possible victim of the drone attacks."

"What do you mean 'possible victim?' I thought you lot had tightened surveillance."

Aaron's paced quickened. "We have. But the victim was found outside the clan's lands, where our surveillance doesn't reach."

Gregor made sure to match Aaron's strides. "Is Lewis already there?"

"No, he's in the middle of a minor surgery and can't leave. Since Sid's still resting from the frenzy, you're our second choice."

Gregor decided not to comment on Aaron's less-than-enthusiastic tone. "What do we know?"

"Not much. One of the nurses is checking her out now."

"Who's the patient?"

Aaron looked over with a grim expression. "My mother."

He may not know Aaron well, but Gregor still gripped the dragonman's shoulder and squeezed. "I'll take care of her." Aaron's expression was emotionless, so Gregor focused on his new patient. "Why was she outside the clan's lands?"

"There's no restriction to leave, as long as it's in human form. My mum had just returned from visiting friends in Italy. We'd checked the surrounding areas and even had a guard posted with my mother. However, she had the car window open and she was attacked that way."

"If that's so, either there's a traitor inside the clan or people are monitoring who comes and goes."

"I'm aware of that," Aaron bit out.

Dismissing Aaron's attitude due to being concerned for his mother, Gregor followed the dragonman to the back entrance. A dark SUV came into view. On the other side of the vehicle one of the younger nurses, Thea, sat next to the motionless form of a middle-aged dragonwoman on the ground.

Gregor jogged to his patient and squatted down. As he did a quick examination, the nurse said, "Her breathing and heart rate are steady, although her pupils are slitted."

Opening the female's eyelids, he saw her pupils hadn't changed. "What about an entrance wound? The others had slivers in their heads."

Thea shook her head. "I can't find anything. Although there is a residue around her nose and mouth."

Bloody hell. If the attackers had changed the dosage method to an aerial spray that simply needed to be inhaled, that would be dangerous.

Gregor motioned to Thea and another surgery employee. "Take her to the surgery, but make sure to isolate her from the others. I want blood samples as well as whatever residue is on her face. I'll be there shortly to take over for Trahern and allow him to analyze the samples."

Thea bobbed her head as the other surgery employee laid out the stretcher. As soon as they put Aaron's mother on it, they carried her off.

Gregor turned to Aaron. "Was anyone else affected in the car?"

Aaron shook his head. "No. The two others are fine."

"That's good news. It probably means the substance only affects those who inhale it directly, in large quantities. However, to be safe, implement a quarantine on the clan. Until I know exactly how this new attack works, I don't want to risk anyone carrying something with them or leaving to be gassed along the way."

Aaron clenched his fingers. "Will she be all right?"

"As soon as I know more, I'll call you. Just make sure everyone stays put for now and reach out to the Irish clan. If we had another attack, they might have too. The more information I have, the better a diagnosis I can make."

Aaron nodded. "Straight away." He paused a second and added, "And take care of my mother."

"Of course."

With that, Aaron ran in the direction of the Protectors' central command building and Gregor moved toward the surgery.

He hoped whatever had been sprayed on Aaron's mother wasn't contagious. Until he knew for certain, he would maintain distance from Cassidy.

~~~

Aaron tapped his fingers against the desk. Why was Teagan O'Shea taking so bloody long to sign on to the video conference?

His dragon spoke up. *I know you're upset, but try to have patience. It's only been a few minutes since you sent the text message. She's clan leader and may be doing something else.*

Then why would she say she'd be on right away? I don't have time to waste, dragon.

Mum will be okay.

Aaron knew his dragon was right since Molly Caruso was a fighter. After all, she had survived the death of a mate and raised a son mostly on her own, but because of that Aaron was protective of his mother. From a young age, he'd vowed to take care of her. It didn't sit well with him that he'd failed.

His dragon swished his tail, but the face of the dark-haired female leader of Clan Glenlough appeared on his computer screen. Her Irish accent filled the room. "Make it quick, Caruso. I have things to take care of."

He leaned forward. "Was there another attack on your clan?"

Her eyes widened. "No, why?"

He pounded a fist on the desk. "The bastards just attacked my mother."

Something flashed in her eyes, but it was gone before he could make out what it was. "I'm sorry to hear that, Aaron. But I'm not sure what I can do."

"Their style of attack has changed. Our doctor thinks the chemical is shot into the face of the target and they inhale it."

"Do you know this for certain?"

"Tests are being run, but there's no sign of an entry point like with the previous splinters. I would bet money the drug is in spray form."

"What's Stonefire's plan of action?"

Aaron hesitated. He hadn't asked permission to share the latest attack yet.

His beast huffed. *Bram and Kai aren't going to like it if you tell her.*

Ignoring his dragon, Aaron went with his gut feeling that Teagan wouldn't betray them, although he ignored why he trusted her. "We're implementing a lockdown. I'd suggest you doing the same. Even without a second attack, Glenlough was targeted before and could be again."

"Still nothing from Lochguard or Snowridge?"

"No other clan has reported anything. However, it doesn't mean this problem isn't more widespread."

Teagan nodded. "I'll increase security. Let's agree to share anything else that happens related to this problem from here on out. Text me 'pigeon' and I'll find a secure line as soon as possible."

"Pigeon?"

"As in carrier pigeon, like the days of old."

Under normal circumstances, Aaron might tease the Irish leader for the corny password. In the present, however, he grunted. "Fine. I'll be in touch."

Closing the connection, Aaron raced out of the small, private communications room and checked on his team in the command main area. He needed to find out who would attack Stonefire twice but also Glenlough once. There had to be a

177

connection. The sooner he figured it out, the sooner he could stop the bastards who had targeted his mother.

~~~

Gregor finished the appendectomy and scrubbed his hands at the sink. No one had updated him in the last twenty minutes of any changes to Molly Caruso. All they knew for certain was that Molly wasn't contagious.

While he figured Trahern was lost in analysis and blood work, Gregor was going to have to implement some rules about checking in every so often, even if it meant strapping a bloody alarm to Trahern's wrist.

He arrived at the laboratory and didn't bother to knock. Opening the door, he blinked to see Cassidy sitting next to the Welsh doctor. She met his gaze and frowned. "Next time, you had better wake me to help."

It took everything he had not to bark for her to go back to their cottage and rest. Keeping his voice calm, he asked, "What have you discovered?"

"The compound is almost exactly the same as the one found in Dr. Sid's body, with only one or two minor differences," Trahern answered. "However, the formula is less potent and I'm fairly certain it needs to be inhaled in a sizable dose and at close range to have any effect."

"Fairly certain isn't certain," Gregor bit out.

Cassidy sighed. "Stop it, Gregor. I'm perfectly fine. My dragon is sleeping and I was going crazy back at the cottage." She pointed a finger at him. "Next time, you'd bloody well better tell me what's going on. Stonefire is my family."

His dragon spoke up. *I would've told her.*

Not dignifying his beast with a response, Gregor moved to stand behind Trahern and Cassidy. "I'll tell you next time. Now, tell me what else you found out."

"One of the minor differences Trahern mentioned was an increase in the ratio of the unidentified compound to the other elements," Cassidy answered. "The question is whether Molly Caruso inhaled enough to affect her dragon or not. If so, it will probably have a worse effect on her beast than the child on Glenlough."

"Or yourself," Gregor pointed out.

Cassidy shook her head. "My case has too many unknown variables to be used as a standard. It's much easier to compare the Glenlough child and Mrs. Caruso."

"That's all well and good, but this drug might have long-term effects. We need to be vigilant," Gregor said. "Speaking of which, I should check on Molly Caruso."

Cassidy stood up. "I'm coming with you."

Gregor's beast chimed in again. *If you don't let her come, you might push her away.*

Not locking Cassidy away until her dragon was tamed and their child was born was proving harder than he'd ever imagined.

But his beast was right. "Then let's go. Lewis, we'll be back later."

Trahern barely acknowledged their exit. Once they were in the hall, Gregor whispered, "How's your dragon?"

"I told you, she's asleep." He merely raised his brows and Cassidy continued, "She was a pain earlier, but I think she and I are at an impasse until closer to my due date. However, I have a theory."

Gregor raised his brows. "Care to tell me what it is?"

Cassidy lowered her voice. "I think we need to approach my dragon as if she's a teenager. She may be thirty-eight years old, but she hasn't had a chance to grow since we were fourteen."

"Interesting. We can discuss your theory in more depth later, although I'm worried about your dragon affecting your work. Are you sure it's a wise idea to be in the surgery?"

His doctor narrowed her eyes. "Don't try to lock me up, Gregor. Of course I need to be careful, but I don't see why I can't work. After all, I hid my episodes for years with no one the wiser. If anything goes horribly wrong, I'll leave."

He stopped them in the hall and leaned closer to her face. "Just promise me you won't hide anything from me. I'm trying not to be overly protective, but I'll never succeed if you keep secrets."

"I won't ever keep secrets from you again, Gregor. I need you to trust me."

Shit. His protectiveness was getting him into trouble.

His dragon spoke up again. *Just trust her. She will tell us when something's wrong.*

"I do trust you, love." He cupped her cheek. "But also understand that I'm still afraid of what might happen."

Her expression softened. "If we're honest and open, then we can handle anything."

"My clever lass."

She raised her chin. "Of course I'm clever."

He smiled. "Right, then let's use the cleverness for good and help our clan."

"Our clan?"

"Aye, our clan. Not only because of you, but the English dragon-shifters are growing on me."

She snorted. "Don't say it as if you've just smelled something rotten."

He gave her a quick kiss. "That will take some time." He took her hand. "Come on. We have a clan to protect."

CHAPTER EIGHTEEN

A few days later, Sid sat next to Molly Caruso's bed and looked over the dragonwoman's chart for the tenth time.

Molly remained unconscious.

Placing the chart back on the end of the bed, Sid opened the female's eyelid and found her pupil slitted. Not once had they been round when anyone checked.

Her gut said that Molly's dragon was in charge, but unable to wake up. Sid only hoped the situation wasn't permanent. And not just because Molly was part of her clan and Aaron kept threatening to find the bastards who did this on his own, but also because if this chemical was distributed over an entire clan in a high enough dose, chaos would follow. Even if they all fell unconscious, some would eventually wake up and their dragons might be out of their minds.

Proof was the child on Glenlough, whose dragon took charge more often than not. Thinking of the poor boy as he fought with the dragon half he should be embracing and getting to know made Sid clench her fingers. Whoever had formulated the drug must not have a heart. Who in their right mind would target an innocent child?

Taking a deep breath, Sid pushed aside her anger. She needed to use her energy more wisely, especially since she had trouble working the long hours she once had. Gregor's bloody baby was already making her life difficult.

Although imagining a little blond-haired boy grinning as he talked his way out of a reprimand made Sid smile. Regardless of how much trouble their child caused, she still looked forward to being a mother with her Scot at her side.

Her dragon stirred and she quickly wiped her thoughts. She didn't want to fight an unnecessary battle with her beast over their future and use up what precious energy she had.

Just as Sid turned toward the door, the disheveled hair and dark, day-old beard of Trahern Lewis entered the room. He said without preamble, "Snowridge just sent the name of the rare moss Dr. Hughes used in that case we read about as well as Clyde's notes on its uses."

She guided him out of the room and shut the door before she ordered, "Tell me everything you know, including if you think it will help the victims?"

"Clyde seems to think it calms our inner dragons, regardless of the cause. An initial analysis told me it's nontoxic."

"The only question is what the side effects may be," Sid murmured.

"Correct. While I've catalogued the side effects of every known substance I've come into contact with, this moss isn't among them for obvious reasons," Trahern replied.

"And how long will it take before you start discovering them?"

"I don't know. By myself, it could take days, maybe even weeks, if I discount the long-term effects. If Dr. Emily Davies were here, I could pinpoint the main side effects much quicker."

"She still hasn't replied?" Trahern shook his head and Sid studied the dragonman. Her instinct said there was more to Emily and Trahern than former lab partners. But she didn't have time to deal with that. "I'll visit Bram if you hold the fort here."

"What about Gregor?"

"He's talking with Finn Stewart via video conference about staying. He should be back soon."

Or so Sid hoped. Gregor had been away longer than she'd anticipated, but she refused to think Finn would deny his request to stay on Stonefire.

Trahern motioned down the hall with a hand. "Go find Bram and Gregor. I'll go back to my laboratory until one of the nurses fetches me. I can look after any patients that need care."

The dragonman basically lived in the laboratory, so she didn't correct him about it being his. "I'll have my mobile phone if you need me. Also, keep me updated on what you find."

Trahern nodded and turned back toward the laboratory. Sid took that as her cue to leave.

While she should be excited about the possible moss to use for treatment, she was more concerned about Gregor. Conquering her beast would mean nothing if he was forced to leave Stonefire.

Yes, he drove her crazy with his overprotectiveness since the end of the frenzy, but he was already an integral part of her life. She couldn't imagine waking up alone without his heat and scent at her side.

Maybe one day, she would have her mate, her child, and her dragon all living in peaceful harmony.

She blinked. Gregor's optimism was definitely rubbing off on her.

Her beast flicked her tail but remained silent. Sid wasn't sure if her dragon being trapped behind a wall or her being present but silent was worse.

Maybe Trahern's moss would help.

Pushing the thought aside, she increased her pace. She could daydream about a happy future later. For now, she needed to get Trahern the help he needed. Sid needed to talk with Bram before finding Gregor.

She soon knocked on Bram's front door and Evie answered. The human sighed. "Please tell me there's not another emergency."

Sid raised her brows. "Another emergency?"

Evie motioned inside. As soon as Sid was inside, Evie shut the door and whispered, "Two humans showed up at the back entrance about twenty minutes ago."

"Is there another threat? As clan doctor, I need to know that as soon as possible."

Evie shook her head. "No. Bram would've sent a message if they had been."

"Then who are they?" Sid asked.

"Dr. Emily Davies and Dr. Alice Darby."

Trahern's friend had arrived, but something niggled at the back of Sid's mind. "The name Alice Darby sounds familiar."

"That's because she's my friend who's been missing for over a year."

At Evie's controlled tone, Sid asked, "Then why aren't you in there with Bram? Surely he'd want you there."

"Apparently not. Something about emotions and needing answers, such as how the bloody hell they found their way to our back entrance undetected, let alone how the two know each other."

"I'm sure there's a reasonable explanation."

Bram's voice echoed down the hallway. "Aye, there is. Sid, take Dr. Davies to Trahern. Evie, come here."

A short, slightly plump woman with dark hair moved past Bram as he said, "This is Dr. Emily Davies. Dr. Davies, this is Sid, our chief doctor. She'll fill you in on what you need to know."

Sid shared a glance with Bram and he bobbed his head imperceptibly. That was the all-clear to share information.

Emily's Welsh accent garnered her attention. "Nice to meet you. I know I'm here unannounced, but I didn't want to risk the DDA saying no. Showing up was my best option."

At the female's smile, Sid's tension eased a fraction. She'd almost expected another recluse like Trahern. "All that matters is Bram cleared you. So, let's go. I'll fill you in on the way."

Sid nodded at Evie as she passed and hoped the human would fill her in later on how the hell Alice and Emily had made it to Stonefire undetected.

The second they were outside Bram's cottage, Emily spoke up. "I know you have no reason to trust me, but all I want to do is help. I've been fascinated with dragon-shifter biology since I was a teenager. Trahern indulged my fancy for a bit at university, but to come here and live amongst the dragons is like a dream."

Sid glanced at the human. She seemed genuine, although Emily would have to earn her trust before she gave it. "It's also bloody dangerous."

"I know all about the attacks as well as what the DDA could do to me. I don't care."

"Why is that?"

Emily stopped and Sid did the same. "Because I'm tired of hiding my interests and who I am. If being myself and studying dragon-shifter biology lands me in jail, so be it. If I don't take the first step, of being truthful about a human wanting to study dragon-shifters, then who will?"

"You're definitely not what I expected, Dr. Davies."

"Call me Emily. And that doesn't surprise me. Trahern only reveals what's pertinent at the time."

"Okay, Emily. Answer one more question. How do you know Alice?"

Emily shrugged. "There is an underground club of sorts, which consists of humans who are truly interested in dragon-shifters. I met Alice via a message board several years ago and then in person about a year ago. I helped her hide in rural Wales and stay under the radar."

"Wait, what?"

"Not by myself, of course. Several of us took turns finding hiding spots. But over the years, we've become rather protective of each other, even if we rarely meet in person. Alice needed help, so we stepped forward."

The surgery came into view. "You're going to tell me more about this club, later."

Emily shook her head. "I'm not divulging secrets that could cost lives. We consider ourselves a clan of sorts and we stick together. After all, we're the only ones who understand each other."

Sid admired the female's dedication. Still, she wasn't about to completely dismiss finding out more information. From what little Sid knew, Alice Darby knew more about dragon-shifters than any other human. She and the others might have information that could help Sid better take care of her patients.

However, as they entered the surgery, she ignored her curiosity for the time being.

Sid looked to each of her staff as they passed, signaling to halt their questions about the human until later. Once they were out of earshot and nearly to the laboratory, she murmured to Emily, "Trahern is currently working on a special project for me.

While I can't guarantee it, if you can help him with it, I may be able to convince Bram to let you stay."

Emily bobbed her head. "That was my plan anyway."

Sid was already starting to like the confident female.

They reached the laboratory door and Sid opened it to find Trahern peering through the microscope. He raised his head with a frown, but his expression turned stunned as his eyes found Emily's.

When he said nothing, Emily laughed. "Nice to see you too, Trahern."

Clearing his throat, he stood up. "I wasn't expecting you is all."

"Aren't you a little bit curious as to how I'm here?" Emily asked.

"Why? You being here is all that matters," Trahern stated.

Emily took a step toward the Welsh dragonman. "True, but the details are the interesting bit."

Sensing the pair would dance around for a while if left to their own devices, Sid spoke up. "As much as I hate to cut your reunion short, I need you two to get to work. Someone's mother needs our help or she may never wake up."

Trahern moved back to his microscope. "Of course, Dr. Sid. Emily, you can read my notes while I continue my work. When you're ready, you can help."

The human didn't blink twice before sitting next to Trahern. Emily had obviously worked with him enough in the past to follow his order.

Sid spoke up again. "Right, then I'll leave you two to it while I do the rounds."

The pair barely noticed her presence as she exited the room and shut the door.

She'd do her rounds as promised, but then she needed to find Gregor and discover why the hell the meeting was taking so long.

~~~

Gregor growled at Finn's image. "Why are you making this so bloody difficult? You took Arabella from Stonefire. It shouldn't require a negotiation to stay here."

Finn leaned back in his chair. "Since you aren't staying to mate Cassidy Jackson, I have to make it difficult or the bloody DDA will breathe down my neck. Dragon clan transfers require a considerable amount of paperwork."

"It's not that I don't want to mate her."

"Then what?"

He sighed. "She is stubborn and out to protect everyone but herself. Until her dragon problem is sorted, she'll find ways to protect me, which includes sparing my feelings as much as possible."

"Then try harder, Gregor. Believe me, I understand wooing a reluctant lass. My question is how much effort have you put into winning her?"

"We've been pretty fucking busy, as you bloody well know," Gregor bit out.

"Aye, I do. But if the threat is minimal and there's nothing critical you can do, then enjoy an hour with your female. We can't let whoever is attacking with the drones scare us into never enjoying our lives."

"I'm not bloody afraid. There's just so much to be done."

"An hour with your mate will help more than you know. Everyone needs a break sometimes. If I can do it as clan leader, you can do it as a mere doctor."

189

He growled. "A 'mere' doctor does a hell of a lot more work than you, Finn."

"If you say so. You have no idea the amount of paperwork I have to do—"

Gregor cut him off. "Is there anything else? Otherwise, I need to go."

"To spend time with your newly pregnant mate."

"That's my answer. Good-bye, Finn."

Gregor severed the connection and ran his hands through his hair. His dragon decided to speak up. *Finn is right. We've barely done anything but sleep next to our mate for days. You still haven't let me out to play, either.*

Not you, too. Doesn't anyone understand there's work to be done?

There's always work to be done. Trahern can watch over our patients for a while. That's why he's here.

With a sigh, Gregor moved toward the door. *Let me see how things are at the surgery. Maybe we can take Cassidy to lunch.*

Not lunch. Kiss her. Hold her. Let her know we still desire her.

Gregor halted his hand from turning the door knob. *Of course we desire her.*

Does Cassidy know? You've kissed her once a day, when you first see her. Our mate needs more, much more.

At the thought of Cassidy thinking he didn't care, Gregor exited the room and walked briskly down the hall. *Maybe I can spare ten minutes to treasure our mate as she deserves.*

An hour.

Thirty minutes.

His dragon huffed. *Talk with her first and then we can negotiate further.*

His beast fell silent and Gregor turned the corner. He nearly bumped into his doctor. "Cassidy?"

She took his hand and tugged him into an empty room inside the Protectors' central command. After shutting the door, she hissed, "What did Finn want that took so long?"

He tried to touch her cheek, but Sid merely raised her brows. With a sigh, Gregor answered her. "He wants another foster candidate from Stonefire to help even out the numbers since Lochguard hasn't had one since the trade for Arabella last year."

Cassidy frowned. "What? Why? Bram didn't demand anything when Finn mated Arabella."

Gregor decided to tell Cassidy the full truth. "Aye, but Finn mated Arabella."

"And we haven't done so," Cassidy stated.

"I'm not about to rush you. I'll keep fighting Finn to stay here, love. Don't worry about that."

"So, if we mate, he'll stop with the demands?"

"I have no idea. Finlay Stewart often does the unexpected." He traced her cheek. "How about we talk about Finn's demands later? Were you looking for me because of something work related or did you just miss my kisses?"

"Talking with Finn has brought out your charm, I see," she drawled.

He leaned closer. "Just answer the question."

She sighed. "I wanted to see you, yes, but there's something more important you should know. Trahern's human has shown up, along with another female."

"What?"

"Emily Davies is working with Trahern as we speak. I'm not sure what's going on with Alice."

Gregor frowned. "Okay, lass. How about you tell me everything from the beginning?" Once Cassidy filled him in, Gregor tilted his head. "It seems odd that Bram trusted the humans so easily, even taking into account one of them is Evie's friend."

Cassidy shrugged. "I have no idea what went on inside his office. But we should head back to the surgery so Trahern can focus solely on his work."

Gregor's dragon huffed. *I want time with our mate.*

Ignoring his beast, Gregor leaned to Cassidy's ear and whispered, "Are the rounds done?" His doctor nodded. "Then I say we take a break. I have a feeling you haven't eaten since the last time I reminded you." When she didn't say anything, he knew he was right. "Then give me a little time to know you better, lass. I admire you for your work ethic, but I bet there is more to Cassidy Jackson than her work."

"Not much."

He kissed her gently. "I don't believe that. Just an hour, love. I bet even Bram takes breaks sometimes."

His dragon snorted. *You're stealing lines from Finn now.*

Cassidy sighed. "I would say that's irrelevant since being a doctor and a clan leader are different, but I know you'll use our child as an excuse next, so I should just give in now to save some time."

"I wouldn't stoop that low. At least, not until I'd exhausted every other avenue."

He winked and Cassidy chuckled. "Fine, one hour, not a minute more."

"Good, then let's hurry up and get you fed so I can make the most of our break."

"I hope you're not saying what I think you are."

Gregor searched her eyes. "Did you tire of me already, love?"

"No, it's just that…"

192

He jumped in after a few beats of silence. "You feel guilty for doing anything that makes you feel good when others are suffering."

"Mostly. But I'm also afraid of my dragon going rogue."

CHAPTER NINETEEN

Sid checked on her dragon, but her beast was still ignoring her. Maybe one day she wouldn't have to continuously monitor her beast's mood before acting or making a decision.

Even so, Gregor mentioning time together made her heart race in anticipation. If it were truly up to her and her dragon wasn't a problem, she'd take the much-needed break with the father of her child.

But what with Trahern and Emily working on their research and Molly Caruso still unconscious, Sid understood her duty. Unless the clan was healthy and whole, she shouldn't be enjoying herself.

Gregor's voice garnered her attention again. "Let's just take it one step at a time, love. I'm not going to shred your clothes and take you against a tree. Well, at least until you say we can."

He waggled his eyebrows and Sid snorted. "You may hide your randy side well, but I need to remember it's always just under the surface."

"Only for you, Cassidy," he whispered. "Only for you."

For a split second, as she gazed into Gregor's eyes, Sid wished she could spend a week simply getting to know her mate. Yes, she cared for him and he'd wormed his way into her life, but there was so much more to Gregor Innes that she wanted to unravel.

She finally replied, "How about you show me your dragon and then we eat? I haven't seen him yet."

"Why, so you can win him over even more?"

The corner of her mouth ticked up. "Maybe."

His pupils flashed, but the sight didn't make her uncomfortable or send a wave of longing through her body. She wanted all of Gregor, both dragon and human.

Her own dragon peeked over her shoulder at that thought. Maybe, just maybe, seeing Gregor's dragon would help coax out her own.

Gregor took her hand and guided her out of the building. Looking around, he finally tugged them toward a copse of trees in the middle of the clan's land. As they wove their way into the trees, Sid's heart rate kicked up. After so many years of avoiding dragon-shifters in dragon form unless absolutely necessary, it was hard to embrace the change.

Then her Scot grinned over his shoulder at her and she couldn't help but smile back. This wasn't just any dragon she was about to meet, but the one male who already meant so much to her.

Gregor stopped when they reached the empty clearing inside the trees. Sid had avoided the place in the past as it was a common spot for lovers, but the grass and surrounding trees made the rest of Stonefire disappear.

In the isolated spot, it was just Sid and Gregor. No work, no threats, and no responsibilities.

Without thinking, she stood on her tiptoes and kissed her dragonman. Gregor wrapped his arms around her and let Sid guide the kiss.

She slowly stroked the inside of his mouth and reveled in the taste that was Gregor.

Then he nipped her bottom lip and she squeaked. In retaliation, she grabbed one of his arse cheeks and dug in her nails. Of course, her bloody mate merely groaned and placed a possessive hand on her arse.

As she took the kiss deeper, her dragon turned around a little more. Sid half expected her beast to push her aside and take control, but she held back.

Rather than think about why, Sid stroked against Gregor's tongue a few more times before pulling away. The heat in his eyes made her shiver. Even without the frenzy, he truly wanted her.

His voice was husky as he said, "Kiss me like that again and I'll see that as an invitation to take you against a tree."

"Leave it to you to ruin the moment."

"Ruin it? Your eyes tell me that you want me, Cassidy. I'm just trying to give my female what she wants."

The heat of his hand on her arse seeped into her skin. She'd almost forgotten what it was like to have Gregor's rough hands on her body. Memories of him caressing her hip, her thighs, and then between her legs from the frenzy flashed into her mind and a rush of heat coursed through her body.

She wanted to feel his touch again.

Then Sid remembered everything waiting for them back at the surgery. She only had time for one activity before heading back. Getting to know Gregor's dragon was more important to both of them, and not just because it might help Sid. No, she wanted to know everything about her Scot. Sex would have to wait until later. No matter Finn's reluctance, Sid would find a way to keep Gregor on Stonefire.

She stepped back and Gregor let her go. She answered the question in his eyes. "You can take me against a tree later. We don't have much time and I want to meet your dragon."

196

His pupils flashed before he answered, "I would try to convince you differently, but my bloody beast is all but throwing a tantrum inside my head."

She raised an eyebrow. "Well, we have about fifty minutes left. If you want me to eat something, then you'd better hop to it."

Gregor tugged off his shirt and tossed it at Sid. She caught it and instinctively wrapped her arms around the warm fabric that smelled of her dragonman. "Just don't spoil him too much or I'll never hear the end of it."

Sid smiled as she watched Gregor finish undressing. "I'm not known for spoiling anyone, so you should be safe."

Gregor's gaze burned into hers. "As long as you let me spoil you once in a while, my dragon and I can live with that."

Sid wasn't used to people wanting to take care of her, so she brushed the comment aside. "Forty-eight minutes and counting."

Sighing, Gregor closed his eyes. His body glowed a grayish color before his nose elongated into a black snout; wings sprouted from his back, and his tail extended out behind him. A few seconds later, a tall, black dragon stood in front of her.

Sid admired the sturdy and powerful form of Gregor's dragon. He may be a doctor, but the muscles of his back and chest spoke of hours practicing in the air.

Letting out the breath she'd been holding, Sid approached the beast. While it was cloudy, the black hide glinted slightly in the faint light. Much like how her brother's golden hide had during the day at the cliffs.

No. She wouldn't let her past paralyze her. Taking a deep breath, she closed the distance between them and placed a hand on the black dragon's chest. At the contact, the beast rumbled.

Looking up into gray eyes the same color as Gregor's, she let out a breath and said, "You're a handsome beast."

Gregor's dragon gave a low roar before lowering his head to bump his snout against Sid's cheek. At the contact, her dragon turned around inside her mind and tilted her head. Sid was tempted to ask her beast a question but held back. She didn't want to break the spell.

Keeping her hand on the black dragon's hide, Sid slowly made her way to one side and studied his wing. Memories of beating her own wings before diving to the ground filled her mind. The rush of the wind combined with the thrill of pulling up at the last moment was one she'd long suppressed. Would she ever experience it again?

Before she could brush it aside like most of her hopes, her dragon took another step forward.

Unsure of how her dragon would respond, Sid asked, *Do you miss it too?*

For a second, her beast stood still. Then she growled and turned her back again. *I will fly again without you.*

The anger in her dragon's voice cut straight to Sid's heart.

Rather than let it ruin her precious time with Gregor, Sid continued her walk around Gregor's dragon until she was once again in front of him. "Hello, dragon. You're a fine beast."

The dragon stood a little taller before lowering his head and offering his ear. Smiling, Sid scratched behind it and said, "Maybe next time I can bring some oil to ease the dryness behind your ears. If you're not careful, you'll have the equivalent of dragon dandruff."

The black dragon grunted and lightly bumped her chest. She added, "If you want someone to merely compliment you on how magnificent you are, then you clearly haven't been paying attention, dragon." The beast grunted again and she chuckled. "But it has a positive side. When I say something, it's the truth. And you are one of the finest dragons I've seen in a long while, especially considering you're just a doctor."

Irritation flashed in the dragon's eyes, and Sid couldn't resist teasing some more. "Maybe we can hold some contests amongst the dragon-shifter doctors, if we succeed in bringing them together. Then you can see who's the strongest."

The dragon backed up a few feet before his body glowed faintly and began to shrink. A few seconds later, Gregor's human self stood in the clearing.

He rushed her and pulled her close. "I think you want to make my life difficult on purpose, don't you? He won't stop pestering me to become stronger now."

She tilted her head. "It just gives me the excuse to watch your dragon more often."

His expression softened. "You're okay with it, then, love? For a second, I was afraid you'd bolt."

She shook her head. "It was just a memory, but it faded. I loved studying your dragon form. However, what's more important is that my dragon took notice of yours."

He cupped her cheek. "I guess from your expression it didn't end with an embrace and rejoicing."

"No, but I didn't expect her to love me overnight."

"We'll bring her round, I promise."

"That's a pretty tall order."

He kissed her. "Nothing is too much for my mate." He kissed her again. "I would ask you to mate me now, but I know you'll make up some bullshit about protecting my feelings. So, I'm not going to ask you until your dragon cooperates. Once she does, prepare yourself for a grand surprise."

199

Sid wanted nothing more than to mate the clever, determined, and teasing man in front of her. And yet, she couldn't until she knew Gregor wouldn't have to experience losing his mate yet again. "You know me too well already."

He traced her cheek. "I'm a doctor. Reading people is part of my job requirement." He nuzzled her cheek. "And since I'm your doctor, my next order is to find you some food before you step foot back into the surgery. Even if I have to strap you to a chair and force feed you, I'll do it." He moved a hand to her lower abdomen. "You can't neglect your most important patient."

Laying her head on Gregor's chest, she murmured, "It still hasn't completely sunk in, you know. About the baby. Once in a while I'll remember, but then I get busy and forget. It makes me wonder if I'll be a good mother or will I always forget about him or her as the hours tick by at the surgery."

Gregor rubbed up and down her back. "Right now, the bairn is a tiny speck. However, once he or she starts kicking and making a fuss, it will become real to you. That's also when I'm going to be more protective because I refuse to lose either of you."

She looked up at the certainty in his voice. "The risk of a dragon-shifter dying in childbirth is small, Gregor." He opened his mouth, but she cut him off. "However, I promise now that if I need bed rest—as dictated by a second opinion so as to prevent you from just being protective—I'll do it. But we have many more months until then. For now, I can handle you cooking or buying food for me. It's almost like I have a servant."

He raised his brows. "Oh, aye? Glad to see my years of medical school and practice are being put to good use."

She leaned back to meet his eyes and tried not to smile. "Oh, don't worry, I'll let you out to play doctor once in a while."

"Cheeky lass," he murmured before he tickled her ribcage. Sid laughed until her sides hurt and she asked him to stop. Gregor relented, then added, "Maybe I'll ask you to be my servant in bed sometimes. That will even things out."

"Well, my years of medical school will come in handy then. I know a lot about anatomy and how a male dragon-shifter responds."

He tilted his head. "Do you, now? Are you ready to give me my free consultation?"

She hit his chest. "No, we're not having sex against a tree. There's no time for that."

"Maybe not now, but I have a few ideas of how to make the most of our bed this evening."

The image of Gregor licking between her thighs as she moaned his name flashed into her mind. Even to her own ears, her voice was rough. "I look forward to your suggestions."

He chuckled. "There's no need for the formality, lass. I plan to make you scream my name a few times and I'm not going to be shy about it."

Her dragon lifted her head. *I want him.*

Those three words brought Sid crashing back to reality. She'd put off sleeping with Gregor again since the frenzy to remain in control. She might be good at hiding it, but she wanted him with each breath.

Her Scot's voice rumbled. "What's wrong, Cassidy?"

She shook her head. "Just my dragon. But I'm determined to win her over."

"And I'll help you in any way I can, love. Just ask."

Touching Gregor's cheek, Sid wanted to tell him how she felt. She'd never had someone care so much for her welfare or stand by her side whilst knowing all of her faults. Bram had her back, but not even he knew all of her secrets.

Gregor did and he supported her anyway.

Not wanting to cry about nearly having what she wanted but not being able to grasp it, she cleared her throat. "Right now, I want food. Preferably something greasy and unhealthy."

After gently kissing her, he stepped back to pick up his trousers. "I would run to the nearest restaurant right this second, but then I'd be sharing this glorious body with the entire clan."

"Which isn't going to happen."

He raised his brows as he zipped up his fly. "As a doctor, and dragon-shifter to boot, I didn't think nudity would bother you."

She took a step toward the path out of the clearing. "It doesn't. But I don't want to scare the others."

Gregor growled and Sid dashed down the path. Her years of running paid off as she stayed ahead of Gregor for a few minutes before his long legs finally caught her from behind. He whispered into her ear. "Caught you, which means I can demand my prize tonight."

She looked over her shoulder. "We'll see, Doctor. We'll see."

He took her lips in a rough kiss. As she reveled in the heat and taste of her mate, Sid only hoped Gregor had time to see through his claim later in the evening. No matter if she burned out from fighting her dragon, Sid wanted to make love with the male she cared about more than any other.

For once, she wanted to do something for herself and she wanted Gregor Innes.

CHAPTER TWENTY

After lunch, Gregor walked with Cassidy into the surgery and headed straight for the laboratory.

He usually loved returning to work, but a small part of him wanted more time with his female. Spending an hour with Cassidy had shown Gregor a glimpse of what he'd missed out on since his first mate died.

His dragon spoke up. *Then learn to delegate better. I want her to scratch my ears again.*

Before I allow that, I want her naked and in bed. Then we'll see about your ears.

His beast perked up. *Yes, yes, I want a turn in bed, too. I want to be in control next time.*

No, Cassidy is mine for at least one night.

At the steel in his voice, his dragon sulked and remained silent. Gregor rarely ordered his dragon around with such force, but he wouldn't be denied in this.

All too soon they reached the laboratory's door. Opening it, he found Aaron conferring with Emily and Trahern.

They stopped talking and looked at him. Gregor asked, "What's going on?"

Aaron answered, "The boy on Glenlough's condition has worsened and O'Shea wants us to take care of him. Kai and a few others are bringing the boy to Stonefire. Since you two were gone, I was just conveying Bram's orders."

Cassidy jumped in. "What's wrong with the boy?"

"He's tenuously close to losing control and going rogue. Nothing Glenlough has tried has helped. Once the O'Sheas heard we might have a solution, the boy's parents volunteered him."

Gregor frowned. "Wait a second. We still don't know all of the ill effects. The previous patient was nearly an adult and the boy is only eight years old."

Trahern replied, "The boy's parents are still willing to try. It's the only option left, apart from keeping him continually sedated."

"Which is no way to live," Cassidy murmured.

Gregor squeezed her hand in his and looked to Aaron. "When will they arrive?"

"This evening. Bram wants all of you working on this together," Aaron stated.

So much for spending time with Cassidy later in the evening.

His dragon growled. *The child is more important and you know it.*

Of course I do, but I wish life was a little less exciting. At least for a few months, anyway.

Cassidy jumped in. "Right, then I want Trahern and Emily to keep working on the moss and its side effects. The more information we have, the better the boy's chances. Gregor and I will keep an eye on the other patients and get as much work as possible finished before the boy's arrival." She moved her gaze to Aaron. "Keep in contact. Not just for the boy, but also in case your mother wakes up. We have no idea what will happen and we might need your decision straight away."

Aaron nodded. "Of course."

"Good," Sid said. "Now, everyone back to work. We don't have much time and a lot needs to be done."

His female was bloody fantastic. Some males might resent a female taking charge, but Cassidy knew her clan better than he. Only an idiot would allow their ego to get in the way of brilliance and efficiency.

Everyone murmured their assent before Sid tugged his hand toward the exit. Once in the hall, she sighed. "At one point, things were fairly quiet on Stonefire, if you can believe it."

"I do, as it was the same on Lochguard. But things will eventually calm down." He leaned down to her ear and whispered, "My only regret is that I'll have to wait to hear you scream my name. I don't think either of us is going to have the energy tonight."

Cassidy placed a hand on his chest and her touch seared through his shirt. "I'm slowly learning that I need to embrace what time I have and not put things off." She nuzzled his cheek. "When we have a little down time, you're mine, dragonman."

He moved to look into Cassidy's eyes and was surprised to find her pupils flashing. He only hoped her dragon wasn't going to make a fuss. "Then that's an added incentive for me to work as hard as possible."

~~~

Sid's dragon paced inside her mind and finally said, *I want to embrace things. Nine months is too long to wait.*

Even though Gregor was staring at her, Sid focused on her beast. *There are many things we can try together, if you give me a chance. That way you won't have to wait.*

205

Her dragon remained silent for a few beats before she replied, *Why do you want to share anything with me when I told you I'm taking control of our body and our child after he or she is born.*

Because I think you remember our time before, when we were teenagers and worked together. It could be that way again. Her dragon grunted and Sid continued, *Think about it. After we save the Irish child, we can try something, if you like.*

I won't interfere while you try to save the child, but I won't make any promises about the rest.

Her beast retreated to the back of her mind again and Sid sighed. At Gregor's inquisitive look, she murmured, "We shouldn't have any distractions while working on our latest assignment. Even my dragon wants to help the boy."

"That's progress."

"I suppose." Sid started walking and Gregor followed. "Let's check on Molly Caruso and make the rounds from there since Ginny said no one had an appointment for another hour."

They made their way down the hall and entered Molly's room. The dragonwoman was tossing and turning on the bed.

Sid let go of Gregor's hand and rushed to the woman's side. She was still asleep, but the change in her behavior might mean the female was ready to wake up.

Taking hold of Molly's shoulders, Sid asked, "Can you hear me, Molly? If so, I need you to wake up so I can help you."

Gregor was on the other side and checked Molly's pupils. They flashed between slits and round ones. She hoped the change was a good sign.

Her mate ordered, "Molly, fight your dragon. We need you awake. Now."

The older female muttered something unintelligible. Sid found a specially formulated vial of smelling salts and held them under Molly's nose. The female turned her head away, but Sid followed her. After a few more seconds, the female shot straight up in bed. "What's going on? Where am I?"

Molly's pupils were round.

Gregor checked her vitals as Sid said, "You're in the surgery, Molly. Do you remember what you were doing before?"

"I was…in the car. That's the last thing I remember."

"Good. Now, how is your dragon?" Sid asked.

Molly took a second before replying, "She's unconscious." Her eyes met Sid's. "Why can't I wake her?"

Keeping her voice cool and collected, Sid answered, "You were given a strange drug that probably affected your dragon. She's actually been in control for days and is probably just exhausted."

"Days?"

Sid nodded. "Yes. Now I know this is disorienting for you, but I need you to answer a few questions so I can help you get better. Can you do that?" Molly bobbed her head and Sid continued, "Can you wiggle your toes and fingers?" Molly complied. "Good. Does it hurt anywhere?"

Molly placed a hand on her temple. "I have a massive headache, but that's it."

Gregor spoke up. "We'll take care of that for you, lass. And if you're up to it, we'll call your son."

"Is Aaron all right?" Molly asked.

"He's fine," Sid answered. "No one else was attacked."

Molly sighed. "Thank goodness. Aaron didn't want me to come back just yet, but I fought him and won. I wouldn't want anyone else injured because of my stubbornness."

Gregor's voice was light as he said, "Stubbornness runs rampant with dragon-shifters. Although I would advise you to stay on Stonefire until further notice. You inhaled a strange substance and we're not sure what the effects are. No matter how small a change, you tell us everything, aye?"

"Yes, Doctor."

Gregor smiled. "Good." Ginny entered and Gregor motioned toward the nurse. "Since all of your vital signs are normal, Ginny will stay with you until your son arrives. She'll also give you something for the pain."

Sid shared a look with Ginny and the nursed nodded—she would try to find out more from Molly and keep prodding her gently.

After a few more reassuring pats, Sid and Gregor exited the room and headed for Sid's office. As soon as they were inside, she said, "I wasn't expecting that result."

Gregor shrugged. "Maybe her dragon raged and fought for so long that she passed out? It's entirely possible."

"But why then is she okay and the boy is not? Trahern said the differences in the formula weren't that significant."

"Even the minutest change could produce a different result, especially if we're not dealing with an expert."

An idea flashed into Sid's mind and she went to her computer. Pulling up Trahern's notes, she scanned the chemical makeup of the substances found in the Irish boy, Sid, and Molly. All three were different, albeit in minuscule ways.

Gregor stood behind her. "What are you thinking, love?"

Sid tapped each of the chemical recipes. "I don't think these were made by the same person. While a scientist would change one variable in small amounts for each trial, each of these have differing amounts of the main compounds that are basically a sedative."

"Aye, I see that."

Sid turned to look up at Gregor. "I think these were made by three different amateurs."

"But wouldn't Trahern have mentioned that?"

"Maybe, maybe not. He's focused on pinpointing the mysterious element. Given what we know of him so far, he might've jotted down the differences somewhere to share later and then moved on to the next test."

"Say you're right and amateurs did this—how do we use that to our advantage? Stonefire has a decent list of enemies. The dragon hunters have become a lot more cautious over the last year and I doubt they'd do something so risky."

"I agree. But the hunters aren't our only concern."

Gregor frowned. "The Dragon Knights? But I thought their main force was captured on Lochguard after their last attack."

"I don't know all of the particulars, but I know that only some of the knights were taken and all of their leadership escaped unscathed. We need to talk to Bram and maybe even Grant."

Grant McFarland was Lochguard's head Protector.

"You go, love. I'll run the surgery so you as well as Trahern and Emily can do your work," Gregor said.

Sid stood. "A lot of males would've resented babysitting."

"Aye, but I'm not most males. I believe in you, Cassidy. It's your theory." He kissed her quickly. "Now, go. Each minute we spend chatting gives the bastards more time to strike again."

At that moment, Sid fell in love with Gregor. He would always have her back and would never truly try to curb her freedom. He also realized the importance of her work and didn't try to dismiss it.

Her dragon perked up at her thoughts but didn't say anything, which was good since Sid didn't have time to deal with her beast, let alone her feelings for Gregor Innes. "Right, then I'll be off to Bram's first and return as soon as possible. If anything happens with Molly, don't hesitate to ring me."

"Aye, Doctor. Now, go."

Giving Gregor one last kiss, Sid raced out the door and down the hallway. Once she was outside, she picked up her pace until she was jogging.

Even if she were right, she wondered if they could do anything with the information. The Dragon Knights attacking so soon again was a long shot, especially with their depleted numbers. However, Sid needed to at least try to help. She wouldn't leave any avenue unchecked.

She reached Bram's cottage and pounded on the door. Stonefire's leader opened the door. "What is it, Sid?"

"Not here."

Bram motioned her inside and into his office. Once the door closed, he spoke again. "We're safe here, lass. Tell me what's wrong."

"Not wrong, exactly." She explained her theory about the amateurs making the compound and attacking. When she finished, she added, "While I know you need to talk to Kai and Aaron, you might want to ask Arabella to search online for any Dragon Knight activity. She knows all of the secret corners of the internet where they like to hang out."

Bram nodded. "If there is somewhere online giving out a recipe for this thing, as well as ideas for improvement, attacks could become more prevalent." He took out his mobile phone and typed a text message before adding, "Good work, Sid. If you're right, then Arabella might be able to find the mysterious compound and Trahern can help formulate a cure."

"It's a big if, Bram. I wouldn't get your hopes up too soon."

Bram met her eyes and crossed his arms over his chest. "Speaking of which, I'm going to be straightforward with you, Sid. I know you've been putting aside dreams of the future. First, I thought it was because of your silent dragon, but later I think it also had to do with these episodes testing your sanity. However, if you always think negatively, you'll never have the chance to enjoy the gift you have. As much as the Scottish doctor irritates the hell out of me, I've seen how he looks at you. If you want my advice, give him a chance and make a future."

"Bram—"

He put up a hand. "I know you're going to say this isn't my business. And maybe even toss in an excuse or two about your dragon being unstable. Or, how you don't want to hurt Innes. But I guarantee he's strong enough for anything that happens."

Sid raised her brows. "Can I speak now?"

Bram snorted. "Go ahead."

"What I was going to say is you know full well my parents died trying to find a way to save me. I can't have that on my conscience again. Gregor would do something daft if it meant I would live. I'm a doctor. My job is to save lives."

"Aye, and you do a fine job. But let me just ask you one thing—if you could do anything to save Innes's life, would you?"

"Of course," she answered without hesitation.

"Then try explaining why you can risk your life to save someone but someone else can't do the same for you. You're worth the world, Sid. Start believing that."

She opened her mouth and promptly closed it. She hated when Bram was correct.

Before anyone could speak again, someone knocked on Bram's door. He shouted, "Enter," and Nikki Gray walked into the room.

The female Protector looked between them and said, "I can tell something serious is happening. Care to tell me why you called me here, Bram?"

"Aaron is with his mother and Kai is busy with another task. You're more than capable of handling this and get along well enough with Arabella."

Nikki tilted her head. "What's going on?"

As Bram explained the situation to Nikki, Sid's mind wandered to Bram's words: *Try explaining why you can risk your life to save someone but someone else can't do the same for you.*

Damn Bram and his words of wisdom. Sid liked logical explanations and he knew it. She'd never be able to dismiss the reasoning now.

There was only one thing to do—be honest with herself and Gregor. When Sid had a moment alone with her dragonman again, she was going to take the plunge and tell him how she felt.

CHAPTER TWENTY-ONE

Gregor finished the splint on the young red dragon's wing and looked at the teenager named Miles in the eye. "You're going to have to stay in your dragon form until one of the doctors clears you. I know you think you're invincible at sixteen, but if you want to fly without pain for the rest of your life, you need to heed my orders. Aye?"

The male dragon bobbed his head reluctantly. Gregor patted his snout and said, "I know you were trying to impress a lass, but believe me, females prefer you alive and well over lying prostrate on the ground. Displays of stupidity rarely work as well as respect and maybe a wee gift." Miles grunted and Gregor snorted. "As you wish, lad. But if you try to fly before you're cleared, I'm not above chaining you to the ground."

His dragon spoke up. *You're giving the same advice the doctor once gave us. It didn't work then. I doubt it'll work now.*

Maybe so, but unlike Lochguard's old doctor, I'll actually chain him to the ground if it means I can save his wing.

Good luck convincing his parents.

Oh, they may be more open to it than you'd think, given what I've heard about this lad getting into trouble.

As the teenage dragon settled on the ground, Gregor put away his supplies inside the tent used for dragon-shifters in their dragon forms and moved to the exit. He gave the lad one more stern look before entering the main surgery building.

He hadn't taken more than two steps inside when his mobile phone rang. Answering it, Bram's voice came on the line. "Kai and the others just arrived and they'll bring the boy to your surgery. Be ready."

Gregor barely managed, "Aye," before Bram hung up.

Dashing toward the receiving entrance, he arrived just as Cassidy entered alone. She met his gaze. "Bram told you, too?"

"Aye, he did." He studied his female a second and noticed her tapping her hand against her thigh. "What's on your mind, love?"

She shook her head. "Now's not the time."

Warning bells went off inside his head. "If it's to do with your dragon, then tell me."

"No, it's not my dragon. It can wait for later. The boy needs all of our attention. I promise to tell you once we help him."

He lightly brushed Cassidy's arm and nodded.

They stood in comfortable silence until Kai and Quinn entered the surgery with a boy on a stretcher between them. The black-haired boy was bound at the wrists and ankles, but unconscious.

The sight of an eight-year-old boy tied up made Gregor want to punch a wall. He hoped Cassidy's earlier idea bore fruit. The bastards responsible for the attack needed to be caught and tried for their crimes.

Cassidy asked, "How is he unconscious? I thought he was out of control."

Kai answered, "He was drugged before we left with the dragon slumber drug."

Gregor shared a glance with Cassidy before an unknown dragon-shifter stepped into the hallway. The male said, "My name is Ronan O'Brien. I'm the junior doctor from Glenlough and I'm here to watch over my patient."

"Great, you think we're going to kill him," Gregor drawled.

Cassidy shot him a look before saying, "Ignore Gregor. I'm Dr. Sid. Tell me what you know, Dr. O'Brien."

Gregor directed Kai and Quinn to the closest room as Ronan replied, "Brendan has nearly lost control to his dragon. In order to transport him safely, he was given two shots of the dragon slumber drug."

"No more," Cassidy ordered.

Ronan raised his brows and Gregor chimed in. "An overdose can lead to permanently silencing someone's inner dragon."

"He's stable for now, so that shouldn't be an issue," Ronan said. Kai and Quinn transferred Brendan to the bed and he continued, "My clan leader seems to think you can help him. I'm a little less certain."

Gregor opened his mouth, but Cassidy beat him to it. "Look, I know clans have been secretive and distrustful for more years than I'd like to admit, but I assure you we only want to help Brendan. If you can't accept that, then you can wait inside the Protector's central command. I don't need any extra negativity hindering my work."

As Gregor stared at his lovely lass with fire in her eyes and her chin raised, he loved her all the more for standing up to the doctor who was several stones heavier than she.

He blinked. Love?

Yes, as he watched his mate glare at Ronan, Gregor admitted he loved everything about his female; from her strength to her stubbornness, even her dedication to the clan. Aye, she was bonny as well, but Gregor loved more than her beauty.

His dragon spoke up. *It took you long enough.*

Hush, dragon. We don't have time for an argument.

Taking a deep breath, Gregor bottled up his feelings. The young lad needed his help; his own feelings and claiming of Cassidy would have to wait for whenever things finally calmed down.

Kai's voice garnered his attention. "There's no time for fighting. Focus on the boy. The more doctors he has on his case, the better chance he has of survival."

Ronan finally muttered his assent and then added, "Then let's hurry up and exchange information since I have no idea how long he'll be out. This is the first time I've ever used more than one shot of the dragon slumber drug."

Ronan held out the file he'd been holding and Cassidy took it. Gregor read over her shoulder.

As the boy twitched for a few seconds before relaxing again, Gregor hoped they could help. No, he wasn't going to hope. Gregor was going to find a way to save the lad. Because the sooner he did that, the sooner he could finally ask Cassidy to be his mate. There was no way he was ever leaving her side.

~ ~ ~

Trahern Lewis was trying his best to focus, but every time Emily leaned toward him to read the results on the computer screen, he caught her sweet feminine scent, which made his dragon wake up bit by bit.

With a yawn, his beast finally spoke up. *Her?*

Yes, Emily. Our friend.

216

His dragon sighed and lowered his head again.

Trahern wanted to shake his dragon and ask why being friends with the clever, beautiful female at his side was such a problem. But Emily tapped something on the computer screen and said, "Another negative result. I'm starting to think the moss won't harm a dragon-shifter."

He focused. "A gut feeling isn't scientific. We need to be certain."

Emily looked at him askance and it took everything he had not to lose himself in her deep brown eyes. "Even with decades of research, side effects are never certain. All it takes is one person with a rare reaction to add something new to the list."

"Decades of research is one thing. A few hours is another." As Emily continued to read the results, he added, "Why are you here, Emily? I know you're close to your family and by coming here there's a chance you might not see them for a while."

"They moved to Australia. I won't be seeing them anytime soon," she stated.

He wanted to know more but sensed Emily wasn't going to disclose anything else from her tone. All he could do was focus on his work.

He'd barely set up the next test when the phone rang. He answered and a female's voice in a Northern English accent filled the line. "Trahern Lewis, I'm Arabella MacLeod. I'm bringing something up on your screen."

"What—"

A new window opened for a program he'd never seen. A forum-like page with several replies filled the screen. Before he could read anything, the female's voice continued, "This is a dark website used by Dragon Knight recruiters."

"Dark website?"

"It's a secret part of the internet that an average person can't access. I found something you should look at. Read the first post."

Trahern looked at the post:

Want to be a part of the Dragon Knights and rid the UK of our dragon problem? Then take these ingredients and figure out the best recipe to make a dragon-shifter's dragon go insane. With heightened surveillance, we only take dedicated members now. Find the solution, document proof, and we'll be in touch.

The rest of the post was a basic formula, minus the proportions. Trahern read down the list. At the last ingredient, he tapped the screen. "This plant must be the mystery element."

Arabella replied, "I looked up the scientific name. When you translate the name used by the locals in the Amazon, it's called dragonsoul in English. It's indigenous to the Amazon rainforest."

Emily, who had been listening next to Trahern, jumped in. "I've never heard of it. If the attackers are getting their hands on this plant, it must be via a black market."

Arabella answered, "I'm looking for sources now. If these bastards are using a forum on a hidden site, they know their way around the dark web, where you can find and buy almost any illegal item. As soon as I find where they're getting it from, I'll let you know."

"Good," Trahern said. "I'll see what we can find elsewhere. There has to be a specific compound that affects inner dragons. If I know what it is, I might be able to neutralize it."

"You'll hear from me again later," Arabella said before she hung up.

Trahern glanced to Emily, and she nodded as she moved to her laptop. As she typed, she glanced at him. "We're one step closer, Trahern. Tell me the second you find anything and I'll do the same."

He nodded and went searching. While he didn't have a way to contact any of the Amazon dragon clans and ask if they know how to counter the effects of the dragonsoul plant, he might be able to find something buried in a research journal somewhere.

~~~

Sid sat next to Brendan's bed and gently brushed the hair off his forehead. Since there was nothing to do but wait, Gregor had gone to check in with Trahern while Sid stood guard with the Irish doctor. She still didn't know enough about Ronan O'Brien to pitch ideas of future cooperation. However, she needed to work on it since adding Clan Glenlough to her network would be a boon for both her and Bram. Sid didn't follow clan politics too closely, but she knew Bram wanted to add the Irish clan to his list of allies.

Brendan sighed in his sleep and she focused back on the boy. Sid wondered if she had also been restless when she'd been unconscious as a teenager. She knew her parents had never left her side. Brendan's parents hadn't been able to come because of the Irish DDA's more restrictive rules when it came to movement between clans outside of Ireland, but Sid would take their place for now. She would fight for him until her dying breath.

Maybe it was selfish, but she hoped her own child never went through something so traumatic. Although, given he or she would have two doctors for parents, the child would have a better chance than most.

She half expected her dragon to growl and say the child was hers. But for once, her dragon merely sat and observed. She was keeping her promise to not interfere until the boy was better.

Just as Sid thought about how working with children might help her get along better with her beast, Dr. Ronan O'Brien spoke up from the opposite side of the boy's bed. "Earlier, Dr. Innes was adamant about too much of the dragon slumber drug permanently silencing an inner dragon. I've never heard of that before. How do you know it's true?"

Sid looked at the Irish doctor and saw genuine interest in his eyes. At one time, she never would've shared her secret with a near-stranger. But if there was to ever be openness and collaboration in the future between clan doctors, Sid needed to take the first step. "Because it happened to me twenty-four years ago."

Ronan frowned. "Your dragon is silent?"

"Was, as in past tense. But I did go twenty-four years without my beast."

Ronan raised his brows. "But you found a way to bring her back, right? Shouldn't we be able to use that with the boy, if it comes to it?"

Sid shook her head. "No. It took the mate-claim frenzy to bring her out, which won't work with a child."

Ronan's pupils flashed. "Ah, yes. You smell like the other doctor. You must carry his child."

Her dragon spoke up. *My child.*

Interesting. When others mentioned the baby, her dragon claimed it.

Ignoring her beast, she answered the question in Ronan's eyes. "Yes, my dragon is back as I'm sure you just noticed with my flashing pupils. However, she hates me for the imprisonment. It's not something I wish on anyone."

Ronan paused a second before replying, "I see. Then let's try to find another way."

She smiled. "I like your dedication. Your clan is lucky."

The Irish male averted his eyes and studied the sleeping boy. She'd hit a nerve, but Sid wasn't quite sure what about.

Before she could ask a question, Gregor burst through the door. "Thanks to Arabella, Trahern and Emily know the mystery ingredient. They're working on a counter-formula."

Sid stood. "That's good news."

"Mostly. It's difficult to obtain what they need, so it may take a while."

Sid looked at the sleeping boy. "We may not have a while."

Ronan moved toward them. "Then let me help your team. I've done my fair share of chemistry over the years."

The Irish dragonman couldn't be much more than thirty, but Sid didn't know his story. "If you think you can assist, then Gregor will take you to the laboratory."

With a nod, Gregor guided Ronan out of the room. She trusted Gregor to fill her in once he returned; she wasn't about to waste time asking questions when Ronan could be helping to find a way to help Brendan.

Her dragon grunted in approval.

Her beast's mood swings were giving her whiplash.

Careful to keep that thought to herself, Sid returned to the boy's side. Taking his hand, she hummed a tune her mother used to hum when she was a child. To her surprise, her dragon soon joined in.

As Sid and her dragon hummed the old lullaby, she tried not to read too much into her dragon's actions. But maybe, just maybe, helping this child would bring them closer together to the point where her beast didn't hate her outright.

However, before Sid could think of ways to do that, the boy's eyes opened. His pupils were slitted and he hissed. "Free me."

As the boy wiggled in the bed and tried to sit up, Sid pinned his shoulders and managed to keep him down with one arm as she hit the call button. Then she leaned down until she was a few inches from Brendan's face. Putting every bit of dominance she possessed into her voice, she ordered, "Look at me." Brendan's gaze shot to hers and she continued, "If the dragon half takes control and you shift inside this surgery, others could die. Not only that, I won't be able to try to save you both if you fly away. The DDA will go after you. Even if you survive their capture, you'll spend your life trapped inside a prison. Is that what you want?"

Some might say her direct manner was too much for a young boy, but Sid was trying to reach the dragon half, which would need the straightforward manner. That was one of the first things a dragon-shifter doctor learned during their training.

The boy's voice was gravelly as he replied, "I will fly free." One of Brendan's fingers turned into a talon. "No one will stop me."

Sid moved out of the way of Brendan's talon. "The DDA has powerful weapons to shoot you out of the sky. However, if you work with me, then I might be able to save you both."

"I don't need saving."

She raised her brows. "What about your human half? Are you going to imprison him for the rest of your life and never let him out?" Dragon-possessed Brendan's confidence faded a fraction. Sid pushed on. "He's your best friend. You'll miss him when he's gone."

Brendan's pupils flashed again. Sid continued, "Let Brendan come out for just a little while. He's probably scared and missing your parents. Don't you want to help him? Dragons treasure children. Even you should know that and want to take care of your own human."

Indecision filled the boy's eyes. Sid might've convinced him.

Brendan's dragon finally answered, "Only for a little while. I won't let him always be in control. There's too much to do and he always holds me back."

"Just a little while."

Sid held her breath and waited.

Brendan's pupils finally turned round and stayed that way. "Who are you? Where's my mam?"

Stroking the boy's forehead, Sid answered gently, "My name's Dr. Sid. As for your mum, she's back home. We're trying to get you well so you can go back to her."

Brendan looked around. "I want Dr. O'Brien."

Her dragon spoke up. *Calm him. I don't like him scared.*

"Dr. O'Brien will be back as soon as he can. He's trying to find a medicine to make you better."

The boy stared for a few seconds before replying, "Why is my dragon so angry?"

She released her arm that had been pinning him down and touched his bicep. "He isn't truly angry with you. He's just been given a strange drug and it changed his behavior."

"Why would someone do that?"

"I wish I knew, Brendan. I wish I knew." Noticing the tension in Brendan's body, Sid needed to do something or the dragon may try to take advantage of the boy's weakness. "How about we play a game while we wait?"

"What game?"

She searched his eyes as she undid the straps restraining him to the bed. "I used to love charades as a child, but I'm not sure you're up for it."

223

As soon as the last strap came free, Brendan sat up in his bed. "I like guessing. You act something and I can guess."

With a smile, Sid stood up. "Okay, although I'm a bit rusty. Hopefully you can guess."

As she tried to think of what to do, her dragon chimed in. *Pick a children's movie. It will be easy for him.*

Taking a chance, she asked, *What do you suggest?*

I like Pixar movies. Use one of those.

Sid barely resisted blinking at her dragon's comment. Sid had seen maybe two Pixar movies in her life, both times with one of her patients. However, if her beast remembered them enough to name them, it might be a way to win her dragon's good graces later to watch a few more.

Picking an easy one, she said, "Kid's movie."

Holding up one finger, the boy said, "One word." She nodded and put her hands up as if holding a steering wheel. Turning this way and that, she made her way around the room with over-the-top movements. Brendan clapped his hands. "I know! Cars!"

Sid grinned. "Yes. Shall we try another one?" Brendan nodded enthusiastically. The happiness in his eyes reminded her of why she loved helping people.

Her dragon spoke up again. *I have another idea. Let's do the pyramids of Egypt. I always wanted to see them.*

Me, too. Maybe one day we can go.

She waited to see if her dragon would huff and turn her back, but she merely said, *We'll see.*

Those two words sent a tendril of hope through her body. However, not wanting to break the spell, she said to Brendan, "Famous place."

Cured by the Dragon

As she went through the motions, Sid forgot about everything but making the little boy smile and laugh at her silly antics. She might be cheering up the boy, but Sid couldn't remember the last time she'd had so much fun.

225

CHAPTER TWENTY-TWO

Opening the door to Brendan's room, Gregor grinned at the sight in front of him.

Cassidy was making motions with her body and the boy was guessing. Not wanting to disturb the fun, he merely hung back and watched.

His dragon spoke up. *Maybe we don't need a special medicine to help the boy. His pupils are round and he's laughing.*

Aye, but we'll see how long it lasts.

The boy shouted, "Cat in the Hat!"

Cassidy nodded. "Five in a row. Are you sure you've only played this twice before?"

Brendan opened his mouth, but then caught sight of Gregor. "The other doctor is here."

Cassidy turned around. Between the flush on her cheeks and joy in her eyes, she was the most beautiful thing he'd seen in a long time. And one he wanted to see every day for the rest of his life.

Placing a hand on her hip, Cassidy demanded, "How long were you standing there?"

He shrugged. "Long enough. I love watching you move about and play charades."

As he gave her a slow once over, her cheeks turned pinker. "Well, I'm nearly out of ideas. So maybe you can take a turn for a bit?"

He walked up to her and gently touched her cheek. "Later, love." He moved his gaze to Brendan. "One of the nurses is bringing you some soup."

The boy scrunched up his nose. "I don't like soup."

He moved closer and lowered his voice. "This soup is different. It'll make you strong, which means you can be out of that bed sooner."

Brendan searched his eyes. "Is that the truth or is it just a lie to make me feel better?"

He blinked. "Why would I lie to you?"

"Adults sometimes lie to make children do things."

He placed a hand over his heart. "I swear on my life that I'm not lying to you. There's some medicine to help you in the soup. If you eat it all, you should be well soon."

The boy hesitated. "What about my dragon?"

Gregor gripped the boy's shoulder. "It will help him, too."

Cassidy spoke up. "If Dr. Innes says it'll help, then believe him."

Brendan looked between them. "You have to say that as he's your mate. You smell of him."

Gregor chuckled and Cassidy shot him a look before turning back to Brendan. "Your parents are mates, right?" The boy nodded. "Does your mum always do what your dad says?"

He shook his head. "No. She sometimes calls him an eejit and Dad backs off."

Gregor bit his lip to keep from laughing. The lad was observant. No doubt, Cassidy would call him an idiot many times in the future, too.

227

"Well, I'm the same way," Cassidy replied. "If I didn't like Dr. Innes's idea, I'd say so. But I trust him. Will you give him a chance?"

Brendan studied Gregor for a few seconds before replying, "Okay. But if the soup doesn't help me, I won't eat any more."

"Fair enough. I also want you to tell me the truth when I visit again later, okay?" Sid said.

Brendan gripped the sheets. "You're leaving?"

His mate was probably wondering what was going on with regards to the soup, but obviously wanted to stay. Gregor chimed in. "How about I talk to Dr. Sid for a few minutes out in the hall once the nurse gets here? That way she'll be close by in case anything goes wrong. Won't you, Doctor?"

Cassidy bobbed her head. "Yes. And I'll come back in as soon as we're done talking."

Brendan looked from Cassidy to Gregor and back again. "Okay. But don't stay away too long, Dr. Sid. My dragon listens to you and I might need your help again."

Cassidy ruffled the lad's hair. "I'll stay as long as you need me, Brendan. I promise."

A knock on the door prevented the boy from replying. Ginny's smiling face came in with a tray. "I have a very special soup for a very special guest."

As Ginny settled the food on a tray and swung it over Brendan's bed, Cassidy spoke up. "Ginny will stay with you for a few minutes whilst I talk with Dr. Innes. I'll be right back, okay?"

Brendan nodded quickly. Ginny took the cue and waxed on about the importance of finishing every last drop.

Gregor pulled Cassidy into the hallway. Before she could open her mouth, he pulled her close and kissed her. While he didn't have a lot of time, he stroked slowly against her tongue until his female sighed. With great effort, Gregor pulled back and murmured, "I love you."

Sid blinked. "What?"

He cupped her cheek and stroked her soft skin. "Our time alone is short and I couldn't wait any longer. Seeing you in there, playing charades with that boy, only strengthened my feelings for you. You're a rare breed, Cassidy Jackson. You're kind, determined, devoted, stubborn, and yet tender at times, too. With you at my side, we can accomplish anything."

Cassidy played with the edges of his lab coat, and Gregor wondered if he'd miscalculated. Not that he'd take his words back as he meant them with every bone in his body.

Just when he was about to ask a question, Cassidy whispered, "I love you, too."

~~~

When Gregor had said he loved her, Sid had frozen. She'd known he cared for her, but hearing the words made it a reality.

While she should be happy he felt the same as her, Sid waited for her dragon's response.

At first, her beast merely sat and said nothing. Then after a few more beats, she spoke up. *Don't lose him.*

She should play it safe, but Sid was tired of tiptoeing around her dragon. *Why?*

Her beast stood up. *He is good for us.*

Us?

Her dragon grunted. *You heard me. What's good for you is good for the baby. Don't chase him away out of fear.*

I'm more concerned about you leaving him, once the baby is born.

I won't leave him. I like him.

Sid chose her next words carefully. *He will only stay if we work together. I thought you wanted to take the child and flee?*

Her dragon paused and then murmured, *I liked the game. If I go out alone, it will be boring.*

So you're reconsidering?

Maybe, maybe not. Just don't lose him.

The importance of her dragon's statement wasn't lost on Sid. She might actually have a chance.

As she stared into Gregor's gray eyes, she could tell he was nervous about her reply. While the conversation with her dragon was a huge step, it paled in comparison to how she felt about the dragonman in front of her. Tired of always playing it safe, she took the jump and whispered, "I love you, too."

The corner of his mouth ticked up. "Are you sure about it, lass? I can give you some more time, if you need it."

She frowned. "Here I am taking a chance and you're teasing me."

He cupped her cheek and his rough fingers against her skin eased some of her tension. "You tensed up as soon as your pupils started flashing. I wanted to help you relax a little. After all, I'm your personal physician."

"Right now, stop being my doctor and just be the man who loves me. He should be kissing me right about now."

Gregor leaned down until his lips were a hairsbreadth away from hers. "I wish we had time for more than a kiss, but just know this is a taste of what's to come."

He prevented her from replying by pressing his lips to hers. At the contact, her dragon hummed and Sid wrapped her arms around Gregor's neck. Tilting her head, she opened her mouth to accept his tongue. He teased and stroked and with each pass, Sid melted a little more against her dragonman. The instant her nipples touched his chest, she moaned.

Gregor took her arse and pressed her against him. The feel of his hard cock against her abdomen sent wetness rushing between her legs.

With a growl, Gregor pulled away. Sid blinked a few times before asking, "Why did you stop?"

"Because if I had kissed you any longer, I would've carried you to your office, ripped off your clothes and taken you."

The image of her sitting on her desk with her legs wide as Gregor pounded into her made her skin even hotter.

Her dragon spoke up. *But the boy.*

At the mention of Brendan, ice flushed through her veins. Clearing her throat, she whispered, "We are definitely going to try that later, but not until we sort out our young patient."

"Exactly, love. Otherwise, not even a thousand dragon hunters at the gates could've stopped me from claiming you."

She raised her brows. "I somehow doubt that's true, but we'll discuss better hyperboles later. For now, I need you to tell me what's so special about that soup."

Gregor lightly squeezed her arse cheek. "Your dedication to your patients is one of the many reasons I love you."

"Gregor," she growled.

"Aye, the soup. Trahern found some information on the dragonsoul plant through some sort of botanical research organization. He's confident he found the counter agent."

"So it's not guaranteed? Will it hurt Brendan?"

Gregor shook his head. "No. Even if it doesn't counter the drug from the attack, it's harmless to dragon-shifters."

"How quickly will it act?"

"He's not exactly sure."

"And Trahern said to try anyway?"

He nodded. "Aye, thanks to that human female. His perfectionist tendencies seem to fade when she's in the room."

Sid tilted her head. "I have my suspicions about them, but now's not the time."

"I agree. I plan to claim you long before we take up time discussing Trahern and his human." He nuzzled her cheek. "Ginny will also be bringing you a batch of the same soup."

"But what about the baby?"

"Since it's used in other formulas, we know it's harmless," Gregor stated.

Sid spoke to her dragon. *What do you want to do?*

I'm surprised you asked me.

The dragon slumber shots and your imprisonment were out of my control, and yours. This time, I want you to have a say.

Her beast paused and Sid wondered if she'd undone all the progress she'd made.

Her dragon finally flicked her tail. *Even from my prison, I watched you go to medical school and then practice medicine. The counter agent should be safe. Try it.*

Thank you.

Huffing, her beast settled down and remained quiet.

Sid looked back up to Gregor's gaze. "We'll try it."

Gregor smiled. "Aye, well, then we'd better head back into the room. The sooner Ginny doesn't have to stand watch, the sooner she can fetch your dose."

She nodded. She loved the fact Gregor didn't offer any guarantees or false hope.

Sid was lucky when it came to her true mate.

Gregor looped an arm around her waist and guided her back into Brendan's room. Her heart pounding, Sid wondered how she would be able to keep the boy's spirits up until Ginny brought her dose. But then she saw Brendan's scrunched up nose as he ate a spoonful of soup and she had to bite her lip to keep from laughing.

Ginny said, "Now, now, the soup isn't that bad. Back when I was a child, our doctor gave us all kinds of foul things to try. You should be grateful."

Brendan asked, "Just how old are you?"

"Old enough. Now, eat your soup. It tastes better warm than cold."

Sid added, "She's right, you know. I'd hurry up and eat it if I were you."

"You have to say that," Brendan replied. "But if it's so good, why don't you have some?"

"Oh, I will be as soon as Nurse Ginny fetches me some." Sid nodded at Ginny and the nurse left the room. "Do you want to be friends with your dragon again?" Brendan nodded and Sid continued, "Then each spoonful of that soup should help."

"Okay," he muttered before taking a large spoonful.

As Sid stood next to Gregor, watching the little boy, she could easily envision them doing the same with their own child when they were sick.

And for the first time, Sid truly believed she'd be there for her child at Brendan's age.

~~~

Five hours later, Sid could barely stand up straight. Even though the soup had made her sleepy, she'd carried on to help Brendan and then Molly Caruso. Both patients were stable and reported that their dragons were nearly back to their old selves. While both of them would stay for another few days to ensure the cure was permanent, Sid was confident that they would be okay.

She would miss Brendan, but she wasn't about to keep him from his parents longer than was necessary.

Besides, she just needed to be patient. She and Gregor would have their own handful before they knew it. Even if Sid hadn't had the chance to check on her own dragon, which was snoring at the back of her mind, she was hopeful.

As she arrived at her office door, Gregor stood waiting. "I'm taking you home."

Before she could nod, Gregor scooped her up in his arms. She frowned at him. "What are you doing?"

"You're not only exhausted, you're experiencing the effects of the medicine. As your doctor, I say you need to be off your feet."

Too tired to argue, Sid leaned against his chest and murmured, "Just this once I'm not going to put up a fight. I feel as if I could sleep for a thousand years."

"Let's hope you don't sleep that long, love. You'd miss not only the birth of our child but their entire life."

She sighed. "Stop being so literal. It's irritating."

Gregor chuckled. "I'm never going to stop teasing you, Cassidy."

Snuggling into his chest, she replied, "For whatever reason why, I hope you don't, either."

"I may have to bring that up to you later. I have a feeling you won't remember what's happening right now."

"I will," she mumbled. It became harder and harder to keep her eyes open. "Just take me home and hold me close, Gregor. I think we deserve that much after a day like today."

"As my female wishes." He kissed her forehead and whispered, "Now, rest. I'll look over and protect you until you're better."

Surrounded by her male's heat and scent, Sid closed her eyes. As she listened to his breathing and the beat of his heart, she fell fast asleep.

CHAPTER TWENTY-THREE

The next day, Sid opened her eyes to the faint light streaming through the window. She had no idea what time of day it was, but she quickly forgot about that as she gazed at Gregor's sleeping face.

He was turned toward her, his mouth open and eyes closed. Even asleep, he had his hand on her hip in a simultaneously protective and possessive gesture.

And Sid didn't mind. Gregor was her true mate and her love. She wouldn't deny his dragon nature completely. She trusted him to know when to act alpha and when to let her loose. He'd more than shown he was capable of that since his arrival, not balking at taking a less exciting task to let her do what needed to be done.

Of course, she would have to compromise, too. As her pregnancy progressed, Gregor would grow uneasy. Allowing him to be extra protective might help him come to terms with what had happened to his mate. Sid would need to take care of herself, too. Luckily she had plenty of extra help at the surgery these days.

It was amazing what several weeks could do to her old routine.

Sid's dragon stretched in the back of her mind. Pushing aside all other thoughts, Sid held her breath. She had no idea if it was too soon to determine if the medicine she'd taken was working or not.

Her beast yawned and spoke up. *I know you're awake. Why aren't you saying anything?*

I wasn't sure you wanted to talk to me.

Her dragon paused and finally asked, *Can I be honest?*

I want that more than anything.

While I'm still upset over my imprisonment, my anger towards you has faded. You were unconscious when the others gave us the dragon slumber drug.

Sid paused to gather her thoughts. She didn't want to sound needy or too hopeful. *If I had known what was going to happen, I never would've allowed it.*

I believe you. I'm not sure why I was so vengeful before. I made noise and roared to let you know I was there and that I wanted to be free. Once I was free, I should've been happy.

It was the drug from the Dragon Knight drone that affected your emotional state. But none of that is important. I'm just looking forward to what we can accomplish in the future.

We will have our mate and child. That will keep us busy.

Sid smiled. *That it will. Although, we'll make sure to have some fun, too. You deserve it.*

Gregor's voice interrupted any reply. "You're smiling whilst talking to your dragon. That's a good sign."

After so many years not talking with her beast, Sid debated whether she should ask Gregor for some time alone with her dragon or enjoy her precious free time with her mate.

Her dragon chimed in. *I will be here. We haven't spent enough time with our mate. I say tease him and make him beg.*

She laughed. *I like that idea.*

Gregor spoke again. "What's so funny?"

Propping her head on her hand, she answered, "My dragon."

237

He searched her eyes. "So things are better?"

"As you'd say, aye, they are." Sid moved her free hand to Gregor's hip and stroked. "My beast also has another idea."

Gregor moved his hand to her arse cheek. The heat of his hand burned her skin and shot straight between her thighs.

Her eyes moved to his full mouth and she could almost taste her mate.

Her dragon growled. *Don't take too long.*

Her Scot's husky voice filled the room. "I hope this idea involves you and me in this bed."

He rolled until he was on top of her. Since they were both naked, she couldn't miss his hard cock pressed against her belly. "Maybe," she answered.

Running a hand between them, he caressed her breast, kneading gently. "The time for games has passed, love. It's been too long since I last claimed you." He pinched her nipple and Sid sucked in a breath. "But unlike the frenzy, I plan to take things slowly this time."

Her dragon hummed. *Yes, yes, hurry.*

Opening her legs, she rubbed against Gregor's cock. "Then you'd better get started, Doctor."

With a growl, he kissed her.

~~~

As Gregor played with Cassidy's breast and stroked the inside of her mouth, all he wanted to do was thrust into her and make his mate scream his name.

However, drawing on every bit of restraint he had, he pulled away to stare into his mate's brown eyes. "I love you."

She smiled and ran her hand through his chest hair. "I love you, too." Her hand continued downward until it gripped his cock. He hissed as she squeezed lightly. "Now show me how much."

His dragon growled. *Stop wasting time and devour her properly. For once, dragon, I'm in agreement.*

He nipped Cassidy's bottom lip. "As soon as you release my cock, I'll suck your hard nipples and work my way down. Your orgasm is in your hands."

She snorted and released him. "I hope not."

He grinned. "Maybe next time." She opened her mouth, but he leaned down and drew her nipple into his mouth before she could reply.

As he nibbled and licked the taut peak, Cassidy moaned and arched into his touch. Not wanting her other breast to feel abandoned, he released her and moved to the other one. As he teased and nibbled, he used one of his hands to roll her other sensitive nub between his fingers.

With each intake of Cassidy's breath, his cock turned harder.

His dragon hummed. *Yes, keep going. I want to lap the honey between her thighs.*

At the memory of his mate's musky taste, Gregor lifted his head with a growl. Cassidy's pupils flashed and it took everything he had not to ask if she was okay. If something was wrong, she would speak up. He needed to trust her.

Kissing his way down her body, he stopped at her lower abdomen and pressed a lingering kiss over their growing child.

"Gregor."

At the tenderness in Cassidy's voice, he looked up. "I know, love. I know." Rubbing the inside of her soft thighs, he

239

murmured, "Which is why we should enjoy what time we have before we have a bairn crying every few hours."

The corner of Cassidy's mouth ticked up. "Then why are you still talking? Do you need some time to prepare, old man? Forty is supposed to be the new thirty, but maybe not in your case."

He gently bit her inner thigh. "Cheeky wench."

Rubbing his whiskered cheek against Cassidy's inner thigh, she relaxed once more with a sigh.

His dragon growled. *Enough talking. Hurry up and fuck our mate with our tongue.*

With pleasure.

Gregor moved to Cassidy's pussy and blew slowly between her folds. She opened her legs further and wiggled her hips in invitation.

At the sight of her swollen pink flesh, Gregor's restraint shattered and he licked slowly up her slit.

She tasted fucking fantastic.

Yes, yes, more, his beast urged.

Taking hold of Cassidy's thighs, Gregor plunged his tongue into her core and thrust in and out. His mate was hot and wet for him.

And if he had anything to say about it, no other male would ever taste the perfection of Cassidy Jackson.

Removing his tongue, he trailed up to her clit but didn't touch. He circled around the swollen bud a few times before Cassidy growled out, "Stop teasing me."

Rather than answer, he blew slowly over her tight bud. Cassidy clutched the sheets with her fingers and he decided he'd teased enough. After licking her clit once, he sucked it between his teeth and gently worried the swollen flesh. Cassidy moaned, "Harder."

Thrusting two fingers into her pussy, he finally complied. As his mate screamed, she clutched and gripped his fingers as Gregor continued to nibble her flesh. Only once she'd stopped spasming did he stop and quickly lap up her orgasm.

His dragon roared. *We did it your way. Now, fuck her with our cock.*

Gregor raised his head and murmured, "Are you ready to scream my name again, love?"

~~~

Sid could barely string two thoughts together when Gregor asked her if she was ready to scream his name again. Her entire body felt boneless and relaxed in a way she couldn't remember.

Her dragon spoke up. *There's time for relaxing and sleeping later. I want his cock inside us. It's been too long.*

It's only been a few days.

We should claim him every day.

Sid finally answered her mate by widening her legs. "I'm more than ready."

With a growl, Gregor positioned his cock and thrust in to the hilt.

Sid moaned and reached for Gregor's shoulders. He leaned down so she could touch his warm skin. "Please, Gregor. Don't play games. Right now, I want you to fuck me."

Her dragon grunted. *We were supposed to make him beg.*

Sid's reply was cut off by Gregor taking her lips in a rough kiss. He moved his hips and his cock filled her in a delicious way.

He increased his pace as his tongue stroked against hers. Needing to feel more of his skin, she roamed her hands down his

241

back to his tight arse cheeks and dug in her nails. Gregor growled into her mouth and moved his hips faster, to the point the bed shook.

She loved how he didn't hold back.

One of his hands snaked between their bodies and lightly brushed her clit. She moaned as his rough finger rubbed back and forth, increasing the pressure with each pass.

Sid was close.

As if reading her thoughts, he pressed hard against her clit and lights danced behind her eyes as pleasure shot through her body. In the next second, Gregor stilled inside her. His orgasm sent Sid into another one that made her scream Gregor's name.

When she finally came down from her high, Gregor collapsed on top of her.

For about a minute, they both breathed heavily and said nothing. However, Sid slowly wrapped her arms around Gregor's back. He rolled to the side, taking her with him but never pulling out.

His gray eyes were at half-mast and full of love and heat. As he brushed her cheek, Sid realized how happy she was. A male loved her, she had her dragon, she could keep practicing medicine, and soon, she would have a child.

Even a month ago, Sid never would've believed that after twenty-four years of pain, she could finally seize happiness.

Gregor's voice was husky as he said, "Tell me what you're thinking, love."

Laying a hand on his chest, she cleared her throat of emotion before replying, "Just that I'm happy."

"Why do you sound so surprised? You, more than most, deserves some happiness."

"I know. But it wasn't long ago that I prepared myself to die alone and insane." She traced shapes against his chest. "And here I am with the male I love and a future ahead of me. It's going to take some getting used to."

He kissed her gently. "Then I'll just have to try harder to make you smile." He fondled one of her breasts. "I think once things calm down, I may try my hand at erotic statues."

"Gregor."

He lowered his voice. "Ones that only you and I will see, of course."

She shook her head and finally smiled. "I guess I could use it as blackmail, in case you step out of line."

He growled. "You wouldn't."

She grinned. "Of course I wouldn't. But it's fun to tease you."

He nipped her bottom lip. "I might be a bad influence on you."

Running her hand down his side, Sid gripped one of his arse cheeks. "You were exactly what I needed, Gregor Innes. No matter how much I may sigh or shake my head, don't ever change. I love you."

He laid his forehead against hers. "I love you, too, and I plan to show you how much."

As Gregor rolled her back under him and hooked her leg around his waist, Sid couldn't stop smiling.

But then her mate moved his hips as he suckled her breast and Sid lost all train of thought. Clutching his hair with her fingers, she pulled her dragonman close.

It wasn't long before she was screaming his name yet again.

CHAPTER TWENTY-FOUR

Two days later, Gregor and Cassidy stepped into Bram's cottage to find a room full of people.

Gregor recognized everyone but a human female with hair dark on the top and blue on the bottom standing next to Evie.

Cassidy stood up on her tiptoes and whispered, "That's Dr. Alice Darby, Evie's friend."

Bram spoke up. "Aye, that's Alice. Alice Darby, this is Gregor Innes, formerly of Clan Lochguard but unfortunately will probably soon be a part of Clan Stonefire."

"Bram," Cassidy growled out.

Grinning, Gregor squeezed his female tighter against his side. "Don't worry, love. Bram says it with love."

Bram sighed, but Kai Sutherland, Stonefire's head Protector, jumped in. "You two can banter later. Right now, we need to sort out some business."

Gregor met Kai's gaze. "What business? Is it medical related?"

Kai shook his head. "No. Brendan arrived back on Glenlough safe and sound, and Molly Caruso is her old self."

Cassidy asked, "Then just tell us what's going on, Kai. You know I hate beating around the bush."

"First, there's an update with the whole Dragon Knight recruitment assignment matter. Arabella MacLeod managed to take down the message board and track down some of the people who posted to the thread," Kai answered.

Gregor raised his brows. "Not all of them?"

Bram shook his head. "No. More than a few of them knew how to hide their tracks."

Evie jumped in. "But at least the drug cocktail is now offline."

"Aye, it is. But anyone who saw it before it was taken down might concoct their own version and strike again," Bram said. He looked to Gregor and Cassidy. "That's where you two come in. I need you to reach out to as many dragon-shifter doctors as you can and share that drug's cure."

Cassidy frowned. "Our allies will be easy, but the others might take some work."

Gregor added, "But between the pair of us, we'll figure something out. As it is, Cassidy and I want to create an organization where all dragon-shifter doctors share information." Gregor motioned his head toward Trahern. "Provided Lewis stays and helps out at the surgery, we should be able to sort it all out."

"I'm not going anywhere," Trahern stated.

Gregor reckoned it was partly to do with the human researcher at his side.

Bram said, "Right then, that's one thing sorted. The next has to do with Emily and Alice, which is why they're here. The DDA has agreed that they both can stay on a trial basis provided both humans share information with the DDA." Bram moved his gaze to Sid. "I haven't given them my answer yet. I need to know if it's okay for Emily to continue working in the laboratory and share her findings with the DDA."

Gregor wondered why Bram would discuss the two humans' futures in front of them.

His dragon chimed in. *It's a show of dominance and power. Bram is in charge. The humans need to understand that.*

I suppose. Luckily Cassidy doesn't back down just to appease someone's feelings.

Which is why we love her.

Gregor resisted a snort just as Cassidy answered, "The new DDA Director hasn't given me any reason to distrust her yet. However, sharing everything is risky. Emily will have to earn our trust day by day, and there are a few things I don't want the DDA to know about just yet." She looked to Emily. "As you can imagine, some secrets could cost a lot of dragon-shifter lives."

Trahern frowned, but Emily spoke first. "I completely understand. I trust Trahern, but Stonefire still has to earn my trust as well."

Well, it seemed Emily Davies had a backbone. She would probably do well on Stonefire, which could be a problem if other males pursued her while Trahern still fancied the female.

His dragon huffed. *Not our problem.*

Bram's voice prevented Gregor from replying. "Good. Alice already knows what she must do to stay as well, with regards to filing her observations of the clan. That just leaves one last thing to discuss." Bram looked to Gregor and then to Cassidy. "You two need to decide your future."

~~~

Sid knew the topic would come up eventually, but she still couldn't help but frown. "Gregor's and my future is our business."

Bram replied, "Aye, it may be. However, without a mating ceremony, Gregor's transfer will be in the hands of the DDA."

246

Gregor growled out, "The DDA shouldn't rush things."

Evie jumped in. "I think you two need to discuss this matter alone. I'm sure Bram can give you a day to figure it out."

Bram sighed. "She's right. I can give you a day, but no longer."

Gregor took Sid's hand. "Are we done here?"

"Aye, we're done here," Bram said. "But I do need to talk with you two again tomorrow."

Sid nodded. "Understood."

"Then if you'll excuse us," Gregor murmured as he tugged Sid out of the room.

As they made their way to the door, Sid's dragon spoke up. *You should just mate him. He is our true mate.*

I want that more than anything. But I'm not about to make that decision in front of a room full of people.

Good idea. Gregor should work for it.

Sid snorted. Since they were outside, Gregor raised his brows and asked, "What?"

"All I'll say is that you should be glad I'm in charge and not my dragon." Gregor guided them away from both the surgery and their cottage. "Where are we going?"

He grinned. "It's a surprise."

"I never know if I should be happy or worried when it comes to your surprises."

"Oh, you'll like this one. I promise."

She half expected him to take her to the clearing where he had showed off his dragon form. However, Gregor headed instead toward one of the practice landing areas used for the children.

Her stomach flipped. She hoped he wasn't going to ask her to do what she thought he would.

Grunting, her dragon stood up tall inside their mind. *Why not? We both like flying.*

We haven't done it in over two decades. I'd rather not make a fool out of myself in front of Gregor.

He will love us regardless. If anything, he will be our biggest cheerleader.

Thinking of Gregor with pom-poms and wearing an American cheerleader outfit made her laugh out loud.

"I'm not sure I want to know what's going on inside your head at the moment. But I'm glad you're getting along with your dragon again."

Her beast huffed. *Once he sees me in all my glory, he will see how mighty and majestic I am. Then he won't think I'm up to something.*

They turned the corner and Sid stopped in her tracks.

Various carved wooden statues in shapes ranging from dragons to horses to even lions ringed a large area in the center of the practice area. In the middle of them all was a rectangular block of wood.

She looked over to Gregor and he explained, "I'm going to carve your dragon form into that block of wood. But in order to do that, I need to see her first."

"Gregor."

He winked. "After all, it will give me the chance to carve you naked in a respectable way."

She shook her head. "And there goes the moment."

He took hold of her waist and pulled her up against his body. "I'm making moments, love. Anyone can be romantic, but few can do it with a piece of wood and talking about naked carvings."

The corner of Sid's mouth ticked up. "I will say that you're original."

"So, will you share your dragon with me?"

Sid hesitated a second and her beast spoke up again. *I'm ready. Do you trust me?*

In the days since taking the cure to the dragonsoul plant, her dragon had been nothing but pleasant and honest. It would take time to build up a friendship of complete honesty and trust, but one of them needed to make the first step.

Taking a deep breath, Sid replied, *Yes. Let's try.*

Gregor nuzzled her cheek. "Is that a yes?"

She moved to smile at her male. "As long as you promise not to laugh if I can't even jump into the air, then yes, I'll share my dragon with you."

He kissed her. "Love, I will be here to support you. My charm will be out and at the ready. Even if you fall flat on your face, I'll have you smiling again in no time."

"Sometimes, I wonder why I love you."

"Because I'm irresistible and quite the catch."

Lightly hitting his chest, Sid motioned with her hand toward the side. "Just give me room to shift."

After one more kiss, Gregor did as she asked and Sid headed toward the middle of the circle of statues.

Her stomach churned as she took off her jacket and top. She was as nervous as her first time fully shifting as a child.

Her dragon spoke up. *Don't be afraid. I'm sure once you learn, you never forget.*

Just don't do anything crazy. Our muscles will be weak and one wrong move could ground us for days or even weeks.

I know, I know. Stop thinking like a doctor and embrace me.

Sid was about to say taking the doctor part out of her was impossible when she reached Gregor's block of wood. The thought of him spending hours lovingly carving her dragon form and then proudly displaying it eased her nerves. Had he known his gift would help so much?

Her beast grunted. *Probably. He's too clever by half.*

Yes, he is, but neither of us would want it any other way.

Turning to face Gregor, Sid shucked off the rest of her clothes and took a few steps back from the wooden block so that she wouldn't break it. Her male nodded at her and she nodded back. Taking a deep breath, Sid imagined her arms growing into forelimbs, her nose elongating into a snout, and her wings and tail extending from her back.

For a few seconds nothing happened. Then she blanked her mind and let her dragon take charge and her body began to shift.

The combination of pleasure and pain raced through her body as she morphed into her green dragon form. While the change took longer than she remembered it taking as a teenager, Sid finally stood on four limbs and snapped her wings up behind her.

Her beast spoke up. *See? We remembered how to shift.*

Meeting Gregor's gaze, Sid saw how proud her mate was of her. His support gave her the confidence to crouch down and jump into the sky.

Sid beat her wings once, but didn't gain any traction. However, as soon as she allowed her dragon to take charge, their wings beat in a steady rhythm as they ascended into the sky.

She wasn't more than one hundred feet in the air when her wing muscles began to ache. *We need to land again.*

Her dragon growled. *Not yet. It's too soon.*

If we don't, then you won't get the chance to fly again for longer than you like.

After a second, her beast sighed. *Fine, but we need to work on building up our strength again.*

Agreed.

Gliding back down to the landing area, Sid was careful to avoid any of the statues on the ground. The challenge was small, but a good one. When her legs finally touched the surface, a sense of accomplishment flooded her body. *We did it.*

Of course. You need to stop doubting us.

Gregor approached them and patted her chest. "Even your dragon is bonny. I'm a lucky dragonman."

Her dragon preened inside their mind, but Sid ignored her to scoop Gregor up in the talons of one of her forelimbs and brought him to eye level. Gregor didn't so much as bat an eyelash as he petted her snout. "Take advantage of my form now because once you're in flying shape again, you and I are going to have a few challenges." She blew air out of her nostrils and Gregor grinned. "It's not childish. Besides, we need to practice for when our bairn is older. If he or she flies away, then we need to be able to chase them."

Leave it to her mate to find a logical explanation for having fun.

Her dragon spoke up. *I like him. I think he will be on my side in the future.*

Then I'll just have to get our child on mine. However, for now, we have a few things to discuss with our male. Is it okay to shift back now?

I like that you asked me. Yes, if we can't do any more flying, then we may as well. After all, we need to agree to mate Gregor.

I thought you wanted him to work for it?

After his surprise in the landing area, I think he's earned it.

Sid wanted to smile. *Just make sure not to inflate his ego too often, okay?*

Her dragon huffed and Sid took that as her beast's reply.

Placing Gregor back on the ground, Sid motioned for him to stand back. Once he was a safe distance away, she imagined her wings shrinking, her legs shortening, and her snout morphing back into her face. After a few seconds, she once again stood naked in her human form.

Before she could open her mouth, Gregor tossed her jacket around her shoulders and pulled her close. "You did brilliantly, love."

Sid raised her eyebrows. "Are you being genuine? Because I felt as if I were flapping around before I could get into the air. I don't think it'd be all that pretty."

"Perfection is boring, Cassidy. I much prefer watching you strengthen and improve with time. Because you showing me your progress means you trust me."

"Of course I trust you. I wouldn't be standing mostly naked in the middle of a landing area if I didn't."

"Speaking of which, we need to get you inside." He gave her a quick kiss. "We have a few things to discuss."

She tilted her head. "Oh? And what might that be?"

"Don't play coy, lass. I want you as my mate and I'm going to do everything I can to convince you to accept me."

"As I remember, you rejected me before."

"Aye, well, I no longer do. I want you as my mate, Cassidy Jackson. Will you do me the honor?"

Her heart thumped in her chest as she stared into Gregor's eyes. She wanted to shout yes and spend the rest of the day in bed celebrating. However, there was one last thing she needed to address first. "On one condition."

"Aye?"

"Take me home, let me dress, and then tell me more about your sister."

He frowned. "What does Nora have to do with our mating?"

Sid raised a hand to Gregor's cheek. "Everything, Gregor. It's the last barrier between us and I want it gone."

"So if I tell you about Nora, you'll be my mate?"

"Provided you answer everything to my satisfaction, then yes."

"Right, then let's get going. I want to shout to the world that you're mine and ask Bram to set up the mating ceremony as soon as possible."

Gregor scooped Sid up and raced toward the cottage. As she snuggled against his warm chest, she barely noticed the chill. The male she loved was more than she ever could've hoped for. She also couldn't wait to tell everyone that Gregor Innes was hers.

~~~

As Gregor made tea, he waited for Cassidy to come back downstairs to talk. Admittedly, he'd rather not talk about his dead sister, but if it was the only way to ensure they would be asking Bram for a mating ceremony, he'd do it.

His dragon sighed. *You've kept it inside long enough. I know you want to talk about Nora and relive memories. It's not good to keep it all inside.*

I never wanted to burden anyone before.

But with Cassidy, it's different.

Aye, I want to know everything about her and it's only fair I share, too.

Just remembering Cassidy's lovely green dragon form made him smile. It hadn't been easy getting his statues sent to Stonefire without his female's knowledge, but Layla had come through for him.

Thinking of Lochguard's new senior doctor made him a little homesick.

His dragon chimed in. *If we have a mating ceremony, we can see many of our friends again.*

He didn't have a chance to reply as Cassidy appeared in the doorway. She might only be wearing yoga pants and a long-sleeved top, but she was still beautiful to him.

With a smile, Cassidy sat down at the table. "I could get used to you looking at me like that."

He placed a cup of tea in front of Cassidy and then sat down next to her. Gripping the back of her neck with one hand, he said, "Even if you contract some rare disease that covers your face in boils, I'll always look at you like that."

She snorted and took her tea. "Let's hope it doesn't come to that."

His dragon grunted. *Stop delaying the conversation. I want her to agree to be our mate as soon as possible.*

Gregor lightly squeezed the back of her neck. "So, what do you want to know?"

Cassidy searched his eyes. "I just want you to tell me more about her. She was important to you, which means she should be important to me."

"You already know my sister liked to read books and stay inside."

"Yes, but what about when you were children? Did you two ever get in trouble? The little details bring a person to life, Gregor. Since I never had the chance to meet Nora, I'd like to know her through you."

"I think she would've liked you, despite your different personalities." He smiled fondly. "Nora may have been quiet, but she was stubborn. So much so that when she wanted to visit a specific bird colony and our parents refused, she came to me. I was fifteen and she was thirteen. We both felt invincible."

Cassidy tilted her head. "Did you succeed?"

"Not exactly." Gregor grinned. "We got lost and ended up hiding in a forest. Being Scotland, it was raining, of course. It took us a few hours before we finally admitted defeat and called our parents. Let's just say that security was tightened for a few months after our mishap and none of the younger dragon-shifters were happy about it."

Even though Gregor and his sister had been different, they'd been close. The thought of never seeing his sister's smiling face, let alone her daughter who looked just liked Nora, squeezed his heart.

Cassidy's voice garnered his attention. "I'm sorry I won't have the chance to meet her. However, you can talk to me about her anytime you want, Gregor. We'll keep her memory alive."

As he stared into his female's eyes, Gregor fell in love with her all over again. "Thank you, love. I'm going to need some time to fully accept she's gone, but I will definitely take you up on the offer."

Cassidy placed her hand on his bicep. "If we have a girl, we can name her Nora, too, if you like."

"We'll see, love. We have many months to decide on a name. Speaking of which, you should rest. It's been a long time since you flew and your body is going to be sore before long."

She raised her brows. "You're forgetting something quite important, though."

His dragon huffed. *How could you forget about wanting to mate her?*

Gregor replied, "Well, I thought that was already decided. I talked about Nora and fulfilled your condition, hence you agreed to mate me."

"Your romantic tendencies come and go, I see."

Gregor took the cup of tea out of Cassidy's hands, placed it on the table, and then kneeled in front of her. "Oh, bonny lass, would you do me the honor of becoming my mate?"

Amusement danced in her eyes as she answered, "I suppose." He growled and she laughed. "Of course I'll mate you, Gregor Innes. Hurry up and kiss me to seal the deal."

Without another word, he took Cassidy's lips in his and left no doubt that the deal was sealed between them.

CHAPTER TWENTY-FIVE

Sid peeked out of the door on the side of the great hall one more time, but nothing had changed. The entire bloody clan, plus more than a few people from Lochguard, were dressed up and waiting for her mating ceremony to start.

Closing the door, she still couldn't believe she was about to be mated to Gregor. Not only that, but with a baby in their future as well.

Her beast spoke up. *We deserve it.*

I'm not going to disagree with you, but with everything that's happened over the last month and a half, I still can't believe it's real.

I do. It's nice not being locked up.

I'm sorry about that, dragon, I truly am.

Her beast huffed. *Stop apologizing. We've already discussed this and put it behind us. Focus on the ceremony. Once we're done with this, we can spend more time with flying practice.*

Sid smiled. *You and the bloody flying. You're going to be doing daredevil tricks before long, aren't you?*

Of course. I need to beat Gregor's dragon.

She merely shook her head. A knock on the door prevented her from replying. "It's just me, Sid."

She opened the door to let Bram inside. The second the door clicked closed, he spoke again. "I just wanted to check on you."

She rolled her eyes. "I'm not going to faint or fall over if that's what Gregor told you."

"I have more faith in you than that. But a lot has happened recently and I need to make sure my head doctor is fine." His expression softened. "You're the heart of the clan, Sid. If you want to back out, just say the word and I'll chase everyone away."

"You just want to get rid of the 'annoying Scot,' as you put it."

He sighed. "Maybe. Finn is going to drive me to an early grave."

"Oh, stop it. Your blood pressure is better and you've been taking breaks. Evie even mentioned you looking for someone to help you with clan leader duties. Finn won't kill you, although he might annoy you."

"So much for having my doctor on my side."

She raised her brows. "I am on your side. But you can put up with him for a day or two."

Bram smiled. "I'm glad to see you happy and back to your old self, Sid. You've definitely earned today." Someone cued up the bagpipes and Bram winced. "That's your signal. I hope you don't dally. Those bloody things should be against the law."

"I won't. Believe me, I want Gregor Innes for my own."

Bram gripped her shoulder and squeezed. "I'll be in the front row if you need me."

Even though Bram was being protective, she nodded. "Thanks, Bram." The bagpipe music increased in volume. "You'd better go or who knows how loud they'll be."

"Right, then I'm off."

Bram kissed her cheek and exited the room.

Standing tall, Sid took a deep breath. While she worked with people every day, she wasn't used to being the center of attention. Hopefully she could keep her wits about her.

Her dragon spoke up again. *Of course you can. Let's hurry and claim our mate.*

With her dragon's encouragement, Sid opened the door and walked toward the dais at the front of the great hall.

~~~

Gregor stood to the side of the room in his kilt-like traditional outfit, waiting for Cassidy to make an appearance. Since the ceremony had been scheduled to start at noon and it was a few minutes past, he hoped she wasn't having second thoughts.

His dragon sighed. *Of course not. See Bram coming out of the room? It's his fault.*

Bram met Gregor's eyes and nodded. Gregor reciprocated the gesture. The two men were coming to terms with each other, although Gregor was aware he'd never be as close with Bram as he was with Finn.

His beast chimed in. *That's fine. Even if Bram's not a close friend, he'll always protect us. He cares for Cassidy like a sister.*

I know. It's just different is all.

Before any other doubts could creep into his mind, Cassidy stepped out of the side room in her deep blue traditional dress and he stopped breathing.

The dark blue dress slung over one shoulder, leaving the shoulder of her tattooed arm bare. The color also made her pale skin glow. When she met his eyes, they were full of love and a touch of amusement. As the bagpipe music increased in volume, the corner of her mouth ticked up.

He walked up to her and tucked one of her arms under his as he murmured, "You look lovely, lass."

"You're not too bad yourself."

They smiled at each other for another second before they walked down the aisle to the dais. Gregor barely noticed his friends and family in the seats. He was about to be mated for a second time.

Not that long ago, he would've doubted his decision or feared for his new mate's life. However, Cassidy had wormed her way into his heart and knocked some sense into him as well. So far, everything was perfectly normal about her pregnancy and she had promised to be careful as it progressed.

Because of her encouragement, he looked forward to his future with his mate and child. He'd never forget his first mate, but he knew she'd want him to be happy.

After ascending the stairs, Gregor and Cassidy moved to the center of the dais, where there was a box open on top of the table. Inside were their silver engraved mating bands.

They faced one another with clasped hands and the bagpipe music died down. The room fell silent and Gregor cleared his throat. Projecting his voice, he said, "I never thought I would be lucky enough to find a second chance. Between walling up my emotions and dedicating my life to practicing medicine, I was determined to be alone for the rest of my days. But then a no-nonsense female came into my life and try as I might, I couldn't resist her strength. She had a will few could only imagine and her own inner battles to deal with. Yet despite all of that, she was determined to help me. Soon, we were helping each other and I knew she would steal my heart. And it wasn't long before I fell in love with the clever, dedicated, and caring female in front of me. I imagine a future where we work together in all areas of life—from practicing medicine, to forcing each other to take a break, to even trying to outdo each other with ridiculous contests."

A few people chuckled in the audience, but Gregor barely noticed. "I love you, Dr. Cassidy Jackson. Would you do me the honor of accepting my claim and becoming my mate?" She nodded and joy raced through his body. Somehow he managed to pick up the silver arm cuff engraved with his name in the old dragon language and gently put it on the bicep of her tattoo-free arm.

Both man and beast liked seeing their name on their mate's arm—Cassidy Jackson was theirs forever.

Cassidy stood tall as her voice boomed out. "To say I was a workaholic was an understatement. However, since I care deeply for my clan, I didn't mind. I never expected to take a mate, let alone be a mother. I had long accepted that, but then one particular Scottish dragonman entered my life and I had a hard time forgetting him. He even came to help when I needed him most. He not only captured my heart, but my dragon's as well. I wouldn't be a whole dragonwoman today without Gregor Innes. I love that he works with me rather than try to take over my practice, and yet he isn't afraid to tell me when I need to take a break. With him by my side, I enjoy life again. The thought of raising a child with him is one of my greatest gifts."

A few people cooed in the audience, and Cassidy continued, "I love you, Dr. Gregor Innes. Will you accept my claim and become my mate?"

"Of course I do, love."

Smiling, Cassidy slid the silver band engraved with her name in the old dragon language around his bicep. The second she was done, he pulled her close and kissed her. While he may not be the first male to do so, he would be the last one. He was never letting his doctor go.

~~~

Sid's heart thundered in her ears as she slipped the mating band around Gregor's bicep. She had no regrets, but standing in front of the clan was testing her nerves more than she would've thought.

However, as Gregor's lips touched hers and he gently nibbled her bottom lip, her heart slowed. The crowd faded. Gregor Innes had her full attention.

As he pulled her closer to his body, she calmed even further. She didn't think twice of his hand roaming down her back until he lightly cupped her arse cheek. She broke the kiss to whisper, "Stop it."

He winked. "I couldn't help it. I needed something to tide me over until later."

Unable to resist a smile, she murmured, "Just don't do the same thing in front of our leaders or your niece."

At the mention of Gregor's niece, Fiona, he nodded. "We should probably face the crowd again and make the rounds. The sooner we do, the sooner I can whisk you away."

"Don't even think of carrying me out of the great hall."

He winked. "It's hard to sneak when carrying another person. You're safe this time."

She snorted and her dragon spoke up. *He always makes things fun.*

Don't encourage him too much.

Before her beast could reply, she and Gregor turned toward everyone gathered in the hall and cheers rose up.

Everything else was a blur as they descended the stairs and were instantly accosted by Bram and Finn. Finn spoke up first. "Glad to see you made it through without Sid running away."

Gregor grunted. "A 'congrats' would've sufficed."

Finn punched his arm. "Congratulations is boring." He moved his gaze to Sid. "Although I will say congratulations to the lady." He lowered his voice. "And keep watch over our doctor, okay? He needs to learn to loosen up every once in a while."

She smiled. "Considering his fancy for scarfs and naked statues, I think he knows how to relax."

Finn grinned at Gregor. "Oh, aye? This is the first I heard of it."

Bram jumped in. "Given your penchant for teasing, I'm surprised anyone shares embarrassing things with you at all."

Finn motioned toward Bram. "Don't worry, Bram. I'm still working on you. Not that Arabella is any help in that department."

Arabella had been forced to stay on Lochguard because of her advanced pregnancy, so Sid decided to keep a check on Finn in her place. "There are far more important things in life to worry about, such as you handling triplets whilst also running the clan."

Finn sighed. "Of course you'd bring that up."

Gregor wrapped his arm around Sid's waist. "As much as I'd like to keep chatting, there are a lot of other people we need to talk to."

Finn placed a hand over his heart. "You wound me, Gregor." He winked. "But keeping Bram occupied will entertain me. Just make sure to see me again before you disappear with your mate. I'm going back to Lochguard in a few hours so I can keep watch over Arabella."

"Don't suffocate her, Finn," Sid stated.

"I try not to, although I can't completely control my nature." Finn motioned toward the crowd. "Go. There are some special guests waiting to talk with you."

Sid knew he meant Harry and Fiona Chisolm.

"We'll see you later," Gregor replied before guiding Sid away from Finn and Bram.

Sid looked around and spotted Evie with Melanie and Tristan MacLeod. All of their children, minus baby Eleanor in Evie's arms, were playing at their feet.

As she watched Gregor scan the crowd from the corner of her eye, Sid decided she would catch up with Evie and Melanie later. Her mate wouldn't be at ease until they talked with Harry and Fiona.

Gregor pointed to the edge of the room, where Harry sat with his daughter, and murmured, "Let's catch them before they try to escape. Even if they're going to be living here, Harry will still find a way to hide."

"Of course. I'm just happy they were able to come."

"It took some convincing by Finn, but in the end, he managed it. For all his teasing nature, he really cares about the clan."

She leaned against him. "Don't worry, we'll try to visit Lochguard as often as we can."

He glanced down at her. "Have I told you lately that I love you?"

"A few minutes ago." Sid grinned. "But you can say it as often as you like, within reason. If you start saying it nonstop, I will punch you. I know how to take down a grown male, after all."

He raised his brows. "Oh, aye? Care to give me a hint so I can better prepare myself?"

"Not a chance. I need a secret weapon or two."

Gregor kissed her cheek and whispered, "I really do love you, Cassidy," before guiding her the last few feet to Harry and Fiona.

Harry stood up and nodded. "Hi, Gregor."

"Is that the way to greet family?" Gregor released his hold on Sid to engulf the younger man in a hug.

The little girl standing next to Harry tugged on Gregor's outfit. "What about me, Uncle Gregor? You promised me an extra big hug if I came."

Gregor released Harry and crouched down. "Aye, I did. Come here."

Watching Gregor hug his niece tightly, Sid couldn't help but notice the girl was smiling in her uncle's arms.

Moving to Stonefire would be good for them.

Her dragon spoke up. *Of course it is. We'll look out for them. They are family now, too.*

Her beast was right—Sid had new members to her family. She would make an extra effort to help Harry and Fiona live through their grief and hopefully find happiness again.

Gregor let Fiona go and the girl looked up at Sid. "You're my new auntie, right?"

She crouched down. "Yes, I am. You can call me Sid."

"I'm Fiona," the girl said before hugging Sid.

Squeezing the little one tightly, Sid finally released her. "Now, Fiona, would you like to meet some of the other children? There's a group of kids about your age toward the back."

Fiona stood on her tiptoes. "Are they all boys?"

She bit her lip to keep from laughing at Fiona's disgusted tone. "Most, but not all." She lowered her voice. "But just act in charge with the boys, and usually they'll listen."

"Really?"

She nodded. "Really. Remember, you're the new girl and everyone will want to chat with you. First impressions are everything, so don't let any of the boys try to intimidate you."

"Aye, I'll try to remember that." Fiona took her hand. "Will you take me there?"

Sid glanced at Gregor. With his eyes full of love and warmth, she knew he wouldn't mind her taking a few minutes of their mating day to settle his niece. "I'll be right back."

"Aye, love. Just don't be away too long."

After one more loving look at her mate, Sid guided Fiona toward the children's play area.

Between her mate's love, Fiona's faith, and Sid having her dragon once again, she was one of the luckiest dragonwomen in the world. Her battle had been hard fought and she would never take her happiness for granted. But she'd be damned to let it slip through her fingers again.

After all, her happily ever after had just begun.

EPILOGUE

A little less than eight months later

Sid tucked the blanket tighter around her newborn son and murmured, "We're nearly home, Wyatt."

Gregor rubbed her back. "He's a braw lad and can handle a few minutes outside. If he catches a cold with that many layers of blanket around him, then it was bound to happen anyway."

She managed to tear her gaze away from her son long enough to frown at her mate. "Considering how you pretty much kept me on bed rest for the last two weeks, I'm surprised you're so laid back about Wyatt."

Gregor brushed their son's cheek. "You're both alive and well. Besides, you've drilled into me how I worry too much. I'm trying to follow my doctor's orders."

"I sure hope this complacency doesn't last long. It makes me uneasy."

"So little faith, love."

He pulled Sid tighter against his side and she sighed. "At least you didn't bring up yet again how our son might one day become a gunslinger."

"That was our deal—we'd name our son after your brother, but I have free license to tease you about it."

She traced the shapes on the blanket around Wyatt. "The Wild West print on the blanket is a tad much."

"Oh, that's just easing you in. I have a surprise for you at home."

"What did you do, Gregor?"

He winked. "Just wait and see."

Her dragon spoke up. *I like surprises. Gregor has the most unusual ones.*

And that's what worries me.

However, they arrived at the door to their cottage before Sid could question her mate further. He opened the door, but as she peered inside, the hall hadn't changed from when she'd gone into labor. "Where's this surprise of yours?"

Gregor chuckled. "Someone's impatient." He guided her toward the stairs. "Come."

As they ascended the stairs, Sid murmured to her son, "Welcome home, Wyatt."

Her baby was fast asleep, but Sid vowed right then and there that their son would always have a loving home. No matter how annoying Gregor could be at times, he was her best friend and true mate. Together, they could do anything.

Gregor stopped in front of Wyatt's room. "The surprise is in here."

Since they'd both been busy and unable to decorate Wyatt's room, it should have been empty. "If you managed to decorate that whilst I was in labor, I might just be impressed."

He placed a hand on her lower back. "Of course I'm impressive. Sometimes it just takes you a little while to realize that."

She shook her head, but couldn't stop smiling. "Just open the door."

"As my lady wishes."

Gregor complied and Sid blinked at what was inside.

A mural painted on the wall depicted what she assumed was the Arizona desert, complete with cacti and horses running wild in the distance. A few cowboys rode hard near the front of the picture, but unlike most human depictions of the old west, dragons also flew in the sky.

After taking in the mural, she noticed the furniture and a few of Gregor's animal carvings posted around the room. However, when she saw what was on the dresser, she stopped to study Gregor's newest carving. It had three dragons posing for a family photo and each of them had on a little cowboy hat.

Her beast huffed. *A dragon would never wear a hat. And most certainly not a cowboy hat.*

That's what makes it so special.

If you say so.

She looked up at Gregor and he raised his brows. "So, what do you think? I had to call in a lot of favors, but I think it turned out brilliantly."

"It may not have been my first choice, but knowing you went to all this trouble, I love it."

Her mate beamed. "Harry told me I was crazy, but I knew you'd grow to like it." He motioned toward the dragons in cowboy hats. "Fiona suggested the hats. I thought it was a great idea."

She chuckled. "Fiona would suggest that." The little girl had started to come out of her shell a few months ago and nearly had the run of Stonefire's younger children. "But as much as I enjoy your surprise, I want Wyatt to sleep in our room for a little while. While I know it's irrational, I don't want to let him out of my sight just yet."

Gregor cupped the top of their son's head. "I couldn't agree more. Besides, he needs time to get to know us, too."

As they stood together and stared at their son, Sid blinked back her tears. Even though they were tears of joy, it would upset her mate.

Besides, despite her exhaustion and soreness, Sid wanted to enjoy this moment as long as she could. Standing in a room full of dragons and cowboys with her son in her arms and her mate at her side was more than she ever could've hoped for. This memory would stay with her for the rest of her life.

However, it was just the beginning. Between coordinating with other dragon-shifter doctors and taking care of Stonefire as well as their son, Sid and Gregor had many more memories to make.

Dear Reader:

Thanks for reading *Cured by the Dragon*. I hope you enjoyed Sid and Gregor's story. If you're craving more of this couple, don't worry, they'll show up again in the future. Also, if you liked their story, please leave a review. Thank you!

The next story in this series will be about Aaron Caruso (Kai's second-in-command) and Teagan O'Shea (Glenlough's leader). I'm still working on the title, but the release date is set for May 2017. However, I will have another Lochguard Highland Dragons book out before that in February 2017. It will be about Faye MacKenzie and Grant McFarland and is called *The Dragon Warrior*.

To stay up to date on my latest releases, don't forget to sign-up for my newsletter at www.jessiedonovan.com/newsletter.

Turn the page for an excerpt from one of my other series.

With Gratitude,
Jessie Donovan

The Dragon Guardian
(Lochguard Highland Dragons #2)

Gina MacDonald may be pregnant and on the run, but she will
do anything to protect her unborn child—even go up against a
dragon-shifter. While hiding in the wilds of the Scottish
Highlands, she soon notices the black dragon perched on the
nearby hills. She debates if he is related to her past or not, but
then a pain overcomes her and the dragon finally swoops down
to help. Despite her determination to stay clear of all dragon-
shifter males, his touch not only helps ease her tension, it sets
her skin on fire.

Fergus MacKenzie protects his clan by collecting information
and warning them of threats. When a redheaded American
shows up out of the blue along a nearby lake, he watches her to
find out more. However, when he sees her bend over in pain,
he flies down to help her. Afterward, he should walk away. But
he can't stop thinking about her green eyes and addictive touch.
Both man and beast want her more than anything in their lives.

As Fergus learns more of Gina's past, he knows she will bring
danger to his clan. Torn between protecting his family and
following his heart, will Gina and Fergus be able to find a
happy ending? Or, will danger force Fergus to choose between
love and clan?

Excerpt from _The Dragon Guardian_:

CHAPTER ONE

Fergus MacKenzie sat on top of one of the hills surrounding Loch Shin in his dragon form and adjusted his grip with his talons. Despite waiting for the last hour to see the redheaded human female, she had yet to step outside.

That shouldn't surprise him given that it was January in the Scottish Highlands. The wind and chill in the north wasn't for the fragile. While everything he'd learned about Gina MacDonald over the last few weeks spoke of her strength, she was also heavily pregnant. For all he knew, she could be giving birth right that second.

Fergus's inner dragon spoke up. _Look. Her door is opening. Maybe we can actually talk to her today._

Fergus watched as Gina stepped outside and headed for the chicken coop. The wind whipped her long, curly red hair behind her and the human pulled her jacket closer around her body.

His beast spoke up again. _Today might be our last chance for a while. We should speak with her._

Fergus wanted to talk with the human more than he would ever admit to anyone. Not even his twin brother knew how Gina had invaded Fergus's dreams since the very first day he'd seen her. Dreams that more often than not had both of them naked and tangled in the sheets.

Pushing away those thoughts, Fergus answered his dragon. _We have no claim on her. I can't risk a confrontation with the father of her child._

His dragon huffed. _We haven't been able to find out anything about him. If he's unwilling to protect his female, then he has no claim on her._

Not true. What if he's in the armed forces and currently stationed overseas?

That is a very small possibility.

It could still be true.

Fergus debated returning to his home on Clan Lochguard when the female gripped her belly and hunched over. Without thinking, Fergus glided down to Gina's house. The sheep ran to the far side of one of the pens and he landed. Imagining his wings shrinking into his back, his talons changing into fingers, and his snout taking the shape of a human face, Fergus stood in his human form five seconds later. Uncaring about his nakedness, he rushed over to the female and shouted, "Are you all right, lass?"

The woman glanced over. Her eyes widened before quickly darting down to his cock and back up to his face. Taking a deep breath, she stood up and frowned. "You're the dragon who's been watching me for weeks."

He took a step closer. "That doesn't matter right now. If you need help, then tell me. I can ring a doctor or your husband."

"I don't have a husband." Gina rubbed her belly and then let out a sigh. "But the damn spell has passed, so care to tell me why you're standing in my yard buck naked?"

Just like the first time he'd heard her speak, he found her American accent foreign yet endearing. "Aren't you in labor?"

"No. I was trying to keep my food down. The smell of chicken scat makes me want to puke."

His dragon chimed in. *Get her inside. I don't like her out in the cold.*

Fergus had asked the same question a million times before, but decided to try once more. *Why do you care so much?*

Just get her inside first.

276

Fergus motioned with a hand toward the door. "Let's get you out of the cold, get me a blanket or a towel so I can cover some of my nakedness, and I'll answer whatever questions you might have."

The corner of Gina's mouth ticked up. "Oh, really? Whatever I want? I can't wait to make the big, bad dragonman squirm."

Ignoring her tease, he moved to her side and placed a hand on her lower back. Despite the layers of clothing between her skin and his, a small jolt shot up his arm. He couldn't remember the last time that had happened with a female. "I assure you I don't squirm. Now, let's get inside. It's bloody freezing out here."

Gina started walking and humor danced in her eyes. "Are you going to use that as an excuse for the size of your penis?"

He blinked. "What?"

"Well, just about every guy I've ever met says the cold makes him shrivel." She paused and leaned over. "But in your case, that makes me wonder just how big you are when it's warm."

Fergus cleared his throat. He wasn't about to allow the lass to disarm him. "The first time I met you, whilst in dragon form, you said you knew the dragon clan in Virginia back in America. I'm fairly confident the rumors about dragon-shifters and their cocks are the same there as here."

"Maybe. But I like the idea of making you uncomfortable."

He frowned. "Care to tell me why?"

Gina laid a hand on her stomach. "It's fun. And believe me, it's been months since I've had any fun."

~~~
277

Gina MacDonald wasn't sure what had come over her. The black dragon constantly watching from the hills had irritated her over the passing weeks. Who was he to spy on her? Not only that, but he never had the balls to talk with her so she could find out why he was there. She didn't think Travis had sent him.

No. She refused to think of that bastard.

And yet she was spilling her guts to the Scottish dragonman. Sure, it was true she hadn't had any fun since her mother had shipped her off to Scotland, but it was hardly something you told a stranger.

The dragonman pushed lightly against her back and Gina nearly moaned at his touch. She would give her left arm for a massage.

The mysterious dragonman spoke up, his yummy Scottish accent making her want to shiver. "Aye, well, sometimes fun has to wait. You're about to have a child, so get used to it."

She glanced over at the tall Scot at her side. "What, do you have a brood of five kids at home and are speaking from experience?"

"I don't have any children."

His tone was a little too controlled. The smart thing would be to drop it, but Gina didn't like unanswered questions. "But you do want them someday."

The dragonman faltered in his step. His dark blue eyes met hers and she drew in a breath. It seemed dragon-shifters were attractive on both sides of the pond.

Clenching her fingers, Gina pushed aside her attraction. After all, that was what had landed her in the current situation.

They reached the door and the dragonman turned the knob. Gina debated the negatives of inviting a strange man into her house. But then the wind gusted. Longing for warmth, she decided to trust her gut that the man wouldn't hurt her, and she stepped inside. "Come in, then, Mister...?"

"MacKenzie. Fergus MacKenzie."

Gina snorted. "You can't get much more Scottish than that."

Fergus clicked the door closed. "Fergus is a strong name. It means man of strength or man of force."

She put on a mock Scottish accent. "Aye, and it's a verra bonny name, too."

She didn't think it was possible, but Fergus frowned deeper than before. "We're doing accents then, aye?" His voice turned into a high-pitched Valley Girl accent. "I'm, like, so super cool. And, like, you're hella crazy."

She managed to keep it together until Fergus waggled his eyebrows and Gina barked out a laugh. "You should talk like that all of the time. It suits you."

His voice returned to normal. "But Americans love it when I roll my 'r's."

Not wanting to acknowledge it was true, Gina turned, picked up a blanket and tossed it at Fergus. "Cover yourself and I'll pour some juice."

From the corner of her eye, she watched Fergus wrap the blanket around his lean hips. The tattoo on one of his upper arms bunched and flexed as he did it.

Dragon-shifters really were too attractive for their own good.

Not now, Gina. We learned our lesson, remember? Keep it together.

Clearing her throat, she went into the kitchen. Just as she was about to lean against the counter and take a breather, Fergus waltzed into the room as if he owned it. Spotting her against the counter, he muttered, "Bloody stubborn female."

Before Gina could reply, he was next to her. Picking her up as if she weighed nothing, she cried out, "Put me down."

Fergus adjusted his grip. "No."

She slapped his chest. "As I told you when we first met, I have ways to defend myself against dragon-shifters."

"Aye? Well, if carrying you to a chair offends you, I wonder how any male came close enough to get you with child."

"Are you trying to insult me?"

Fergus gently rested her on the kitchen chair and remained bent over so his eyes were level with hers. His pupils flashed to slits and back before the corner of his mouth ticked up. "Lass, I have a younger sister and a twin brother. Believe me, when I insult you, you'll know it."

She opened her mouth and Fergus pressed her lips together with his warm, rough fingers—fingers that no doubt could do wicked things to her body.

Gina blinked. She needed to get Fergus MacKenzie away from her or she would most definitely do something stupid. Given her track record over the last year, she really didn't need to add any other mistakes to her list.

And spending time with Fergus would be a mistake she couldn't afford to make. Not with a child on the way she needed to protect.

Want to read the rest?
The Dragon Guardian is available in paperback

For exclusive content and updates, sign up for my newsletter at:

http://www.jessiedonovan.com

Author's Note

Many people were rooting for Sid to find her happy ending and I hope I did her justice. Originally, I didn't think she'd get her dragon back. But the stubborn beast wanted to step into the limelight, and so she fought her way out. I truly had no idea when I wrote the no-nonsense doctor back in *Sacrificed to the Dragon* that she'd have a silent dragon, let alone that she would find her true mate in a Scottish doctor. It just goes to show you that my imagination has a mind of its own! Oh, and I apologize for any mistakes made regarding scientific and/or medical practice. I did the best research I could, but I'm not a doctor or a scientist. :)

As always, I have a few people to thank with regards to getting this book out to my readers:

- My editor, Becky Johnson, and her entire team at Hot Tree Editing really make my stories shine.
- My cover artist, Clarissa Yeo of Yocla Designs, is amazing as always. She truly captured Dr. Sid on the cover and I can't wait to see what she comes up with for my next book in this series.
- My three beta readers—Donna H., Iliana G., and Alyson S.—are amazing women who volunteer their time to read, comment, and find the minor inconsistencies and/or typos for me. I truly value and appreciate their hard work.

The next dragon-shifter story will be Faye MacKenzie and Grant McFarland's book (*The Dragon Warrior*, LHD #4) with a target release date of February 2017. The next Stonefire Dragons books will feature Teagan O'Shea (the Irish leader) and Aaron Caruso (Kai's second-in-command) and should be out in May 2017. I'm still working on the title, but if you want to stay up-to-date with release information and news, then make sure to subscribe to my newsletter on my website at www.jessiedonovan.com.

As always, a huge thanks to my readers for their support. Without you, I wouldn't be able to write these wonderful stories and revisit characters that have become like family to me. Thank you!

About the Author

Jessie Donovan wrote her first story at age five, and after discovering *The Dragonriders of Pern* series by Anne McCaffrey in junior high, she realized people actually wanted to read stories like those floating around inside her head. From there on out, she was determined to tap into her over-active imagination and write a book someday.

After living abroad for five years and earning degrees in Japanese, Anthropology, and Secondary Education, she buckled down and finally wrote her first full-length book. While that story will never see the light of day, it laid the world-building groundwork of what would become her debut paranormal romance, *Blaze of Secrets*. She became a *New York Times* and *USA Today* bestselling author in late 2015.

Jessie loves to interact with readers, and when not reading a book or traipsing around some foreign country on a shoestring, can often be found on Facebook. Check out her pages below:

http://www.facebook.com/JessieDonovanAuthor

And don't forget to sign-up for her newsletter to receive sneak peeks and inside information. You can sign-up on her website:

http:///www.jessiedonovan.com